INHUMAN INTENTIONS

MASON MANTHOUS

WARRINGTON
PUBLISHING

Danbury, Connecticut

Inhuman Intentions
Copyright © 2025 by Mason Mathous

Published by Warrington Publishing
Danbury, CT
www.warringtonpublishing.com

Printed in the United States of America
First Edition
ISBN: 978-1-944972-84-4 (paperback)
978-1-944972-83-7 (ebook)
978-1-944972-85-1 (hardcover)

Book cover designed by JD&J Designs
Edited by Mike Waitz of Sticks & Stones Editing

Dedicated to everyone who accepted me

–CHAPTER 1–

IN WAIT

Even the sky was barren in the frontier. Sparse clouds drifted carelessly above. The land was dry and desolate; an apathetic savanna of long, flat expanses populated by little more than brush, grass, and the occasional rolling hill. Nestled against one such hill, Aaron knelt, watched, and prepared to hunt a monster.

It was poor cover, but the best he had. He and his team. They were nine in total, each of them camouflaged and arrayed to allow no blind spots in their formation. Blindness was death, and so they covered each other while waiting for their target.

There was tension in his limbs. Weeks on the hunt had turned humor to sand. They, the members of S-0, knew the wastes. They respected the emptiness. That didn't make it pleasant. A bleak place of few landmarks and resources, the ground did little to absorb heat from the sun, and nights arrived with a chill that gnawed at his limbs. When he shifted his weight, dust pinched his skin in a dozen different places, having snuck through his uniform despite all efforts. The spots scratched like centipedes crawling over his limbs.

Perhaps worse for Aaron was the silence. So far out, all of the sounds that told him of life and existence were painfully absent. Trees were withered with few leaves, barely stirring in the breeze. Mice and other rodents were a rarity. It had been days since he'd seen a bird. The only noises that provided him with comfort were the breaths and heartbeats of his companions.

At his left hand, Durham shifted, tugging at the mask over her face. Ever restless, the quiet was torturous for her. "No sign of them yet?" she asked, her voice the first all night. "How long has it been?"

His lieutenant, Dalton, answered softly. "Four hours."

A fitting counterpart to Durham, he was a statue of a man, and as comfortable in stillness. His words were spoken in a controlled and even tone, never shifting his eye from the scope of his rifle.

"There's still time, though."

Sif, who functioned as Dalton's spotter, ran her fingers over a handheld map. "It's possible we overshot during the day. They could have changed directions. The target could have as well."

Aaron doubted it, having spent the day reviewing the map himself. "I don't think they would turn around. The beasts are aberrant, but they've followed a pattern so far. These ruins are the next closest in their path, and where they go, he'll follow."

A quiet murmuring of agreement rippled through the group, and they returned to their watch, looking out at the sight before them with renewed vigilance.

What had been built in that unforgiving emptiness was too small and simple to be called a town. It was a few hundred buildings at most, depending on how one defined the word, but it stood taller and prouder than anything for miles around. Those plain, rugged structures were not built to impress or captivate. In truth, they were constructed from the ruins of another insignificant attempt at civilization that was discarded some uncounted years ago.

At the end of the world, territory in the wastes was gained and lost. Towns were constructed in times of expansion and then abandoned in times of hardship, to later be reclaimed in the decades or centuries that followed. Aaron wondered when this one had been lost. There were fragile young trees and the remnants of farms to the south, and a small river for water. The architecture was unfamiliar and eroded, but it had a beauty to it for all of that. It was the beauty of defiance.

Brook spoke next, looking down her nose at the ruins with the superiority of a bird of prey. "If he doesn't show himself tonight, then we should turn back. We've gone beyond our limits in more ways than one."

Nobody responded at first, least of all Aaron, for whom the remark was directed. Brook was a scion to an old family and never afraid to question his judgment, but her point was valid. Home was far behind them. They had known they might test their boundaries when they set out on their hunt, but as time dragged on and the sights of endless ruins assaulted them, it wasn't strange to consider the alternative.

But it was not an option. "If we give up now, we'll never have the chance again," he answered.

"That's not all there is to it," Brook continued, undeterred. "We're running out of supplies for a protracted hunt."

"We have enough supplies," Aaron assured her. Though it was true that they were beginning to ration food, they had enough to return home with days to spare.

It was Rista who objected next. "That's assuming all goes well. Plan for the worst, sir, so that you're never disappointed."

Though tactful, it was still an objection. Aaron shifted his position to better observe Rista, whose shadowed eyes tracked his every movement like a poised cat.

"It's not a failure if we retreat, Captain," he pressed. "Why not just let the wastes take him?"

It was a sensible question. *"Wastes take you"* was a common way of condemning one to death on the frontier. There were few worse places to be stranded than the barrens at the edge of the map. It was so tempting that Aaron almost took them up on it. Still, it was unacceptable.

"Dalton, how many people has our target killed?" he asked.

"Six, Captain," his lieutenant answered. "That we are aware of."

The number brought forth the memories of the corpses, so thoroughly defiled that he hadn't been able to tell their number at a glance. The casual depravity reserved for a rancid breed. Too cruel to do better. Too proud to want to.

"Yes," he said. "That's why we see it through to the end."

Durham laughed aloud, prompting a heavy-handed glare from her peers. "Keep your voice down!" Lenz hissed, nearly invisible among a cluster of shrubbery.

"Sorry, sorry," she said with a dismissive wave. "He just sounded a lot like one of the Paradisers for a second. You know, the paladins who whine about damnation while staking people with silver."

Discomfort rippled through the group, not necessarily for the thought itself but for what it reminded them of. The purported haven of humanity in a verdant and thriving land was little more than an insult to the people of the frontiers, not because it was a fantasy but because it was real, and unattainable all the same.

"Please don't make jokes," Aaron said. "We're a long way from Paradise."

Gavin, who had been so silent that Aaron nearly forgot he was there, nudged him lightly. "You're from there, though, Captain."

The reminder was even more unpleasant, riling distant and chaotic memories of a crumbling castle in a place far away by more than just distance.

"That was a long time ago."

"Movement!"

The discussion was dropped. They took up positions to better observe their quarry. The few clouds fell over the moon, as if heralding their arrival, and the members of S-0 shifted soundlessly in response. Drawing back her sleeve, Durham pressed a finger to her forearm, resting it against the mark of her pact. In response, it shimmered faintly. Slight as it was, the magic was potent, and Aaron saw her eyes and the rest of S-0 take in the results as it enhanced their vision in the darkness.

"Almost wish I hadn't," she muttered. "These things are not a pretty sight."

Aaron looked out at them, nodding agreement. He had never seen a nightmare worth looking at.

There was no true "breed" to the things they called nightmares. The beings had no bloodlines to observe. Some hunted alone, and some formed groups. There were those considered ordinary, and there were those nebulously categorized as aberrants. The creatures were as varied in appearance as their namesake would suggest, and all were monstrous. Moving in a loose pack, the misbegotten and deformed creatures took slow trudging steps across the waste. Only some could actually manage it, though.

Aaron counted twenty-two of them, and not one of them had a face. They came in every color, but all appeared washed out and muddled. They were amalgams, with some covered in leathery hide and some clad in scales or fur. A few of them blended between the states, and some seemed to shift between them from moment to moment. In place of eyes, they had horns, growths, empty sockets, or mouths. Each had one or many gnashing, chittering maws, all filled with teeth suited for tearing flesh.

S-0 took in the sight calmly. "Leader in the front looks bigger than the rest," Brook said.

There was a silent agreement, but it was brittle. Aaron understood. Even for him, the reaction was difficult to control. To look at nightmares was to look at something unnatural, and to experience them for too long was to degrade one's own sanity. Training could only discipline the mind so much when faced with creatures that defied reason. Even in the seconds that they watched, the beings were in transition, horns and scales sprouting from joints, spines elongating or compressing. It made the viewer feel like they were going mad rather than witnessing a creature of flesh and blood.

Rista reverently touched the pact etched into the back of his hand. It was a habit of his. There was a comfort in it, and in controlling even a fragment of magic. The pact was otherworldly, to be sure, but it was an exchange made. Nightmares were creatures that only consumed.

Aaron traced the creatures' path, knowing their destination already. They had moved through two sets of ruins to get this far, and this would make the third. Sure enough, when the nightmares caught sight of the old buildings, they hurried their pace, uneven limbs rolling over each other to move toward the empty husk of civilization.

"What's the plan, Captain?" Gavin asked.

Aaron considered, speaking aloud what all of them knew to be true. "We wouldn't want to engage them at night. Even with the pact, it's not ideal."

"Except for you, Captain." Durham chimed in.

He ignored the comment, true as it was. "Still, there aren't so many buildings here. Once the nightmares leave, it won't be long until the target arrives. We can wait and ambush him."

"A fine plan," Dalton said, adjusting his scope as the nightmares made their way into the ruins. "But what do we do if they find the truck?"

The captain considered it. "Nightmares aren't inclined to kill what isn't alive, but they're aberrants; they might act outside of our expectations. Still, I highly doubt they'd turn around. Lenz, you'll track their movement once they leave. If they risk running into the truck, we'll split into two teams."

He twitched. Something prickled at his ears. His hearing was acute, even more so in the silence of the wastes. Something had disrupted that silence. He closed his eyes and sorted all he could: heartbeats, breathing, the sound of the nightmares' uneven movements in the ruins. The sound was something higher-pitched than that. It was a keening, eerie sound.

His eyes snapped open. It was a hunting cry. But before he could vocalize it, the members of S-0 snapped to attention as a scream tore through the quiet.

Within the ruin, tiny, dim lights sprang to life, and the crack of gunshots filled the empty night. More screams followed, and the shrill call of the nightmares was replaced by rasping bellows and the breaking of wood and stone.

"It's populated!" Moore hissed from his cover, half hidden beneath the dirt. "This far out?"

"They'll ruin everything," Rista said.

"Or make it better," Brook considered. "The target is practically guaranteed to show now."

Gavin adjusted his cap. "The chaos will make it hard to locate him, but it keeps the odds of being discovered low. We need to adjust the plan."

But Aaron had already done so. "Lenz, get the truck."

All eyes were on him instantly. It took only a second for them to understand his intention. Lenz said nothing, moving with haste to fulfill the command. The rest extricated themselves from their positions and improvised camouflage for what was to follow. There was little to do to prepare. They had all been ready to fight. But Aaron saw the expressions and their thoughts on the matter. Only Brook voiced her disapproval.

"Captain White, you need to reconsider. This puts our mission in jeopardy."

"Our mission is always to save lives," he declared.

"*Respectfully*, sir, our priority is to exterminate," Brook retorted. "This is not our land. This is Lord Sterling's territory. Those are his people, and if they learn who and what we are, then there will be violence."

Aaron stared at her. Six and a half feet tall, she was one of the few people who stood eye level with him. He drew his shaded glasses from his jacket. He had little need for them during the night, but donned them anyway. She had a point. The people there were not necessarily on their side. Better not to risk any of the citizens seeing him for what he was.

"Those are people," he said. "And to nightmares, they're all the same. Nephilim, too." He didn't convince her. He saw it in her eyes. Nonetheless, she obeyed his order and grabbed her rifle, falling in with the rest as they made to move in.

–Chapter 2–

Nightmares Made Real

S-0 advanced through the village in pairs, taking turns moving forward while under the watchful eyes of their teammates. Two would dart from one point of cover to the next at a time, guns trained for any sign of sound or movement. The rest would act as support, ready to strike first if a nightmare made itself known. All except for Aaron, who strode forward in the middle of empty streets as a challenge to any who would threaten them.

"Use the pact," he ordered. "And cover it up. We don't want anyone seeing it."

Those who hadn't done so already complied. Each drew on the contract they had been gifted, the small scraps of magic granting them sight in the darkness and sharpening already honed senses to their limits. Aaron had no need of his own, which served a different purpose than theirs, but drew strength from the connection they shared. When battling nightmares, control over the self was vital.

The buildings they navigated were poorly maintained and in varying states of disrepair, from broken windows to holes perforating the walls. They had the telltale signs of abandonment and recapture. Aaron noted the differing styles of architecture between houses built adjacent in space but decades apart in time.

He saw intricate windowsills and pillars carved with the likeness of wolves, the calling card of the warden's house of Sterling that ruled the region. These had been eroded and worn away by time until some of them were little more than dark smudges in the stone, replaced by newer construction of a simpler, more streamlined likeness. These too had suffered over time, painting the village in different shades of calamitous history.

They followed screams and the clamor of desperate fighting. The smell of blood was in the air. Aaron turned a corner, and slumped against a well in the center of the street was the first of the bodies. It still had the lean shape of a man, but little else remained of its appearance. The wound that had killed him looked to be a claw to the throat, and the blood that sheeted down his side would have been more than enough to doom him on its own. But with nightmares, that was never enough. His body was covered in wounds like pockmarks, each location a chunk of flesh ripped free and consumed in a ravenous frenzy. Normally, they would eat until every piece was gone, but the allure of fresh victims had undoubtedly kept the creatures engaged.

S-0 walked over the corpse without a word, their pace neither accelerating nor faltering. Aaron longed to throw himself into the fray against the creatures, but to rush into combat was to rush into death, and he resolved to honor the fallen man with the destruction of his killers, and he hoped, the salvation of his kin.

Continuing forward, the gunfire that had been distant grew louder with each step. Aaron could make out individual voices that became more frantic by the moment. Hastily lit lamps were scattered across the streets, as were more bodies. It was then that Aaron saw the first of them up close, hunched over its latest victim.

The nightmare stood on double-jointed legs, gray skin clinging to thin bones. One of its arms was longer than the other, ending in a ridged spike and dragging against the dirt road. The other held the body and fed on it with the frenzy of a starving beast. It possessed no eyes or nose with which to observe them.

In their place was a single gaping mouth filled with teeth like needles that sank into the victim with relish. Behind those teeth, Aaron knew, was only darkness, a hungry void that would never fill. It was as empty as the wastes, something from a dark fairy tale that ended in tragedy and children who were never seen again.

A half-dozen marks were drawn on the creature, but Aaron stopped them with a hand. "Quietly," he said. "Don't want to alert the others." The creature would notice them in a moment, but either due to its lack of visible sensory organs or simply being lost in its gruesome feast, it hadn't yet done so. Aaron holstered his pistol, instead quietly drawing his sword. His stride quickened as he approached the nightmare, breaking into a low run. It barely had time to turn his way before he brought the blade down on it in a strike that cleaved its oversized mouth in half.

He wrenched his blade out the side of its neck, drawing back with a dark spatter. Another two-handed strike decapitated the vile thing. It dropped to the ground, limbs twitching and flailing. "It's neutralized for now," Aaron said. "We'll clean it up later." He observed the wretched mass of limbs in disgust, its severed head slowly leaking blood thick as sludge.

The next turn was even more crowded with corpses. Buildings showed signs of restoration, only to be stained with blood or cracked and broken. Glass from windows and lamps was shattered on stone walkways, and freshly planted trees were torn with claws and talons. Still, the sounds grew more prominent.

"They're just ahead!" Aaron declared, though the rest of S-0 could certainly tell that for themselves. The street they moved up grew wider and more maintained, only to abruptly turn toward the center of the cluster of what they had thought were ruins. It was when he turned the corner that Aaron saw the full horror of what was occurring.

The village square was spacious, built over a neat cobblestone road. The buildings were larger than those that made up the outer structures and were constructed from smooth stone rather than brick or wood. More defensible, people had taken up residence there and made it a bastion as the nightmares attacked.

There had clearly been a plan in place for that eventuality. It wasn't an unthinkable situation, after all. Those on the frontiers prepared their whole lives for it. Parents sang songs of the nightmares' evil to babies bouncing on their knees. Schoolhouses read stories of such horrors, and children were taught to fight back before they were taught how to read. People in the frontiers didn't survive by being weak, but Aaron knew from experience that no number of speeches, sermons, or time spent fearing the day would prepare them for just how chaotic the attack would be.

It was a vicious melee. Denizens of the little village ran, screamed, fought, and were savaged by the nightmares. There were dozens of people in the square, surrounding their killers as well as they were able. Some had guns, but the majority were armed with shovels, axes, hammers, and other makeshift weapons. Most fierce was the fighting around a great statue, some fifteen feet tall, that occupied the center of the space.

The wooden monument had a twisting, coiled appearance, wrought in the likeness of a great snarling wolf. Its rippling fur was lovingly carved from polished lumber of one of the ancient Atsali trees that could be found in the frontier. It was a monument of loyalty. The people were ruled by and under the protection of the nobles of House Sterling after all, but they were also pioneers. As far out into the wastes as they were, even if the Sterlings knew of their little town's existence, they wouldn't be coming to help them in time.

The fight was a desperate one for survival, and the citizens clearly knew it. Men, women, old, and young took up arms in defense of their homes. All the same, it was a losing battle. The people hacked and slashed and shot at the nightmares, but the effects were minimal.

That was not to say the creatures were unaffected; they simply didn't care. Nightmares were monsters bereft of souls but still with physical forms. They could be struck, even hurt, but ending them was a different story. Aaron watched one of the monsters, a hulking biped covered in sickly molting scales, take an axe to the head, and simply continue as if the tool weren't buried in its skull. It shook itself, snarling from mouths in place of eyes, and lashed out with a great taloned hand, tearing into the man who had dealt it the superficial wound. Another, a twisted humanoid with a mouth splitting its torso in half, staggered and screamed when struck, but the wounds did nothing to stop it.

They continued forward, shambling but undeterred and insensible to pain that would render other creatures immobile. That was why S-0 did not consider nightmares something to be killed, merely destroyed. Aaron recalled an old rhyme of the church of Paradise. *They may bleed but do not die, for they were never true alive.*

But there was more to it. Aaron saw it in the people's eyes: hysteria. They were not trained soldiers. They were staring death in the face, and they were losing their will. Against nightmares, even the instinct for survival could be dulled in the wake of overwhelming fear. When it took hold, chaos would destroy the only hope they had left, and then it would be over. They would go from fighting to being slaughtered, running only to catch the attention of another monster.

"Gavin," he ordered. "You first. Use the stake driver."

"Yes, Captain," Gavin replied, taking a place at Aaron's side. "The big one?" he asked, looking at the scale-covered brute that had led the abominations and now flung a man backward through a window.

Aaron nodded. "Fire when ready."

Gavin took a knee and patiently lined up his shot. The stake driver was a heavy crossbow that sacrificed the speed and stopping power of regular guns for silence when firing. It was a valuable tool when picking off stray targets, and it worked well in the chaos in front of them. Where the loss of speed and power might hinder the killing potential of a projectile, the loss was minuscule for their intended target. The nightmare didn't even notice when the bolt buried itself in its neck. It twitched as if bitten by a fly, only to shudder and shake as the true weapon took effect.

Nightmares were soulless creatures, and that made them formidable. They would continue past when any ordinary creature would fall and die. They were an assault on the sanity of those who perceived them. But they were hollow beings, and the touch of silver was anathema to any creature without a soul.

The bolt fired by the stake driver was tipped with that silver, and once lodged in the nightmare's throat, set it aflame like dry tinder. The monster convulsed, twitching and lashing out with arms as wide as a man. Its malleable form mutated, scales and skin splitting to reveal grooved spines pushing their way into the air. Bones snapped and splintered inside its body, and a sunset glow built in the back of its throat.

The nightmare unleashed a hoarse bellow, only to be cut off as a gout of flame ignited in the air. The mouths it had in place of eyes leaked smoke, only to erupt in fire that consumed its entire hideous head. It staggered, sickly scales blackening as the sanctified metal incinerated it from within. Talons clawed at its head, shredding flesh in an attempt to tear the bolt free. With a gasp, it fell to the ground, flame hungrily creeping along its body.

By this time, both nightmares and humans had taken notice of S-0. For their part, the monsters had no emotions to show, merely sensing the arrival of fresh meat. That worked out well enough. S-0 had already taken up positions. Gavin took the moments of the first monster's death throes to reload and fired once again.

The second shot, still practically soundless in the midst of the ongoing melee, seemed to tip the nightmares off that what had appeared was actually a threat. They immediately disregarded their victims and approached the new foe. Townsfolk were sent reeling as clawed limbs smashed them aside for the monsters to sprint in the direction of their enemies.

This was by design and ensured that the creatures were in motion directly toward them. This made it easier for the members of S-0 to hit their respective marks. The most important thing when fighting nightmares was to control the engagement.

A half dozen piles of limbs faltered and fell as silver bullets penetrated their skin and set them aflame. Skin cracked, glowed, and turned to embers, blunting the wild rush. One of the creatures brought up an insectoid limb as the bullet struck it, and the limb flew off once the joint started to burn. The nightmares didn't die immediately, but they slowed to a degree that they were run down by their own fellows.

Aaron remained still, letting the monsters maul their own. Meanwhile, the denizens of the village were not idle. Despite the terrible losses they sustained, the arrival of allies who could kill the aberrations emboldened and restored hope to them. They fell on the creatures as they turned away, attacking from behind and knocking, slicing, or breaking limbs to hinder their movement.

The nightmares came closer, and a second volley of fire ripped into them. The members of S-0 targeted the chest and head. The purpose of the shots was to strike the nightmares with silver bullets that would lodge within them. Aaron met the few that made it close with deft swings of his blade. He knocked aside burning limbs ending in claws, hooves, and eyes, severing them with heavy slashes that forced the frenzied creatures away long enough for them to be shot down. He never went for a killing blow, instead striking and deflecting the creatures around him in such a way as to keep himself rooted. His teammates knew the dance, and so long as he maintained his position, he knew he wouldn't be shot.

The nightmares were cut down with cold efficiency, screaming and heaving what passed for their final breaths. It was swift because it had to be. They weren't as simple as mere beasts and possessed a twisted cunning that allowed them to learn and adapt to hunt their prey. If they weren't slaughtered all at once, they would quickly scatter, either fleeing the village or hiding to wait in ambush. Removing them would become far more difficult after that. Thankfully, their attack had put them into a state of frenzy, and by the time whatever passed for reasoning made them realize that this new threat was fully equipped to deal with them, they were already burning into ash.

Aaron heard the truck approaching well before it arrived. Lenz veered into the town square with a speed that pushed the boundaries of common sense. Bringing the massive, armored vehicle to bear, he slammed into the nightmares from the side. The bulk of the transport sent them tumbling in a mess of their own gore. Lights glared to life, sensory overload providing a welcome stopgap for the members of S-0 to reload their weapons.

They were finished off quickly after that. Aaron watched his team inspect each smoldering pile of flesh individually, executing with precise, practiced shots those that looked like they might still be capable of moving.

It was almost too perfect to be true, but there was no time for relief. "A successful counterattack, Captain," Dalton said as he inspected his rifle. "You've exterminated the nightmares. Now what?"

"This much damage won't go unnoticed," Aaron replied. Even amidst the smell of smoke, he was nearly staggering at the scent of so much blood. "We'll post up at the edges of the town. Wait for him to arrive. Once he makes his way in, we'll tighten the net and ambush him."

Dalton snapped a fresh magazine into place. "That could work. He won't be able to resist. That just leaves the townsfolk."

Aaron adjusted his glasses, making sure they covered his eyes. "Not that you need me to say it, but stay calm. We'll be gone before it's a problem."

Now that Aaron got another look at them, he was better able to assess the state of the survivors, who couldn't have numbered more than two hundred. They were dressed simply enough, with many of them still in their nightclothes. Those who'd had time to equip themselves were outfitted in the unadorned browns and blacks of laborers and farmers, with some heavier leather and thicker cloth for the cold nights that the frontier brought. There were dozens on the ground, mutilated and bleeding out or dead, with more dropping in exhaustion with each passing moment. Of those who were still whole and healthy, half were attending to their fallen, while the other half stood still, pale and shell-shocked. A few looked in awe at the members of S-0, and a handful had their hands clasped in recitation of a silent prayer, though to Lord Sterling, or the Church of Paradise, Aaron was unsure. Still, it was better that way, that they were distracted. The fewer people who took notice of the specifics of his team, the better.

One stood out from the rest. He was the oldest of the crowd who was still alive, with a silver beard and pinched face covered in scars that wrapped around the side of his head. He must have once been a soldier. His body was lean, but what Aaron saw of his arms was built muscle that hadn't left him with age.

He approached S-0 slowly, leaning on an axe wet with tar-like viscera. The man scratched at his head and seemed to be looking for words to say to them. Aaron prepared an introduction to put the man at ease and distract him from any potentially uncomfortable questions, only to be interrupted before he could begin.

"What the hell did we walk in on?" Durham barked, striding forward. Half a head shorter than Aaron, she made up for it with the volume that accompanied her, no longer having to keep quiet. "You bring these people all the way out to this shithole without any silver to defend yourselves?" It was a magnitude less polite than what Aaron had planned to say, and clearly took the man aback. Nothing he planned to say survived first contact with Durham, and she pressed him. "Well? Spit it out. What's your name, man?"

Something was triggered in the old man, and he stood at attention. "Apologies, ma'am. They call me Frey now. I was once Third Company, Fang of Vexin. I speak for these people."

Durham nodded, going along as if she knew what the title meant. "At ease, man. Your people just got bloodied. But the world isn't ending yet, which means it's got to keep spinning. You clear?"

Aaron stepped forward, putting a hand on her shoulder. "What she means is, the night isn't over. You've got wounded to tend to, and the nightmares might not all be exterminated. We're going to sweep the area and make sure they're cleaned up. In the meantime, keep your people directed and keep them here. Can you do that?"

Frey inhaled with renewed focus, the direction clearly helping him cope with the shock of the night's events as well. He started calling out names, rousing a few other men and women who appeared to have more of their wits about them. They filed into nearby buildings, coming out with improvised bandages, organizing groups, and creating order from the chaos.

Aaron nudged Durham. "You're really keeping me on my toes here."

She shrugged. "Better to put pressure on to keep him from asking anything we can't answer. This'll keep 'em busy and out of our way. Like you said, right? We'll be gone before it's a problem."

Nightmares burned quickly; their bodies crumbled into bright coals within minutes of the silver piercing them. In a ritual born of necessity, S-0 inspected the smoking piles of ashes, fishing out the precious silver that was their greatest weapon. Despite the damage it inflicted on the soulless creatures, they picked it up without harm, collecting it to be repurposed for the future. While they did, Aaron and Dalton cataloged the bullets they had expended and considered the best locations in the town to take post.

"Ideally, we'd have two sets of eyes to watch for approach," Aaron said. "He'll follow from the north, and we can catch him when he enters from one of the ruins."

"He may go around the long way," Dalton considered. "He has to keep a distance from the nightmares in case they attack him."

Aaron frowned. "Maybe. He was known for stealth before he defected. We should assume he'll be close behind. Killing doesn't gain him anything when there are fresh bodies everywhere. I think he'll go for the low-hanging fruit."

Dalton looked back at the way they arrived. "We could appropriate a few. There's plenty of bodies to lure him out."

"No," Aaron said sharply. "Respect the dead."

"To respect the dead is to make use of the dead, Captain," Dalton countered. "That's how humans operate." Aaron winced. It was a fundamental truth, both on the frontier and in Paradise. He had never enjoyed it, even if it was how he survived. Moreover, to hear it said so matter-of-factly was almost as uncomfortable as the truth itself.

As it happened, they didn't have time to come to a conclusion, as their discussion was interrupted by Frey walking over to them. "Pardon, officers," he said. "If you're to sweep the rest of the town, can you stop by the old mill at the south wall? A few of our boys went there when the nightmares showed up. We've put up residence for its proximity to the river. The nightmares would probably have missed them, but they'd be sure to be buckled down there."

"Of course," Aaron said, seizing on the opportunity. "We'll sweep it last, since the nightmares will be unlikely to have found their way there. We'd be likely to hear it if that were the case."

In truth, he was quite certain that they would be fine. Having counted the creatures before they entered the village, he knew that they had been thoroughly dealt with. This was further reinforced when Lenz confirmed exterminating the one they left behind earlier.

So, why was he hearing something?

Aaron's hearing was his greatest tool, sharper by nature than even what the pact could provide. It was a prey-seeking sense, serving him to pick out life and individuals across space and through barriers. Even if he wasn't conscious of what it was, he could sense a disturbance when it was nearby. Frey was about to speak, but Dalton silenced him with a look. He turned to Aaron, having noticed his change in bearing.

Aaron shut his eyes in concentration. He filtered through the heartbeats around him, the weeping and wailing of the mourning townsfolk, and searched outward in the empty night. *Kill the truck,* Dalton ordered, and the sound faded away to clear Aaron's focus. Whatever it was, it was coming from the south, and it wasn't the bellow of a nightmare or scream of a last stand. It was faint, casual even, but stood out like a stain in the darkness.

It was the sound of laughter.

Aaron's eyes snapped open. "Form up!" he ordered. "We're moving south. Lenz, have the truck ready!"

S-0 was complying before they even considered why. He broke into a run, a hound off its leash. Pulling his radio for the first time, he issued further orders.

"Teams of two. Fan out and surround the mill. Lenz, be on standby. Weapons ready." His teammates fell into formation behind him despite lagging in speed. All but Durham, who paired up with him as the only one who could keep up.

"We didn't miss any, did we?" she asked him.

"We did," he growled. "The most important one of all. He snuck in through the confusion. The target's already here!"

–CHAPTER 3–

NEPHILIM

Unlike during their arrival, Aaron did not pace himself as he ran through the town. He dashed aside stalls and barrels full of supplies for restoring the old ruins. The refurbished houses that made up the heart of the little village quickly gave way to the dilapidated exterior that had led him to believe the place was empty. He would have thought it pointless were he not able to hear what was occurring.

"We underestimated the bastard," Durham said. "Never thought he could keep so close to nightmares without being turned on. Even for a nephilim, he was always closer to them than to us. No offense."

"No, you're right," he said. "But it ends here."

He checked to make sure his sword was secure in its sheath and drew his pistol. He had saved the silver bullets for their target, knowing that for all the horrors the nightmares might inflict, what they hunted was something even more dangerous.

Nightmares were a plague, a wound in the universe. They were roaming hoards, and as the little village had shown, a group unprepared to slay them faced extinction at their hands. In the frontier, they were the greatest threat to human life, and the soulless monsters were completely incapable of being reasoned with. But where nightmares were the deadliness of a landslide, nephilim were the deadliness of a serrated blade.

They were beings between human and nightmare; myth and legend given form through the abuse and mutative properties of magic. Millennia of conflict had given rise to a variety of species, but they were invariably long-lived and powerful. Most importantly, they drew that power from only one thing: human lives.

The mill came into view, and Aaron drew to a halt. It was a tower several stories taller than the rest, and wider than the houses he had passed. Outside it, two men lay lifeless on the ground, blood pooling beneath them from ragged tears in their necks. Aaron listened for heartbeats, for breath, and heard nothing. He stepped around the corpses, still listening intently. Within the mill, he heard hearts beating; their terror made them beacons to him.

The laughter was gone. Curtains were drawn over the only windows, and so he gestured to Durham with a hand. She understood it, falling into standby behind him. She would cover the door while the other members of S-0 made to surround any other possible exits. He knew that if he needed her, she would be ready to back him up or cut off escape.

Aaron smashed the door with a kick, in the process breaking a crude barrier that had been set up behind it. The room within was as simple as the rest of the town. A stairway led upward to the second floor. Furniture was scattered, and a small lamp had been overturned. A pot of flour rested on the countertop next to spilled salt and water, perhaps to prepare bread for the day.

There were no bodies, but Aaron smelled blood. He climbed the stairs, pistol leveled, and took in the scene.

From above came the muffled sound of turning metalwork, and in his nose, the scent grew more potent. The room was more spacious than the downstairs one, occupied only by a pair of beds. Leaned up against one was a woman. Still dressed in her nightclothes, she was huddled down and turned away from him, coughing. She heard his approach and turned, squinting.

"Who's there!?" she called.

"A friend," Aaron answered calmly.

He approached at a measured pace so as to not startle her. He knew that in the night, he would be little more than a silhouette to untrained eyes. She looked to be in her early twenties. Her hair was a mess, and there were cuts on her shoulder. She was shaking, and when he looked around her, he saw why.

Beneath her was a young man. He was bleeding from his stomach, and she was applying pressure to the wound with a tightly drawn bed sheet. Worse was his face, which was raked across and bleeding more still. Either she wasn't aware of the damage in the darkness, or didn't even know where to start helping him. One eye was intact, but the other was likely beyond saving. Knowing Aaron's target, his skull was also damaged. His breaths came slowly, but his heart was beating.

"Please." The woman's voice was hoarse as if she'd been strangled. "Under the bed. Rammi, go with him. Rammi?"

Her voice cracked at the lack of response, and another fit of coughing took her. Aaron saw no injury to her throat. Sickness? That alone might have spared her. With a hand, he lifted the bed, but there was nobody there. Above him still was the sound of the mill's machinery.

"He's still here," Aaron said.

The woman shook, a ragged prayer on her lips, and he placed a hand on her shoulder, avoiding the wound. "It's going to be all right," he whispered. "Stay here and stay with him. I'll bring her back."

Aaron left her there. It was cruel, but necessary. The man did need help, but moving him would be unsafe, and at least they were out of the way. Readying himself, he climbed to the next level. He took the stairs two at a time. There was no need for stealth. His presence was already known.

Turning gears and dusty furniture greeted him. In the center of the room, the mechanism turned around what looked like a massive screw. His pistol was heavy in his hand.

"Where is the girl?" Aaron asked the darkness.

No response. A low whistle carried through the room as wind found its way through cracks in the old walls. He had been prepared for the nephilim to be able to hide from him, but not the human too.

He settled on boldness for his tactic, clearing his throat and speaking with confidence. "There's no point in hiding. I know you're here, Silas."

At his utterance of the name, the wind changed directions. It carried with it the chill of the night, and a smooth, sensuous voice unbothered by the death left in its wake.

"I thought I smelled something rotten. You lackeys are persistent."

"And you're more cowardly than I realized," Aaron retorted. "I never thought I'd see a nephilim hiding behind a child."

"So, the cattle told you," the disembodied voice answered. "But how do you know she's not dead?"

Aaron continued to scan the room, not moving too far from the stairwell. It was disturbing that they were still hidden from his senses: unnatural. He pressed further. *Keep him talking and wait for him to slip up.*

"I don't think so," he said. "If you wanted a meal, both the man and woman downstairs were larger, and there's no point in a dead hostage. The only explanation that comes to mind is wanting to bargain with the townsfolk. I don't think you'd stoop so low, but considering you're following nightmares around like a carrion feeder, I shouldn't be surprised."

"They make fine hunting hounds, so long as you do not impede their natural function." Silas laughed, a halting, cruel sound that ended in a snarl. "I don't expect you to understand, though!"

The wind blew faster, and Aaron blinked. As if stepping from behind an invisible curtain, Silas was there.

The vampire might be mistaken for a human in the dark, but Aaron's vision was unimpeded. He had a handsome face with chiseled features, a strong jaw, and windswept brown hair, but those were just distractions from his true nature. His eyes were darker than a nightmare's throat, the same color as the clawed nails on his hands in which he held his hostage. She was a skinny little thing, with wild black hair and eyes bulging wide with terror. He covered her mouth, nails pricking the skin of her cheeks, but she was otherwise unharmed.

Silas smiled, but there was no pleasure in it, only the contraction of muscles and long fangs still red with blood. He breathed in deeply through his nose.

"I smell her magic on you. I remember you now. Yes…" He drew out each vowel in his speech. "White. I'm surprised to see you stray so far from your master."

Aaron put on a mask of composure, acknowledging his name with a slight nod. In his mind, however, he was not so calm. He knew what had just happened was not a mere trick of the light.

Keeping his tone casual, he replied, "Imagine my surprise, then. I didn't know you could use magic. I heard rumors you were a noble's bastard, but I never took them seriously."

In truth, he'd studied the target extensively. Nonetheless, Silas scowled, gray skin tightening in anger. "There are worse fates. You're nothing but a housebroken pet!"

"Pets that aren't housebroken get put out, and pets that bite get put down."

Aaron knew it was dangerous to antagonize the vampire, but it was even more so to let him remain calm. He needed to keep Silas on the back foot. Magic that could be used at will was rare, even for nephilim, and he was no longer certain of the target's capabilities. Thus, he poked and prodded, waiting for an opening.

"What the hell are you even doing out here?"

Silas's grip tightened around the girl, nails drawing blood. Aaron didn't look at her, didn't acknowledge her as an individual. That was the only way to protect her. He adjusted the aim of his pistol in response to the question, keeping the pressure on Silas to act. That was the way. She was a foreigner, not his concern. He knew that if Silas thought for even a second that he could use her as collateral, her life would be over.

It worked for the moment. The threat of the pistol kept the vampire's eyes locked forward. "Ah, yes, I'd forgotten your *proclivities*. Humans were never enough for you, were they? You only find thrill in hunting us."

"Is that why you betrayed Lady Baal? A thrill?" Aaron's finger rested on the trigger. Still, he didn't acknowledge the girl. "This is the only chance you'll get. Surrender to me now and you'll receive a fair trial."

Silas's lip curled, long fangs bared in limitless malice. "So arrogant. You're just like her. No, I didn't find them thrilling prey at all. I killed them because I wanted to. Because I labored too long for a commoner masquerading as a queen. I am Silas, son of House Bleakshroud, and I am no one's slave!"

Silas threw the girl straight at him with unnatural strength. He caught her out of the air, the force of the nephilim's throw nearly knocking him from his feet. He leaped sideways to avoid an attack, but none came. Silas simply made for the stairs.

Rolling to cushion their impact on the ground, Aaron had only an instant to aim and fire. The shot grazed but didn't pierce. The vampire snarled in pain but fled down the stairs.

"Stay here!" Aaron ordered the screaming girl and sprinted in pursuit.

Aaron cleared the flight of stairs in a single stride, the scent of the vampire's blood putting fire in his veins. The situation worked for him. He would herd the prey outside, and then Silas would be cut down by the members of S-0 watching in wait. That was his plan until he reached the first floor, and the air in front of him shifted. He saw it more clearly then, the space distorted as if it had become a physical surface. Silas wore it like a cloak, hiding himself from sight until the moment he struck, lunging at Aaron like an animal.

Clawed fingers sank into the hand that held his pistol, wrenching it from his grip. Aaron twisted into a punch that snapped Silas's head backward and broke a hole in the wall. He struck again with his elbow, aiming to stun and disorient, but was grabbed instead. They pushed back and forth with Aaron attempting to lock Silas in place, but he was taken off his feet and slammed into the stairwell instead, the sound of the cracking wood like a gunshot in his ear. He resisted the vampire's attempts to bite into his neck, only for Silas to throw him across the room and through a table.

"A disgrace," Silas hissed, picking up the pistol from the ground.

His lip was split from Aaron's strike, but in seconds, the flesh flowed like water and knit itself together. Unlike the nightmares, a nephilim was more than capable of recovering from any superficial damage. Wiping the blood away, it was as if the wound had never existed.

He pointed the gun at Aaron with vengeful satisfaction. "A taste of your own silver!"

His face then grew even paler, and he ducked aside to avoid Durham taking his head off with a swing of her sword. He tried to turn the gun on her, but he was clumsy with it, and she cut into his wrist, forcing the weapon from his hand.

Silas struck, hissing, but she danced out of his reach, delivering another slash that opened his chest. It was just a flesh wound, and mended in seconds, as did his arm. But it gave Aaron time to stand and draw his own sword, leaving the vampire surrounded.

"Running out of options, bloodsucker," Durham purred.

Silas threw his cloak at her. It was a desperate move, but effective. She couldn't risk him getting hold of her, so by blocking her sight, he forced her to retreat. He darted around her, and even though her blade cut into his side, he didn't slow. Aaron grabbed his pistol from the ground and pursued him. It was still in accordance with their plan: herd the prey. Silas would walk into their line of fire.

That was when he heard the townsfolk.

"Jess, Micah, Rammi? Are you there?" one of them called.

"No, no, no!" Aaron burst from the mill behind Silas, only to catch sight of a dozen of the citizens getting their first look at the corpses the vampire had left. "Get away!"

He tried to warn them, but it was too late. Worse, it was an admission of distress, and Silas was as sensitive to it as he was to the scent of blood. He sprinted straight toward them. In the group, Frey was the only one to realize the danger. He brought up a hunting rifle and landed a single, well-placed shot in Silas's chest. But not being silver, it didn't even slow him down.

He killed the first of them, a muscular woman with a shaved head, with a swipe to the throat. His hand passed through her flesh as if it were insubstantial, and she hadn't even fallen when he smashed aside the man behind her. The vampire's strength cracked the man's skull and sent him tumbling backward into the dirt. Frey tried to batter him with his rifle, but Silas broke the weapon and threw the old man backward, ripping through the chest of the screaming woman behind him, laughing all the while.

The people reeled in shock and horror while Aaron brought up his pistol to try to get a shot. Silas darted side to side, slipping between and grabbing a pair of gangly teenagers too brave or stupid for their own good.

"Take your shot, Aaron," he taunted from between their terrified faces. "Don't tell me you're feeling sympathy for some humans!"

Aaron looked at the two boys. Both had wild, curly hair, the same thin eyebrows, and olive skin. They might have been brothers. He couldn't ignore them, but couldn't let Silas go. His hand shook, and Silas noticed the weakness, his face twisted in disgust.

"You truly are a waste of blood, Aaron White. She will tire of you, and your death will not be gentle." He tightened his grip on the two. "Or maybe I'll just kill you here-"

The sound of a gunshot cut off his words. Silas twitched, not understanding what had occurred. Then he screamed. Silver didn't affect nephilim as harshly as it would a nightmare. He did not ignite outright. But the effect was the same as touching something red-hot, and unlike nightmares, the vampire felt pain.

Silas threw the boys away, scrambling and flailing to remove the bullet from his body. Whatever strange magic he commanded wrapped around him like a wound in space, blinking him in and out of vision with disconcerting silence. But he had been shot in the back, and not only was the sorcery failing him, but his healing factor was also impeded by contact with the hallowed metal. Now with a clear shot, Aaron put another round into his chest.

It drove the breath from him, and Silas backpedaled in a futile attempt at escape. Aaron took slow steps closer to him, Durham approaching alongside at a leisurely pace. She laughed at his pain.

"I like you better this way. You can still beg for forgiveness, you know."

Smoke was beginning to leak from the wounds. Aaron smelled burning flesh as strength ebbed from the proud nephilim. Silas looked at them with burning hatred, spitting his next words. "I will never kneel again!"

"Then die standing," Durham said with a shrug. She took his head with a single swing of her blade, swift and merciless. His body crumpled to the ground, and she put a bullet in his skull for good measure before grinning at Aaron beneath her mask. "Surrender complete."

He nodded, eyes on the pair of boys who had nearly lost their lives. They were panting on the ground. One of them threw up. It could have been worse. He approached the prone Frey and offered him a hand. "I told you to stay."

–CHAPTER 4–

PAINFUL TRUTH

Aaron hauled the old soldier to his feet, and Frey shook his head, still dazed. "You took off in such a hurry, I figured something was wrong. You came to our aid. I won't let you fight for us alone." He looked at the decapitated corpse and spat. "Filthy monsters. One day, Lord Sterling will wipe them all out."

Aaron affirmed him stiffly, uncomfortable with the thought. A small crowd had followed their leader and gradually picked their way through the ruined buildings behind him. He clicked his tongue, suddenly and acutely aware that they were on a timer.

He checked that his glove was still secure before reaching for the corpse of Silas. Frey made a sound of discomfort as he removed the silver bullet. It smoked and steamed in contact with the vampire's blood. He handed it to the elder man. "If you want to keep this place, you'll need a few more of these."

Frey took it reverently. He appeared to struggle to choose his words as he looked down at it. "We only had a few. Only ever seen the like in small groups and figured we could handle any nightmares we found out here. A buddy of mine who knew one of the Sterlings said they come in waves, ebbing and flowing with the decades. You believe it?"

"Only makes sense," Aaron muttered, preferring to keep any information to himself.

"It's not been so bad lately. The breach was what, twenty years ago? Only right that it gets worse now." Frey noted Aaron's expression and shook himself. "You're right, shouldn't mention the damn thing. Bad luck."

Aaron agreed while he took stock of his teammates. The hell breach was a taboo topic, but it wasn't what occupied his thoughts. They assembled before him, taciturn and regarding the living and dead citizens coolly. Dalton met his eyes in a moment of silent understanding, and he blinked acknowledgment.

"We're going to run a patrol of the village, just to be safe," he lied.

Frey shifted foot to foot. "Of course. For the best. You really came just in time, y'know? If there's anything we can do for you-"

"It's nothing," said Aaron. "We're the ones who should be helping you."

"I'm serious," Frey insisted. "Haven't seen soldiers this far out in ages. It's all we can do to..."

He slowed. Aaron didn't realize why at first. In the moment of confusion, he finally turned his attention fully to Frey and faced him. The old soldier was looking up at him, brow furrowed in concentration. Dalton took a step forward, but it was in vain. Frey squinted, tilting his head.

Something changed. Frey's eyes snapped open, his lips curled back, and his heart skipped a beat. A strangled shout of rage filled his throat. The hand that held the bullet clenched, drew back, and he punched Aaron in the face. It was a good technique, with the full weight of the man's body behind it. It knocked Aaron to the ground and split his cheek open. The pain bloomed hot and sharp. He heard the footsteps that followed and threw out an arm to keep Durham from moving past him. She had advanced, her sword still at the ready.

Frey's shoulders were shaking, his face radiating fury. "You. You're one of his kind! You're a nephilim too!"

Aaron stood, lightly inspecting the damage to his face. The pain faded quickly; his body healed automatically, reducing the wound to a dull throbbing bruise that vanished after a few seconds. He heard a collection of inquiries and gasps. It was only then that he realized he'd lost his glasses in the mill. Without them, his eyes were plainly visible, and Frey had only needed to see them to realize the truth.

"Your Lord Sterling is a nephilim as well," he reasoned. "That doesn't make us enemies."

But Frey was too smart for his own good. Aaron could see him figuring it out in real time. "But you're not a Sterling, are you? The only nephilim who serve alongside him are his own family. You expect me to believe another vampire?!"

Aaron sighed, still thinking he could defuse the situation. He pulled back his lip with a finger to show his teeth. "I'm not a vampire. No fangs, see?"

But that did little to curb the tension in the air. The people of the town were rallying behind Frey. Likewise, he heard the members of S-0 taking up positions behind him. Their mission was complete. If they couldn't use the town, then they had no need for it.

Durham adjusted her grip on her sword. "Remember, we're the ones who saved you. You're the fools who came to this place with no means of defending yourselves. Don't blame us just because you're the ones who got bled."

Frey still held the remains of his broken rifle. "You defend this thing? Do you have any idea what his kind has done? He's not a lord, not a warden! He's a vulture, picking at the dead!" His breath came heavily as he came to the realization. "Shit, that's why. Of course you knew they were coming…You're Baals! You used us as bait!"

"We were only hunting the vampire," Aaron explained, trying to keep the situation from getting bloodier. "We had no idea this place was occupied."

Throwing back his head, Frey laughed without humor. "Of course it is. That self-styled queen of yours who turned on the other wardens saw to that! Worse than the church of Paradise; at least they didn't leash monsters!"

He reached for a knife at his waist, and Durham took a step forward, fully prepared to take his life as she had Silas's. Only Aaron kept her from doing so.

"Don't do this," Aaron said. "There's no victory you'll win."

Frey looked at him with implacable hatred, then at the crowd gathering behind him. He ground his teeth together, warring within between the duties to destroy his foes and protect his loved ones. When he met Aaron's eyes again, the fire was still there, maybe even hotter than before, but it was contained.

"Get out," he said. "Leave, and never come back."

Aaron sighed, grateful for that at least. Lenz pulled up the truck, no doubt having waited on Dalton's command. He waited until each of the other members of S-0 were in it before boarding himself.

"Take care," he said, but they were no longer looking at him, having turned their backs to return to the ruins they had tried to make home.

–CHAPTER 5–

GRIN

The fire pit provided welcome warmth to the group. Though the sun was rising, it would be the afternoon before the cold of night left the air. Between the fighting and the rushed departure that followed, none of them had gotten much sleep in the last few days. The bunker they took shelter in was old, a remnant of the conflict between Lady Baal and Lord Sterling. Built under the roots of a great Atsali tree, it was an ideal shelter.

The vegetation that grew at the edge of the world was, like everything else there, scarce and resilient, and the Atsali embodied these ideas more than any other. The one they sheltered under was a modest size, some few hundred feet tall and nearly so wide, with roots wider than a man was tall and bone-white leaves shot through with scarlet veins. Their ridged bark was stronger than steel and sharp enough to cut a man with a touch.

When threatened, the trees would shake and tremble, sprouting human-sized thorns that impaled anything foolish enough to touch them. They were the product of wild magic, something as untamable as the nightmares but with none of their malice. It was all the security the team could hope for while trying to find rest.

Aaron tracked the movements of the teammates in his peripheral vision; they each had their own ritual after a hunt. The long silence in the wastes had been a heavy burden, and he wished them nothing more than the peace to lift it. Rista and Lenz liked to smoke everything they brought with them, idly bantering as they did so. He indulged them only so long as they kept by the window.

Brook reclined, stretching her long legs while she fiddled with a screw. She had an odd penchant for carving on small canvases, like bullet casings. It looked unbearable to work on, but she never showed any expression other than intense focus. Moore drew on scraps of paper, and Aaron deemed his current project inappropriate for work. Sif's eyes were closed, hair a mess over her face in an approximation of sleep. Though looking at the restless twitching of her finger, he knew this to be false. As for Durham, she was usually…

"Damnit, watch where you're touching!" Durham hissed as she squirmed. He had discarded his gloves to better assess the depth of her injury, and his thin fingers examined the area surrounding the damage as delicately as he could. She winced, but didn't say anything further, tightening the bandage herself.

"Take it easy," Aaron cautioned. "I'd rather be certain that none of your ribs are broken than deal with the consequences."

He leaned back, satisfied for the moment as she slung her jacket over her shoulders. Removing her mask left her mess of sandy hair only slightly more unruly. She looked down her nose at Aaron like he was scum, having long since mastered turning scowling into an art form.

The encounter with Silas had left her with a scratch, but it didn't compare to the many scars around her left eye, nor the largest that ran across the bridge of her nose and over her cheek. The skin, raised and pale white, stood out sharply against her tanned skin. Aaron watched her lip twitch, a sign that her irritation was especially potent.

"See something you like? Just wanna eat me up?"

He chuckled at that. "I appreciate you not shooting at me in the mill. How did the new sword feel?"

Her lip curled into a sneer, then relaxed into something softer as she rested her hand on the weapon. Drawing it slightly from its sheath, she traced a faintly glowing rune at the base of the blade. It resonated with the pact on her forearm.

"Yeah, well, I was going to, but my pact got mad. Always does when you're in deep. As for the sword, not great. Not *pristine*. Supposed to have some magic in it, but it just feels like a weapon you would use. Heavier than it should be and harder to swing. They call it Re-Human, whatever that means. I don't know what they enchanted it with, but it's no good."

"That bad?" Aaron asked, taking the sheathed blade in his hands. Her description was accurate; it was far weightier than it should have been, almost as heavy as his own.

As a nephilim, wielding silver was dangerous for him, but it also posed risks to the weapon due to his abnormal strength. He could easily shatter such a blade with a careless swing. As such, his weapon was forged of steel infused with a material called Hades. The material was rarer than silver and had unnatural properties of its own. Metal forged with it was a magnitude heavier than its size would suggest, but immune to wear or rust and virtually indestructible. He wondered aloud why they would give a weapon like that to a human.

"The Research and Development team wouldn't leave me alone about it. Not often anybody actually comes to me for something."

Reclining next to them, Gavin tucked dust-covered hair beneath his cap, shielding his eyes from the fire. "I'll admit, they're a weird bunch. Some uncomfortable mix of science and sorcery. I don't understand it, but they've spat out some good toys recently."

"Stupid," Durham drawled. "And no nephilim allowed to use it either. Guess that means you can't try it out."

"Even stranger since it isn't silver," Aaron considered, shivering at the thought. Their greatest weapon wouldn't treat him any more kindly than it had Silas. "I heard Lady Baal is interested in the weapons' performance as well. You might get a personal summons."

"Wonderful," she muttered under her breath, only too late remembering Aaron's unnatural hearing.

"Something to say?"

She ruffled her hair with a groan. "What? She's good to you 'cause you're not a potential meal. This ass isn't fond of being considered lunch."

Aaron rubbed his neck, both reveling in and bemoaning her sharp tongue. "I don't know about all that."

Much like the hum of the silver in his presence, she left an echo whenever she came to his mind. Nightmares, like the ones that attacked the little Sterling town, were frightening. Nephilim, like petty, cruel Silas, were frightening too. But Lady Baal was a warden, a ruler of the frontier, and a higher class of vampire. To her, even he was prey. Returning his attention to the present, he noticed the single absence in the room and stood.

"I think I'll get some air."

He left them behind and closed the door quietly. The room was well-insulated, making the sounds of the hallway more pronounced. Aaron wondered to himself how anyone could be so silent. If he didn't hear the man's heartbeat, he would have thought him a ghost.

Dalton leaned against the door, eyes closed but very much awake. His facial hair had grown unruly in their time away from the city, hiding sun-beaten creases that made his face look like a mountainside. His uniform, like the rest of theirs, was covered in dust. The "kiss of the wastes," the soldiers called it. His skin, however, was clean, courtesy of a small water basin set up nearby.

Aaron made use of the basin as well, cleaning his face as well as he could. He examined himself with a small mirror. In a way, cleaning made it worse. Pallid skin, sunken cheeks, and thin lips could be masked by the dirt. Hair fell in a mess over him, wavy and ink-black except for the streaks of white that had given him his name. The dust helped hide that as well.

However, there was little it could do for his eyes. Amber irises stared at him in sclera darker than black. They had given him away to Frey and would forever remain the striking beacon of his inhumanity.

They weren't even the worst part of him to look at. The top button of his jacket had come undone, revealing dark wormlike veins creeping at the base of his neck. He sighed, having only soured his mood, and turned to the silent Dalton.

"I can still smell the smoke," he remarked. "What will your wife think?"

"Not much, I hope. I'd consider it a low blow if you told her."

"You have nothing to worry about from me," Aaron said, taking out his flask.

The contents called to him, silky sweet and tantalizing, yet repulsive if for no other reason than his unnatural want for them. It was partitioned to him and the other nonhumans under Sitri Baal's command in equal measure. Though no vampire, he craved the blood all the same.

He spared a glance at Dalton, but the man's expression hadn't changed in the slightest. It never had, nor had any of the others, when they watched him feed. The drink was taken with silent thanks, not savoring the taste or rush that accompanied it. Setting the flask aside as one might hide evidence of wrongdoing, Aaron returned his attention to the matter at hand.

"Say what you want," he told his lieutenant. "No point holding back."

Dalton paused as if considering his words, though Aaron was certain he had known what he would say well before they left the town. "Nobody told us Silas could use magic. We'll need to have words once we get back. It could've gotten us all killed. Decisive action was essential for the kill. Well executed."

Aaron frowned. Not the issue at hand. "But..." he prodded.

"We shouldn't have been there, Captain White. It wasn't right."

Aaron recalled Brook's protests as they pursued the vampire well outside of their usual limits. "You didn't object when I made the call."

"Brook spoke out of turn," Dalton replied. "Promoting individuality makes us more flexible, but not if it undermines authority. That said, she had a point."

"She's highborn, after all," Aaron said. "But the situation never left my control. Silas was eliminated without a casualty. Someone like him running around with magic at his fingertips is a ticking bomb."

His lieutenant showed no indication that he was moved by the words. "Be that as it may, we crossed the borders without permission. We risked an incident with Lord Sterling. The nightmares and Silas both were his to deal with as soon as they left our territory."

"That town would have been wiped out," Aaron interjected. "And more if Sterling's response was slow. Worse, Silas might have come back. He killed our people."

"You're deflecting the issue," Dalton said. "If there had been any military presence in that little ruin, then things could have escalated beyond our control very quickly. Lady Baal was at war with Sterling not long ago. Let's say you're right and somehow Silas and the nightmares both die: offering foreign aid is-"

"I was out of line," Aaron interrupted. Dalton blinked in response. "You're right. Maybe things could have gotten out of control, but they didn't."

Dalton grunted. "I know why you made the call, and I'm glad we got to them in time. Just keep in mind that there are risks. Partly because of the political situation and partially because of what you are. Sterling may have lost territory in the conflict, but he's no fool. He fought Lady Baal to a standstill, and nephilim don't survive centuries without learning a thing or two about patience. We don't want to give him an excuse to attack, even if it means some lives may be lost. We have a duty to our own people first."

Aaron accepted the council, though it hurt to admit that the utilitarian perspective had merit. "Well, we're leaving now at least. The day you catch me lingering in Sterling's territory will be a desperate one. He doesn't even let other werewolves in if they don't join his pack. And when it comes to Lady Baal…"

He trailed off. How did Sterling respond to Lady Baal? Hate.

Aaron nodded, pulling his journal from his pocket and scribbling the words hastily. *Lord Roman Sterling hates her.* Once they were written, he read them again. The pages were full of short notes like that, jotted memories frozen into ink on paper so they wouldn't flee from his mind. That was his ritual, and though it seemed silly, it brought him a surety he couldn't fully explain. Some were recollections of wildlife that he'd found in the wastes. Some were the sights of ancient battlefields, littered with skeletons and rusted weapons. The latest words joined a hundred other errant thoughts that he deemed significant enough to immortalize despite their simplicity.

"Are you all right?"

Aaron pinched the bridge of his nose, wishing he had his shades as he became aware of a dull throbbing in the base of his skull. "Fine. Just trying to remember something. You saw Sterling in person once, didn't you?"

"That's right," Dalton said, lighting another cigarette. "Met Lady Baal that day, and my wife too."

"Not sure which floored you more?"

The ghost of a smile played under Dalton's beard. "Both terrifying. Thankfully, it died down, and we managed to keep our heads through it all."

"Hear, hear," Aaron said. A pause hung in the air. "Is that when you met me?"

Dalton took a long drag. "You've asked before. No, we were never acquainted. You arrived with most of the *other* special powers at that time, half-starved and two-thirds mad, as the rumor goes."

"So you've said," Aaron muttered, not remarking on his lieutenant's term for the inhuman. "Don't mind me," he shrugged it off with a laugh. "It was a long way from Paradise."

Something made a scratching noise. It was slight, too slight for even Dalton to hear. Nonetheless, it bothered Aaron. It accompanied a muted screeching, like mice in between walls. But the walls of the bunker were metal, and in the wastes, there would hardly be any suitable space for them. The larder was untouched when they arrived, leaving no suspicion of pests. And why did it seem to be so far away? Aaron wondered these thoughts to himself as he approached the bunker door.

"What are you doing?" Dalton asked as he walked.

The scratching was not like that of an animal; it was rhythmic and predictable. Aaron tried to place its location, but the insulation of the bunker worked against him. The wind outside howled, letting a low whistle settle in the air. Aaron took stock of his senses, calling upon them one at a time. He inhaled, tasting the air, pressing his hand to the door in order to feel for motion or heat against it.

"Call it 'fresh air,'" he said. A crash of metal, and the door unlocked. "I just have a feeling."

The door swung outward, and his blood ran cold when he beheld what waited outside.

It was hunched over the door, dwarfing it in height. Its flesh, pale and corpselike, was shot through with dark veins beneath the skin. With muscular legs and thin arms, it appeared oddly bottom-heavy, sporting wide hips and an unnaturally thin waist. A mane of dark hair hung from its head to the ground, but beneath it, Aaron could clearly see white teeth, too many white teeth, set in a rictus grin.

In the moment of silence, it released a quiet breath. Lifting its thin arm, it drew a long, claw-like finger across the frame of the door. It scratched at it quietly, mouth opening to breathe quietly. *"Haaa."*

Aaron slammed the door shut with enough force to shake the bunker, cranking the lock into place as Dalton cursed. His hand went for his pistol before he remembered where it was. "Dalton!" he barked. "Give me silver!"

A massive crash distended the door, knocking loose its reinforcement. Aaron held out his hand, not looking away. A weight settled in it. The pistol was lighter than his own, but it was serviceable. He leveled the weapon at the door. Dalton's heartbeat moved down the hall as he called to the others.

"Nightmare!" Aaron took slow steps backward. A second crash knocked screws free as the door bent further, bolts breaking and falling free. His sword hung at his side, but the hallway would not allow him to properly swing it. He exhaled.

The door flew off its hinges straight at him. Aaron ducked low, ramming it to the side with his shoulder. Despite his strength, it nearly floored him. The nightmare stepped through the now-empty frame slowly, its grin so still it could have been a mask. Aaron aimed for the center of its chest and fired.

The muzzle of the pistol flashed, and the nightmare jerked with the impact. He fired two bullets, placing them squarely in the creature's chest. Ears ringing, Aaron stood once more, trying to get a view of more nightmares before the one before him inevitably turned to ash.

However, that was not what happened. The nightmare did not writhe. It did not scream as the holy metal consumed its flesh in fire like so many before it. Instead, it regained its balance, dark blood leaking from the wounds it sustained. The perforations glowed as the silver burned, yet seemed weak and ineffectual compared to what they should have been doing; what Aaron had seen and experienced himself.

It was less effective than shooting a nephilim, except that the nightmare did not recoil in pain or slow down. Its teeth parted, and a series of clicks loud enough to shake bones assaulted him. He leveled the gun once more and shot again, targeting chest, limbs, and head. The result was the same. *Why?* His thoughts raced as he fired. *Why isn't it working? Is its skin too thick? No, that isn't what's happening. It's resistant!*

He discarded the empty mag, calling out for another, but none came. Only in that moment did he consider just how many silver bullets they would even have remaining, or if Dalton was carrying more on his person. He drew his sword. In the bunker, it was impractical, but better than nothing. A series of breaths, heightened heartbeats, and cursing accompanied the squad's arriving and laying eyes on the nightmare.

It had been reeling from the impact of a dozen rounds in its torso, but with their arrival, its demeanor changed. For the first time, the creature appeared to notice something other than him. It hunched forward and then sprang into motion.

Aaron threw himself toward it. Unable to swing his blade comfortably, he instead settled for driving it straight into the nightmare's heart.

It was stronger than he expected: almost as strong as Silas. It drove him backward with the force of its charge. A pain in his gut. He looked down. The hilt of his own sword had slammed into him. The blade dug several inches into the creature's torso, but no farther. He twisted, but it remained firm, like it was stuck in bone. Another click, and the nightmare tensed.

"Shoot it!" he yelled, and the world changed directions as he was thrown into the wall.

More gunfire helped reevaluate his location relative to the rest of the bunker. He had landed on his head, evident by the warmth running down the side of his face, but he could think straight. He kept down. Much like the nightmares, he had little to fear from conventional damage. But the world was spinning, and standing might mean getting shot with a silver bullet. That would be dangerous.

If any doubts remained that the nightmare was special, they were quashed by what happened next. Another score of bullets riddled it and amounted to little. It bled plainly enough, but whatever inherent resistance it had meant that it didn't combust from the holy rounds. In addition, its frame was highly optimized for its weaponry. Silver itself was the weapon against them. As such, the guns they wielded were designed to be lightweight, maneuverable, and able to lodge the bullets within their foes so that they would burn from within. The nightmare's thin body and limbs made such wounds especially difficult, reducing successful hits to glancing blows. Then, with whatever protection it had, those that did land didn't ignite as they should have. It twisted its head, clicking and chittering. Aaron tried to steady himself, but found only the bent door when he reached out his hand. Though it contorted in the strength of his grasp, it offered no solid ground.

"Oh, for God's sake!" Durham yelled and threw a knife directly into the nightmare's eye.

The creature staggered, letting out a shrill groan. Aaron's hand found the wall, and the team made the wise decision to retreat. They had barely made it around the corner before the creature slammed into it, hurling itself with tremendous speed and power.

Aaron staggered to his feet. His head still swam. He reached into his coat pocket and pulled out his flask. With a grimace, he emptied it. The world came into razor-sharp clarity, shadows vanishing into a haze of red. The throbbing in his skull remained. He picked up his sword and ran.

The scent of sweat and the vibrations of heartbeats led him to the central chamber. He burst through the door to the sight of Durham swinging Re-Human into the nightmare's shoulder. It dug deep, but it stuck on the creature's collarbone. It swung an arm, which Durham avoided, but Rista, attempting to reload his gun, took the hit. It flung him against the wall, and the nightmare moved for him, wrenching Re-Human free of Durham's grip and sending her sprawling.

Aaron swung his sword into the creature's wrist, lopping off the hand an instant before it could latch onto Rista. However, the force of his swing also sent his blade sparking from the floor, shaking his grip and allowing the nightmare to swing its other arm at him.

It knocked his sword from his hands and slammed him to the floor. Rista bludgeoned it from behind with the butt of his pistol, but it was of no use. It lunged for him once again, but Aaron had already recovered and drove his fist into the creature's jaw from the side. He saw a tooth knocked loose.

The creature did not react in pain, and merely turned its attention back to him, fixing him with a curious stare with its single remaining eye before biting into his hand. Pain shot through him, and he struck the thing. It didn't react except to bite down harder. It pulled and twisted, and he did his best to move with it, but couldn't free himself from its grip.

Why won't it die?! he thought as he pummeled the nightmare, but it was not inclined to answer him. He wrapped his free hand around its jaw, attempting to force it open or break it. It only latched down harder, his bones grinding between its teeth. He looked at Durham's knife, still in the creature's eye socket, flesh smoldering around it. It was working, but not quickly enough. He spied the strip of raised surface along its grip, and he gritted his teeth, wishing he still had his gloves.

Aaron reached around the creature's head, grasped the hilt of the knife, and twisted.

"Heee!" It released a sound between a shriek and a roar, one that he wished he could replicate as his arm erupted in agony. The silver ridge along the handle, specifically designed to stop something like him from touching it, was as hot as a flame in his hand. It seared and smoked, sending tremors through his body almost as if attempting to throw him off.

He tightened his grip, drawing out even more pain from the purifying metal, but did so with the certainty that anything less would have caused him to let it go. The nightmare tried to throw him, but Durham delivered another blow with Re-Human to its leg, taking away its ability to properly maneuver. He wrapped his arm around the nightmare's neck. It smelled like death, decay, and his burning skin.

Digging his feet into the ground, he used the thing's momentum against it. Drawing on his inhuman strength, he hurled the creature into the wall, the impact driving the knife out of the back of its skull.

Flames erupted from within the creature's head. Its long limbs twitched and spasmed, yet it slowly sank to the floor, dragging against the interior of the bunker and leaving a trail of steaming blood.

Aaron turned to Durham and Rista. "Where are the others?"

A wave of fatigue struck him as the pain in his hand swelled once more. He breathed in ragged gasps, unable to keep his pain silent. A flickering line of blackened skin marked where the silver had burned him, yet the pain did not stop at his palm; it snaked up his arm towards his body like venom.

"Aaron!" Durham called out while limping toward him, clutching her injured side.

"Where are the others?" he repeated.

"There's another one outside!" she answered. "We're out of bullets, and the pistols aren't doing shit! They went for the truck."

"Understood," he growled, rising to his feet. He spared a glance at Rista, who, while conscious, held tightly to an arm that might have been broken. "Stay together and prepare to move," he ordered. "I'll go deal with the nightmare." He looked at his discarded weapon. His burned hand was unresponsive. "Take my sword. I need something heavier."

He left the bunker not a minute later. His makeshift weapon trailed him, slowing him as he contorted it through the rear exit. It was a bit unwieldy, but necessary for his purpose. Their gear was in the truck, hidden in a small cave formed by the roots on the east side of the Atsali the bunker was built under. It made sense for the team to make for it. Without greater stopping power, he doubted anything short of a shot through the eye socket could down another one.

Above him loomed the towering tree, its bark the color of tarnished brass. It twitched and trembled unnaturally, as if it too was disturbed by nightmares' presence. Aaron dragged his weapon behind him as he navigated the uneven terrain that the colossal roots of the giant created. More gunshots.

"I'm out!" Sif yelled. Aaron rounded the far side of the tree and saw them.

He took stock of the situation. They were separated by about ten yards. The nightmare in question was similar to the first; long and tall, with distended limbs and a twisted head. This one was bald, making it much easier to appreciate its stretched grin and tombstone-shaped teeth. It walked on all fours. Burns covered its side, but didn't slow it down.

Hissing and clicking, it moved at Sif, but Gavin pulled its attention by shooting at it twice. An empty click, not from the nightmare but from the empty gun, dominated the air. Other members of S-0 were trying to make for the truck without alerting the creature. The vehicle had their weaponry, but if it was damaged, they were in even bigger trouble. Dalton pulled out Aaron's pistol.

"Get down!" he yelled as he braced himself.

He handled it well. The gun was stronger than a standard-issue pistol, meant to deal deathblows to dangerous nephilim like Silas. However, the long slide, heavy weight, and extreme recoil made it unwieldy for an ordinary man. The first shot slammed the nightmare's side with enough force to crack bone, but the second only grazed it.

The nightmare let out a shriek. Done with chasing prey, it leaped for Dalton. For his part, his lieutenant only adjusted his aim for the airborne monstrosity that assaulted him, but Aaron didn't wait. He sprinted as fast as he was able, time seeming to drag ever slightly as he came between them. The nightmare didn't even acknowledge him; its lifeless eyes saw only their target. He took great satisfaction in the way they contorted as he swung the steel door into it with all the strength his good arm could muster.

He swatted the nightmare from the air like an oversized fly, slamming it into the loose dirt with the force of a car crash. The echo of the impact left the world briefly silent. Even the nightmare couldn't find a sound to create, though Aaron suspected that was merely the effect of the blunt force. He looked at the door in his hand. The impact had nearly crumpled it, yet the monster was still alive.

It twitched and shuddered, then began to rise. He clubbed it again, and still, it didn't stay down. He looked at the Atsali tree looming overhead, and a thought occurred to him. When it tried to rise again, he braced the ruined door between it and himself and charged the creature, shoving it into the base of the tree's armored trunk. The air groaned as the tree shuddered and shook in outrage, and Aaron frantically backpedaled as a half dozen thorns erupted from the nightmare.

And still, it moved. "I don't care if it's silver or not, just get me a gun that can kill this thing!" he yelled. Brook and Lenz complied. Lenz carried the stake driver, and Brook carried Dalton's sniper rifle. "Positions!" he ordered, and they took aim, moving into places where they would simultaneously shoot without the threat of harming one another.

The nightmare made a final attempt to free itself, a strangled gargling replacing its previous vocalizations. Aaron motioned forward. Wordlessly, two triggers were pulled. Both the bolt and bullet penetrated the thing's head, carving away flesh and bone in an instant. It exhaled, then fell still.

Quiet claimed the air. The members of his squad stood around him, hearts beating rapidly. The bright light of day was oppressive to his eyes, but his burned hand had frozen stiff, and he didn't have his shades anyway.

"Captain," Dalton began, but Aaron cut him off.

"Get the truck ready now," he ordered, for the wastes were vast, and it seemed only he had heard the nightmare's final sound.

Carried on its last breath, a single word. *"Help."*

–CHAPTER 6–

HOMEWARD PATH

In the back of their transport, the members of S-0 sat in agitated silence. Their truck was built for traveling anywhere and everywhere, but with speed came an uncomfortable amount of movement. It was loud and disorienting, requiring constant adjustment if one wished to stay upright. Nevertheless, its passengers were beyond the point of caring. Following their hasty departure, three more of the wiry, distended-limbed nightmares pursued them, and each went down slower than the ones before it.

With a sense of sickness, Aaron watched the wilderness pass behind them. Though his night vision was impeccable, the daytime made the desolation starker. If one ventured far enough east, at the edge of humanity's domain, the wildlife began to fade away. This was not just due to the dry, inhospitable climate, but the nightmares themselves.

The creatures sought out, attacked, and consumed living beings, with a preference for humans above any others. In the absence of humans, they would hunt animals. When they had eaten down to the insects, they would start destroying flora or catch the scent of new prey far off on the horizon.

The team's flight had sent them sharply to the west in an attempt to flee from the monsters. With Rista and Durham hurt, Aaron had no desire to wrestle with these new and dangerous foes, and he wasn't much better off. His hand had begun to heal from the silver, but slowly. He wasn't used to that.

Ordinarily, his body would heal minor injuries in seconds, and anything that appeared serious would usually vanish over a few hours, especially if he was fed. The holy metal was different, and its ache faded in and out of his thoughts, ebbing or swelling in between breaths. Attempting to distract himself, he focused on the returning sight of nature. They began to find themselves passing larger and larger clusters of healthy trees, and hints of wildlife made themselves known to him despite the truck's discomfort.

"This is too much," Durham said with a huff. "You really think it was worth it for a piece of shit like Silas?"

He shrugged, adjusting his position with the latest bump in their path. "They're all pieces of shit. We wouldn't be after them otherwise. But we were able to make a difference. Whether they appreciated it or not, we did save those people."

"I didn't know words could make me so nauseous."

"Nauseated," Aaron corrected. She punched his arm. "Never a bad time for self-improvement," he defended.

"You should 'improve' your tactics unless you're looking to cook yourself," she replied. Aaron gave a halfhearted laugh, but a strong grip on his shoulder took the humor out of him.

He ignored her pointed look. "I'll be all right."

"Get blooded," she said, pulling up her sleeve. "The pact doesn't lie, unlike you."

The mark of Baal glowed on her arm, a pair of spears crossed at the heel before beams of light. Aaron itched at his collarbone where his own was etched. If his eyes had been enough for Frey to throw a punch, seeing the pact would likely have seen the man try to tear his throat out. They were marks of favor granted by highborn nephilim to their subordinates. The nobles used them as contracts, guaranteeing loyalty and granting boons in return.

Lady Baal had made a great many. For the members of S-0, they granted sharpened senses and enhanced endurance to better combat dangerous and cunning foes in their own domain. For Durham, it also granted her something like a sixth sense. She'd always had great instincts, but the mark gave her notice whenever the members of the team were in danger as well. As if on cue, it pulsed in tune with the throbbing in his hand.

"I'm fine," Aaron insisted pointlessly. He flexed his fingers, forcing them to move through the echoes of the pain that burrowed into his veins. A straight line of necrosis had burned into his pale skin. It had been some time since he had been touched by silver. Despite the pain, there was an odd sense of comfort to it. That was the way it was supposed to be.

"It will scar," he muttered, more to himself than her. "But it won't stop me. Benefits of being a monster."

"You're not a monster, you're a freak," Durham jabbed. "Those things were monsters. Have you ever seen anything like that?"

"Haven't even heard of something like that," Aaron said.

"You once said Sitri caught a silver blade bare-handed."

"That's Lady Baal," Aaron said. "Strong nephilim are resistant, but it still burned her. Silver should ignite nightmares on contact. A way to resist it changes the entire dynamic of fighting them. If enough of those things appear somewhere at once, we could end up like that town nearly did. It would be a disaster."

"With bodies like that, we need power," she remarked. "Piercing attacks are no good, but slashing seemed to work well enough. We just need to target joints or the neck. Nephilim are well-suited to it."

"Don't forget crushing," Dalton said. Aaron and Durham snapped their attention toward him, having not even noticed his movement. He looked at them calmly and continued, "I owe you one for that."

It took Aaron a second to find his voice. "Not the most elegant weapon I've ever used, but I needed something heavy."

"At least it was good for something," Durham said. "Both doors caved as soon as they started knocking."

"I noticed that," Dalton concludes. "You don't find that strange? That they found us so soon after the others?"

"What are you implying?"

"Nothing," he answered. "At least, not until we learn more. We lost half a pound in silver bullets just to learn they were ineffective. Silver is life. We can't let that happen again." Excusing himself, he returned to his place beside Moore and Brook, where he sat quiet and unbothered by their motion.

"He's really very serious, isn't he?" Durham said dryly.

It was a shared sentiment. A decorated veteran with more experience than anyone in S-0, the Deadeye had earned his reputation as one of the deadliest warriors in Sitri Baal's employ. Aaron's free hand twitched. It had reached for his flask, but he knew it to be empty, and scolded himself for the wants of his body. Suddenly aware of it, it began to creep on him. It was a scratching in his throat, an illness of his mind. Though he was in control, it was always within him.

When no further nightmares appeared, they adjusted their course more strictly north. Still, travel was slow, the better to remain undetected by any possible agents of Lord Sterling, or worse, a member of his pack. Thankfully, they didn't encounter anyone else and fully escaped through the reaches of the wastes without incident, all expressing unspoken relief when more Atsali trees came into view.

The immense trunks first appeared alone at the edges of their vision like the one they had sheltered under, but gradually grew in number as the group traveled. They rustled as S-0 passed them by, more in response to their presence than any breeze. Other smaller trees joined them until they navigated through woods, then light forestry. Aaron made a note of them in his journal.

It was another day's travel in the truck, but one they could take swiftly. Relief came to everyone when they encountered a paved road. In a world where danger could attack with teeth and claws at any moment, the efficiency of movement was something of unquantifiable value. Lady Baal herself had deemed the construction and maintenance of roads and railways a national priority, but she wasn't a god. They could only reach so much of their own territory, let alone contested zones. A bit uneven and unused, it was still a welcome improvement from the constant, sickening rocking that had plagued them until that point.

Aaron drove the rest of the way himself, moving through the night with the singular thought of their destination. At the dawn of the third day of flight, it came into view.

When Lady Sitri Baal came to power, she made no secret of her intentions to expand. In defiance of the nightmares that threatened her, she had abandoned her own ancestral capital to create a new one. As with most great structures in the frontier, she built on what had once been ruins.

The Spearhead Mountain was once home to a fortress supposedly raised over a thousand years ago when the territory in the frontier was at its most expansive. The Baal ruler at the time had chanced on a vein of silver nearby and leaped at the opportunity to monopolize such a precious resource. Haste had led to disaster, however, and an attack by a swarm of nightmares saw the land laid to waste and hundreds of miles lost. Sitri Baal had made the great effort to reclaim the landmark and turn it into something grander than it ever was before.

The mountain was one in name, but closer to three shorter peaks connected. They formed a point that was its namesake, directed eastward. The castle that had been raised there made for excellent defense on account of its steep position, but the young Baal had grander ambitions, and learning from the mistake of her ancestor, had taken no half-measures in securing her seat. Spearhead used the backing of the mountain as a defensive wall from which to build a city. Sheltered behind the "point" of the spear, the new capital had been built.

One of the benefits of being located so far from developed land was that resources were largely untapped. The silver vein was expansive, and no fewer than three mines were to be found in the area, not just for the holy metal but also for iron used to forge steel. It was a rich bounty, but not without risk. In many ways, it was unthinkable, bringing so many people so close to the flesh-eating monstrosities that sought them. With nightmares attracted to large gatherings of humans and no others of its kind around, the city was under constant threat. But for that purpose, it was also well-fortified.

Nightmares would almost invariably come from the east, and when they did, they would encounter the full might of the garrison there. If all else failed, the defenders could rely on Lady Baal herself, situated in the angular granite keep she called her home. It was that keep that caught the eye as they approached the city, and that called to them with the end of their mission at hand.

They didn't approach from the safer western entrance. To do so would funnel them through the traffic that accompanied more public affairs. Government agents, merchants, and artisans brought in a steady stream of goods to the city year-round, and the Ironblood River, located just west of the mountains, housed an ever-growing number of factories that the working class operated. Military craft instead entered from the east.

The pointed tip of the Spearhead Mountain was the primary shield against the threat of nightmares, and it was appropriately reinforced. Housing a moderate-sized base on its slopes, it served as both the primary garrison for the Baal soldiery and a staging ground for missions into the wastes. As S-0 approached one of the great gates that led to blessed safety, they received their first indication that something was amiss.

The gate was not open. This was not in itself a problem, but Aaron's suspicion began when the guards atop the watchtowers didn't immediately signal upon their arrival. Their truck came to a full stop without any response.

"What are they doing?" Sif wondered aloud, inputting a code into the truck's radio. A moment later, she received a reply. "They said to wait!" she exclaimed.

"No accompanying code?" Aaron asked.

"Code is zero-one-five," she replied. "I haven't heard that one before, though."

"I have," Moore called from the back. "It's an older status, waiting for confirmation. Something is off on their comms, most likely. They're stalling."

A pang in his head. Aaron felt his eye twitch. "Input my personal code," he commanded. Sif nodded, pinging again. The reply was faster this time. "They're working on it."

He was incredulous. Leaving them out with his code was disobeying an order from a superior officer. Normally, the only situation that could prompt such a response would be a nightmare attack. But they could clearly see that no nightmares were to be found around them, and they would have been informed of such a thing besides. "On what grounds?" he asked.

Moore made his way to the front of the truck. "Try this one," he said, handing her a piece of paper. Sif entered the code. Her eyebrows drew together. "They're going to open it."

"Of course," Aaron muttered. "But why would they have waited? What was the code you used?"

"I started in the garrison," Moore answered. "These delays without an explanation mean something's off in the chain of command. A missing lead officer or a conflicting order. That one is the universal reply for not caring. Might make for a hassle later, but you looked like you wanted progress."

Aaron bit his thumb in agitation, cracking the knuckles of his free hand. "That's just perfect. The last thing we need is trouble at home."

The gate finally opened, revealing armed guards to usher them in. The dark uniforms of the city watch had a tendency to blend together, but they were particularly dense that morning. His unease grew worse.

The guards directed them forward while the gate shut heavily behind them. Aaron observed the commotion, noting their haste and urgency. When they finally disembarked, he was met by a man he did not recognize.

His uniform bore an additional stripe that marked him out from the rank and file, but other than that, he seemed quite ordinary. He was young and clean-shaven with a strong jaw and neatly combed black hair. Though the man didn't look entirely comfortable in his role, he greeted S-0 as a whole with due politeness. "Welcome back," he said evenly. "We'll take care of offloading your transport."

"Where is your commanding officer?" Dalton asked before Aaron could get a word in.

The soldier's expression wavered just a hint as he turned his attention to the individual rather than the group.

"Lieutenant Dalton! Apologies, but Captain Barnes is currently indisposed," the watchman answered. "I am receiving all inbound travel in his place."

"Receiving, huh?" Durham muttered, cracking her neck. "You know we just risked our skins out there, right? Your job's to open a door. Not much of a reception, keeping us waiting."

Both the assembled watchmen and the other members of S-0 shifted. Aaron fixed her with as withering a look as he could muster, but it was too late. She shrugged.

The young man didn't react with intimidation or anger, the usual responses to Durham's lack of filter. "Second Lieutenant Durham, is it? Once again, it was the captain's orders that, while he was gone, the gate stayed shut. It just took us a minute to identify your code. It isn't a regulation unit, so—"

Aaron heard her take a breath and decided to intervene before she could speak again. He took a half step forward. "What's your name?"

The man took stock of him directly. The uniforms of S-0 didn't display their ranks, but if the man knew Dalton and Durham, then he undoubtedly knew who Aaron was, too. He also surely knew that Aaron could read the last name on his breast pocket easily enough. The soldier exhaled a breath.

"Warrant Officer Levi Orendal."

It was a well-composed response, if not acknowledging Aaron's name or rank. "Then, Orendal, if something important is holding Barnes's attention, I'd like to hear about it."

Orendal drew in a breath, his pulse picking up. "I have no such information to provide you with at this time," he stated.

A faint stirring caught Aaron's attention, and he turned his head to the noise. Lurking at the fringes of the assembly of humans was another figure. It had avoided his notice, though it did nothing to hide itself. Once he laid eyes on the nephilim, he wondered how he had ever missed her. She was clad in a buttoned black shirt that brought to mind the wealthy merchants and local governors who visited the city. Around her neck, she wore a golden chain choker, while her long silver hair was tied up with a red ribbon. Her fingers ended in long claws, which she was careful to position as she rested her face against her palm.

Her lower body was wrapped about the edge of one of the guard tower's support beams. In place of legs was a muscular serpentine tail covered in copper scales and spotted with dark hourglass markings. Wrapped around her tail and arm were a pair of golden bands, each etched with the Baal family crest.

The two regarded each other for just a moment. Aaron hadn't seen the naga before and didn't recognize her. She showed little emotion beyond light amusement and stretched her arms, reclining to better absorb the morning sun. Aaron returned his attention to Orendal before him, where the man hadn't made a single response to his behavior. *Other nephilim active on guard duty? No code for that, I suppose.* He cracked the joints of his fingers.

"Very well. I'll let you take it from here, then."

Durham groaned. "Boring. I was hoping for a fight."

Aaron excused himself from the situation, leaving the humans to their business. Return from any mission required an inventory of all weaponry as well as a physical on anyone exposed to nightmare activity. For excursions outside populated areas, this was doubly true. But, as a non-human, he was exempt from the latter of the two, and so left it to his team. His mind was too busy and his body too uncooperative to waste more time. The results of their extermination mission, as well as the attack that followed, were to be drafted and reported immediately.

To ease his travel, he boarded a shuttle that would ferry him to his destination. There were two ways to navigate the eastern base camp. He could either go up the roads through the main garrison on the steep mountain slope or travel straight through one of the Spearhead valleys to enter the city proper. He chose the latter, as officially, he did not operate using the east garrison. Instead, the headquarters of S-0 was located at the base of the road that led to Sitri Baal's very castle.

Something was different. Passing through the basecamp to the city itself, Aaron noticed there were fewer soldiers than normal. Not only that, but those he did see watched him with unusual attentiveness. Most preferred to not look at him, and those who did were usually only doing so to reaffirm his appearance. The S-0 uniforms were distinct but undeniably military.

Under normal circumstances, it would end with a once-over, but gazes were lingering on him more than he was comfortable with. Even when they took notice of him watching them in turn, they didn't avert their eyes. It almost looked like they were waiting for something from him, and that was particularly unsettling. His arrival at his barracks provided a welcome sense of normalcy. The guards at the gate recognized him immediately and greeted him, and the gate swung open before he even had to slow down.

The ground floor of the building served as one of several checkpoints throughout the city that stored supplies in case of nightmare attacks and hosted one to two dozen soldiers at any given time. Though its location meant it rarely served this purpose, the rotating personnel were also there to serve as a deterrent for any visitors while the members of S-0 were away. The interior walls were the dark green common to Baal construction, with the ever-present family crest hanging over the front desk. He strode past those present like a shadow, for they had long since moved past acknowledging his existence except to regard him warily.

He climbed the spiral staircase with echoing steps, eyes passing over the spindles shaped like spears before approaching a locked steel door. Though he could enter it with a combination, the most effective key was the mark at his neck, and without a touch or sound, it swung open before he even needed to slow his pace.

The upper floors were more comfortable than the utilitarian ground level, hosting his offices, meeting rooms, and library, as well as rooms for housing, storage of food, weapons, and other personal belongings. Polished wooden support beams lined the ceiling, and several paintings decorated the walls. It had been only one when he was assigned: a dreary landscape set to the bloody rising of the sun. Aaron had taken it upon himself to add others since. Rolling hills, a shadowed forest, and a glimmering lake provided splashes of color that brought a smile to his face.

At the end of the room was a high wooden desk. Though it was unoccupied, Aaron's sensitive ears clearly heard the presence of the other man. As he waited for his arrival, he drew curtains over each of the windows, casting the room in low light better suited to his nature.

He heard the door open and took in the familiar scent of paper and incense. "Eric, is that you?"

"Who else?" replied the man in question as he returned to his desk. Eric walked with confidence, but his expression betrayed the discomfort of his weak leg. Once a member of S-0 himself, he had been wounded in the field and removed from active duty. His cane clacked against the floor with every other step he took. He offered a nod before sitting, one file of many in hand.

"Welcome back, Captain. Did all go well?"

"Well enough," he replied, taking a seat of his own. He listened for others on the main level, but found the building silent. "Is it just us?"

It would be unusual for any other teams to enter their quarters, but not unheard of. Eric kept records of their targets, past and present, and had access to a variety of resources on nephilim and nightmares. That would be fine ordinarily, but at that moment, Aaron didn't want to have their conversation overheard.

Eric sighed. "For now. With the entire team gone, it was just me and a few others. Good thing you returned when you did. It's been a week since you were expected. They were about to send someone out to look for you."

"Yeah," Aaron said. "About that. I want to set up a meeting with Lady Baal."

He expected pushback, if not stunned silence. He received the silence, but it wasn't "stunned." Eric lit another incense candle, placing it off to the side. His heavy brows and hooked nose cast shadows that covered the side of his face. "I don't suppose you could ask for something else? Maybe the sun in your pocket so you can see easier during the day?"

Aaron actually laughed at the joke. "That brings me to my second request. Want to tell me what's happening in the city? We were practically barred at the gates."

Eric sighed, pulling open his desk drawer to procure several bottles of differing liquids. One of them was marked for Aaron, and the contents were so alluring, it all but made him salivate. He bit his tongue, but Eric noticed. He poured a large glass calmly. "Looks like the mission didn't go 'well enough,' as you say."

"Not perfect," Aaron admitted, downing the glass in a moment. The contents stilled nervous tremors of his muscles and lightened his head.

A heat spread through his chest, and the ache in his hand dulled, then gently subsided. "I'll tell you later. First, it's your turn."

"Nothing is certain," Eric said. "All I know is what the rumor mill churns out."

"You wouldn't be saying it if you didn't have proof. What's the news?"

Eric breathed the incense with a serene expression. Then he exhaled and was solemn once more. "The Paradise Church is officially making headway in the East."

Aaron's hand clenched, crushing the glass and driving shards of it into his already injured hand. "Ouch," Eric remarked. "I thought you were past that."

"Sorry, sorry," Aaron muttered. He pulled his glove free in order to better pluck the pieces of glass from his skin. His nails, also evidence of his true nature, glinted a bruised shade in the candlelight. However, having just fed, the pain faded in moments. Eric handed him a towel, and he wiped the blood and glass clean. By the time he was done, the damage was already repaired, leaving only a strip of dark red scar tissue from his prior injury.

Eric whistled. "That looks like silverburn if I've ever seen it. Don't tell me you pissed off Durham."

Aaron flexed the hand, enjoying the freedom of motion that had returned to him. "Well, it was her knife, but that's beside the point. Let's just say things got a bit strange out there. As for the Church, well…"

"A hot mess if ever there was one," Eric said. "It's a load of problems just waiting to happen, and I haven't heard a thing from the castle, but I'd bet anything *she's* in a rage over it."

Aaron shivered. "Not a sight I'd like to see. I hope the castle is all right. Do we know what and why?"

"Their efforts have been purely humanitarian, for now," Eric answered. "They started moving in a few days after you left. A couple of the churches saw some of the Paradise priests show up with food and water and silver; all that shit."

"Not the most unsettling on its own."

"Maybe not on its own," said Eric. "But it was too coordinated. Given their choice of region, there are half a dozen other places they could have chosen, but instead, four of our most westbound towns were occupied, and all of them were hotbeds to begin with."

Aaron raised an eyebrow. "Hotbeds?"

"You know the type, far enough west to benefit from Spearhead's protection, but towns that used to belong to Eydis Nero. Though they lost the war a decade ago, some still live who are old enough to resent the occupation. As for the why…seems pretty obvious, don't you think?"

He stared at Aaron, drilling the point home. He was why. Or, to be more precise, he and everything else like him. Paradise was the safest place on the entire continent, as far from the teeming nightmare swarms as possible. But they and their paladins weren't enough to control the entire world, especially with so many powerful nephilim that might contest them. The Church, rather than waging war against the nephilim, had instead offered them a pact. The oldest and most prestigious nephilim families, often with domains and armies of their own, allied with the faith and became wardens of its borders.

These houses and their supernatural might acted as a shield against the nightmare hordes. Humans who served them wielded the immortals' power in exchange for providing the houses with the offerings that sustained them. The Paradise Church, meanwhile, practiced its worship, creating holy weapons to battle the nightmares on their own terms.

For over three thousand years, this order had operated undisturbed. Amongst thousands and millions of humans, it was a little challenge to provide tithes of blood for a dozen or so nephilim. Major houses acted as wardens while minor houses provided their services to them, but all were paid in the same currency. To many humans, it was a solemn duty. To a select few, it was an honor. To the Church, it was a necessary sacrifice.

But if a house was not providing its services, it was not worthy of existence. Just as new houses might rise to power and offer their services in the interest of survival, so too could houses fall from power and be exterminated. This resulted in the existence of those called rogues: the uncounted unaffiliated nephilim who were hunted both by the paladins of the Church to protect their people and by more highborn nephilim in order to cull their competition.

All until the rise of the current Lady Baal. She, who had watched her house nearly collapse at the invasion of House Nero, looked at these rogue elements and saw nothing more than untapped potential. She had offered a haven for them all, taking in as many as she could and putting them to work. They fought and killed in her name, and if they stepped out of line, they were purged. Fear of her power kept them in line, and those who forgot their place were reminded. This alone would have shifted the balance of power on the frontiers, and that was without considering Baal's annihilation of her one-time rival.

Aaron shook his head. "As obvious as it gets. There hasn't been a ruler like Lady Baal. The only question is whether this intrusion is to get a better understanding of what kind of ruler she really is, or if it's to probe for weaknesses."

"There's a third option, Captain," said Eric. "That this itself is an attack."

Aaron's hand twitched, cracking the replacement glass he had been handed. He placed the glass down, mindful of his strength, which had escaped him while he listened to the old soldier speak. "Well, thank you. I appreciate hearing your point of view."

The man reclined, waving a hand. "Don't mention it. It's not my ass on the line anymore. I'm just here to get you what you need."

Aaron drummed his fingers on the table. "Honestly, more than anything, I could use a shower. Once they're back, get the others up to speed, or just Dalton. You know he'll make them aware. Then do whatever you have to and get me a meeting with the very top."

"This must be big. You never ask to meet with her."

"Exactly right," Aaron said, resting his hand on the hilt of his blade. "S-0 is her force, after all. It's been a while since we spoke, but I need her to hear this. We can't afford to be fighting a war on two fronts."

—CHAPTER 7—

AGENTS OF PARADISE

The intense afternoon sun stung his eyes and scratched at his skin. Nonetheless, Aaron enjoyed the novelty of it. He made his way at a brisk pace through the cobblestone streets of Spearhead. The west side of the city was out of the shadow of the mountains and more open than the military and residential districts. And, unlike navigating the wastes, it didn't fill him with a sense of dread.

It had been a long time since he'd tasted the emptiness beyond, and he had never experienced relief quite like the return to civilization. After seeing the small town that the citizens of Sterling were attempting to resettle, he was even more acutely aware of his fortune at being able to view such a city. Spearhead accommodated its densely housed inhabitants with a swath of wider streets, squares, and parks to allow for leisure. He took in the sights and sounds of people walking, shopping, talking, and laughing. After so much silence, it was an atmosphere he couldn't help but stop and enjoy.

Though, as usual, the atmosphere didn't particularly enjoy him. People parted around him with mixed reactions. Some offered polite deference, acknowledging the Baal sigil on his uniform first and foremost. A few offered him a salute, which was certainly a rarity. He believed it to be because of his pact. Though he preferred to hide as much of his pallid skin as possible, the heat had him undo the top button of his jacket. This left part of the mark visible, and its meaning was plain for anyone to see.

He made a note of it. Not all of the lowborn nephilim were well-regarded in polite society, and the unshakable proof of his loyalty made for a more pleasant atmosphere. Still, some turned their eyes away from him in distaste, and even a few in fear. He presented his best face of confidence and approachability to any who laid eyes on him.

As Aaron walked the streets, he passed the time by finding distractions suited to something like him. The shop from which he had purchased his dark glasses was currently expanding, and he offered his services to the builders. They looked at him like he was insane, likely suspecting a trick of some kind. However, they quickly warmed to the idea, or at least saw the use of him as he lifted a stack of wooden planks, some few hundred pounds, and hefted it onto his shoulder. He shrugged, asking where they should go, and the bravest among them pointed a finger.

He entered the shop after that. It was run by an elderly man and woman. He greeted them with a smile, which they returned in kind. The two had always been pleasant with him. Ironically, they both had issues with their vision, and he suspected that despite their skill with their craft, they sometimes forgot what he was. The two of them engaged in common pleasantries while he browsed for a replacement, asking him about the day and his job, and such. He answered politely, but avoided saying anything that would bring to mind the less pleasant aspects of his work.

Satisfied with his choice, he bought a replacement pair of shades, thicker and stronger than the rest. This served him twofold, both filtering the harsh sunlight more efficiently and being less likely to break. Since his strength sometimes made holding cups a feat of precision, that was essential. Of course, the pair also insisted that if durability was a concern, he should purchase a handmade case for the glasses, and after being convinced to spend twice the money as before in what he could have sworn was a work of magic, he departed.

Aaron used the wide berth afforded to him to move swiftly through the streets. His destination wasn't far, but it was in the center of the district. The city was built on a grid, and intersections of larger streets led to more popular and open shops. At one of these junctions, he approached Dominic's Café. The place was crowded, with tables out in the open air by the streetside and in a spacious interior.

The density of people had a benefit, though. Aaron had several visual tells that marked him as a nephilim, but fewer than most. With his nails and eyes covered, it wasn't easy to tell at a glance, and once he was a part of the crowd, he enjoyed more anonymity than usual. As he walked inside, the bell hanging at the door rang in his ear, followed by the clamor of the staff announcing the arrival of another customer.

He looked around, his acute sense of hearing becoming an uncomfortable burden in the clamor of people. Thankfully, the voice he was listening for had no qualms asserting itself far above the others.

"You're late!" Durham shouted as her palms struck the tabletop. "I swear, how complicated is it to make a straight walk here?!"

Gavin laid a claw-like hand on her shoulder, but it did little to dull the racket she raised as Aaron approached. It was his first time seeing them since the debriefing, and both took the opportunity to escape from their uniforms. Gavin presented himself simply, in a plain black shirt and gray striped slacks. His hair, a mess while in the field, had been cut short and neat, and his skin was a shade lighter when cleaned of the kiss of the wastes. Never unprepared for a brawl, Durham wore a leather jacket while retaining her cargo pants and combat boots. She had straightened her hair as well, an unusual gesture for her. Clearly, his relief at being home was one that all three of them shared.

They sat at his favorite spot in the cafe, tucked in the corner with a windowed view of the main road. He greeted them both with an embrace, accentuated by a pat on the back from Gavin and a jab beneath the ribs from Durham, before the two took up the opposite bench, allowing him the rare opportunity to stretch his limbs. Durham sat with a smirk and pushed a glass of water toward him.

"Don't bother with the menu; we ordered your piss."

"Thank you."

"She means to say that *I* ordered your piss," Gavin interjected pointedly. "This one was busy playing with some poor foreigners."

She feigned innocence. "That doesn't sound like me at all. Besides, did you see how they were dressed? I've been stuck in the wastes with nothing but you goons for weeks. The least I can do is enjoy some of the locals!"

"Didn't we just establish that they weren't locals?"

"Didn't we just establish you can kiss my ass?"

A voice behind them called out, "Hey, bitch!"

Durham turned, just in time for Dominic to come to rest on her shoulder. "You really do respond to it!"

"Just a time saver," she replied, extracting herself from beneath him. "By the way, you've gained weight."

"Can't imagine where you get all those colorful nicknames." Dominic laughed. "Good to see you again, Alice, and in one piece too!"

"Do not call me Alice!" she groaned. "It sounds so wrong now!"

"What, do you prefer bitch?" Gavin asked.

She shrugged. "What can I say? Feels like home."

"And Mr. Jaycen," Dominic continued as if nothing had occurred. His heavyset weight moved lighter than it should have, giving him a disarming speed with which to pull Gavin into a shell-shocked hug to the annoyance of Durham, caught in between. "How's the family?"

"Ah, well," Gavin said as he politely retook his distance. "My foster sister gets married in a month. Our parents are thrilled."

"Very exciting!" Dominic boomed, now attracting the stares of several passersby. Aaron smiled, happy to not be the subject of attention. "Don't suppose the poor sap's met you yet, eh?"

"He seems all right," Gavin said, smirking with Dominic's infectious joviality. "Steady job and a nice family. He might be too good for her."

Dominic laughed and called over one of his employees to bring drinks. A steaming mug was placed in front of Aaron, which he gratefully accepted. "That's a rude thing to say," he said as he sipped the tea, briefly choking at the scalding heat.

"Bit hot?" Durham laughed. "Wait, I thought you said she was annoying!"

"Hot enough to burn my tongue," Aaron gasped as his mouth turned numb. "You're lucky I heal fast. And no, I *agreed* that she was annoying. That's different."

She fixed him with a look of incredulity. "You did not just try to argue that."

"Gotta give it to Aaron on this one," Dominic remarked with a sage nod. "Agreeing and pointing out are different levels of rudeness."

"Don't you have tables to wait on, old man?" she asked.

Dominic was unperturbed. "Actually, I built a business so that others do that for me while I talk to my buddies. Pay attention, babycakes, and maybe you'll learn something aside from slinging silver."

"I'd rather be called Durham," she jabbed. "That gut is the only babycakes here."

Dominic paused, looking down at his stomach and then up at the three of them. "The missus likes it." Having attempted another sip of the tea, Aaron promptly choked on his laughter.

They sat there for a time. Dominic pulled up a chair, his width unable to fit on the bench with Aaron's length. The crowd around the window came and went, with only a few stopping to stare at them. Dominic offered a new import of beer, which Aaron attempted to refuse while Gavin and Durham jumped for joy.

"I swear, I don't know how you stay open with all the crap you give me."

"Give you?" Dominic snorted. "I charge you triple for the folks you scare away with those peepers." Aaron's forehead hit the table. "Ah, relax, I'm just kidding. If not for you, this place might not even exist. You'll pay me back soon enough, yeah? Once you're a big bad lord and you and Lady Baal get shacked up."

Aaron's eyes went wide. "I'm sorry, what?"

"Don't even joke about that," Gavin said while Dominic laughed. "Besides, he's not a vampire. Even if he's made a lord, he'll have to find another broken thing like him."

Aaron groaned. "Should never have told you about that. It's not like it's going to happen tomorrow. Mission aside, I have something Lady Baal will want to hear."

"Sounds interesting," said Dominic. "Do tell. I heard there was a mess with a vampire lately. You stake the bastard?"

Silence. Dominic leaned back in his chair. "Ah, something else, huh?"

"It's complicated," Gavin said.

Dominic took a swig of his beer. "Yeah, yeah. You three handle that off-the-books black-ops stuff now. Forget I asked."

"Let's just say our enemies aren't getting any more pleasant," Aaron said, rubbing his hand. "As long as they keep coming, we'll never be bored."

Dominic nodded. "Amen, brother, amen. God, I don't know how you guys stick it out. Couldn't get away from the service fast enough. How about something a bit more public? You were gone for a few weeks. Heard the big news?"

"What's the latest?" said Durham. "I can't keep track. We leave for a single mission, and everything goes to hell."

"I hear they're in Spearhead now."

She twitched like a predator did at the soft snap of a branch. "No way."

"I'm serious!" Dominic exclaimed. "I heard some folks talking about it yesterday. Two men in white, real paladins! Plus, that church caretaker lady makes three in the city."

"The woman in black isn't one of them," Aaron interjected. "She's been here for a while."

Durham raised an eyebrow while Gavin stirred his glass. "You know her?"

A slight heat rose in his face. He stuffed it down. "Leah, yes. We worked together on a case once before you two were reassigned. She just runs local services, nothing to worry about. The men in white, on the other hand…They could just be envoys, and I hope you're wrong about what you saw. If they're real paladins, then they've come to the wrong place. The Church of Paradise is officially our allies, but that's just what we say to avoid war."

"You're not wrong," Gavin said. "But they've got protection. They can reach out to any place they want to offer aid. Worst case, they might not find us deserving. They'll root out any impurities they see, real or imagined."

Durham sipped her drink. "When you put it like that, I'm surprised Lady Baal doesn't get along with them better. You get that meeting with her yet?"

Dominic turned his head. "Meeting?"

Aaron gestured at the thoroughly unflustered Durham. "You can't just say what we're doing!"

She snorted. "What? Is he going to tell the town that we're killing nightmares? That gonna set the world on fire? Relax a bit. I doubt it would matter even if he knew you were meeting with—"

Gavin's hand covered her mouth, muffling the string of profanity that followed.

Dominic laughed at it, shaking his head and standing. "Fair enough. I'm not about that life anymore. I'll make myself scarce for now. Just wave me down if you need anything."

He returned to work while Durham slapped at Gavin's head until Aaron intervened, long arms reaching across the table to stop her from making more of a scene. Grateful, Gavin adjusted his position to be slightly out of her arms' reach.

"Eric filled us in," he said, more quietly than before. "You managed to get a meeting with Lady Baal?"

Aaron sighed, shaking his head. "No luck. I used as much official weight as I could, but the higher-ups have been in nonstop meetings about what to do about the Church. It's a technicality. We only report to her, but I can't exactly force them to let me in."

"She normally gets your reports, though, right?"

"Not directly. I've never gotten any notices from her faster than a few days. And with things like they are… I don't know."

He had tried a more direct action as soon as he felt able. Aaron told them how he had approached the castle itself, determined to find an audience and report the new monstrous nightmares. But when he arrived at the main gate, he found it less than receptive. An entire squad of armed guards had met him. When he'd introduced himself, he was met with an immediate challenge.

"Nephilim don't make Captain rank."

He had addressed the man calmly, withdrawing the seal of his office and presenting it to him.

"Ordinarily, yes. Maybe this will clarify," Aaron had said, tugging at his collar to reveal the pact of Baal beneath his throat.

The leader of the guards had been surprisingly gracious, seeing the pact and immediately understanding.

"I see. Very good, but I still can't let you in."

He had been stunned. "Can't let me in? This pact allows me access to this castle, soldier. You will allow me in."

But it didn't make them budge. "Ordinarily, sir. But my orders supersede yours. Nobody is allowed in without express invitation. If you're to report to Lady Baal, you'll have to do it on paper. If you have one to provide, I am authorized to take it now. I'll see to it personally that it makes it through the proper channels."

Aaron ground his teeth, remembering it.

"Watch it," Durham cautioned. "You can't afford to break any more furniture."

He unclenched his hand, which had already begun gripping the edge of the table. He shook it off. Further pausing, he pulled out his notebook and scribbled a quick summary of the events.

"They were firm," he said as he did. "It looks like there really is nobody in or out while Lady Baal plans her next move. As a warden, she has contacts in Paradise. Do you think she's getting connected to them?"

Gavin considered it. "Not sure. If those contacts were worth anything, you'd think they would've kept her informed that this whole debacle was coming. But then, as far as wardens go, after the *incident* with House Nero, she's probably public enemy number one to them. Wardens don't like the idea that they aren't invincible. Lady Baal made it clear that they weren't when she wiped the old crone out."

"All the more reason to get in her ear as soon as possible," Aaron asserted. "Those things we killed weren't ordinary, and I don't think for a second that we've seen the last of them. You disagree?" he asked, turning to an unconcerned Durham.

She was busy trying to balance forks on top of one another, creating a misaligned and ugly pile of metal.

"Meh, you worry too much," she mumbled, waving her free hand. "They show up, we blow their heads off. All the same meat at the end of the day."

"Not sure why I asked," he chuckled, leaning back.

"Me neither," remarked Gavin. "Y'know, you could learn a thing or two about not caring from this one."

She rapped him on the knuckle with a spoon, and he recoiled. "It's enough to worry about with you idiots. Don't need any more."

Gavin conceded with a nod. "You did get us moving when those nightmares showed up. Wish I'd had the foresight to ask the pact for something like that."

Her mouth set in a smug grin. "You know why? I've got the *vision.*"

An eyebrow went up, though Gavin's expression remained neutral. "Yeah, you've got something, alright. What was your big ambition, using your retirement funds to work in some seedy gambling den?"

"That's to *own* a seedy gambling den!" she corrected. "And a bar!"

They argued back and forth for a time while Aaron watched. As he did, the din of the cafe gradually grew louder and more pervasive in his ears. His throat itched, not with thirst but with energy that seeped outward into his limbs. Without warning, the two of them ceased their conversation.

"About that time," Durham remarked.

"Hey, Dom, money's on the table," Gavin called, knocking on the polished wood for good measure.

The abruptness of it confused Aaron. "What are you doing?" he asked.

Durham knocked over her cutlery tower. "Getting you moving. You got that stupid look on your face that says you want to do something. If we get it started now, it feels like our idea."

He sputtered. "I-"

Gavin shoved him lightly. "Get a move on, 'Captain.' You're a big, scary nephilim. You've got a reputation to maintain."

Some more sputtering before he accepted that they knew better than he did. "Well, that's that, I guess. Might as well move quickly."

They ushered him up and out the door of the cafe, poking and prodding him all the while as if they were three children rather than a monster and two trained killers. When they opened the door, it bumped into another patron. Aaron reflexively made to apologize, only to be met by a familiar face.

"Rista?"

He remembered his etiquette, taking a half-step backward. His teammate was dressed casually, in a checkered shirt and jacket. He shifted his weight from foot to foot, eyes glancing to judge the distance between them. His injured arm was held in a brace, though his fingers still twitched with his movement.

"Captain," he acknowledged with a tilt of his head.

Aaron looked about, searching for a reason for Rista to be there. Unlike Durham and Gavin, the two of them weren't friends. Though Rista never disobeyed an order he had given, Aaron knew he was one of the more apprehensive members of S-0. Like Brook, he came from a well-connected family of decorated soldiers who had served the Baal line for generations.

That family had known a time when the Baals still had allies in other highborn nephilim, and undoubtedly had some distaste for a nameless one like him. Though the other members may not have enjoyed working with him, they at least put more personality on display when it came to voicing their opinions. Rista never opened up, never tried to get to know him better. In a way, that was even worse. Aaron tried to find words beyond awkwardness.

"I see you got patched up."

Rista examined the cast with a curious expression. "Nothing serious. The pact lets me recover quickly, so I'll be good to go soon enough."

"No need to worry, just focus on recovering for now." Aaron bit his tongue, cursing his own idiocy. *What do you think he's doing?* Aaron thought. He changed the topic. "I don't see you out in the city. What brings you here today? Not spending time with the family?"

"None of them live in the city, sir," Rista answered. Aaron cursed himself again.

"I'm sorry," he said. "I know Dalton's home is here, so I just assumed…"

Something changed in Rista's face, the lines around his eyes relaxed, and he laughed without spirit. "Don't stress about it. I was actually just in the area by chance. I see the gang's all here."

Durham leaned up against Aaron from behind, having to lift her arm high to drape it over his taller shoulders. "Anthony, *great* to see you," she said with mock cheer.

"What the hell do you want?" She stared at Rista with palpable apathy. "Spit it out, don't be shy! You want something, clearly. We know you wouldn't be with the dogs if you didn't."

Aaron swallowed, the pause that followed being brutally uncomfortable. Rista shifted from foot to foot. "I just wanted to thank you. You too, Captain. Back at the bunker, you both really stuck your necks out for me. Thanks for that."

Durham sneered. "Real professional, Anthony. I almost couldn't tell how much you hated doing it. Here's a little tip you pick up in the undercity: if you're only doing it because you think it's expected of you, it just makes you look like more of a rat."

"Easy," Aaron tried to calm her, but she stepped forward past him.

"We're not on duty now," she said icily. "Don't even try to stop me. Hate to break it to you, but we're not all pretty little academy boys here; you don't get points for spraying around politeness. When it's fake, it's worthless. And if that's all you have, so are you."

"Alice!" Aaron exclaimed. "He's here to say thank you; it's not something to condemn. I'm sorry, Rista, but it was nothing. Anyone would have done the same—"

He stopped cold. He'd moved to reach out, perhaps to shake Rista's hand, or maybe clap him on the shoulder as so many did. But the moment he'd taken a step forward, he sensed the signs. Rista didn't move from his position, but the change was apparent. His nostrils flared, pupils dilating as they fixed on him. His heart accelerated, and the arm that rested in its sling clenched in tension.

It might have been invisible to a human, but to his senses, it was overwhelming. The distrust, the fear, and the rejection were complete and utter. It was the same way he looked at the smiling nightmares. He retracted his hand.

"Don't worry about it," he said lamely. "Anyone would have done the same."

Rista shook his head. "Maybe anyone *would have*, but you *did*. I won't forget it, sir."

He offered a stiff salute and excused himself by stepping into the street and vanishing into the crowd with startling swiftness. Gavin exhaled a sigh, while Durham spit. Aaron turned to glare at her.

"You didn't have to insult him!" he snapped.

She didn't acknowledge his anger, instead leaning up against him. Her pulse remained even, and her eyes met his perfectly still. The only thing in her bearing that changed was the way her scars relaxed as the anger bled away from her face.

"Every time I think you're making progress, you say some dumb shit like that. You've got a lot to learn about humans, Aaron," she said. "They talk a lot but don't mean all of it. If you want to live with them, you need to learn which ones are actually on your side first."

The air cooled as they walked, but he didn't pause to enjoy it. The navigation of the west wing of the city suddenly seemed very tedious to him. His fists clenched. That frustration was exactly what made him so unapproachable, he told himself. Then he pictured Durham pointing out his actual appearance and grew ever more frustrated.

They passed street after street at a leisurely pace, though it still dragged with the crowd.

"So, what's the destination then?" Gavin asked him. "Don't keep us in suspense."

They rounded a corner, enjoying a gap in the usual crowds that let them move more easily. His mood lightened. "Well, hopefully, I can introduce you to someone. With the Paradise situation the way it is, I thought we might all benefit from talking to someone with a bit more knowledge than us."

Durham smacked him upside the head. "That's somehow even less helpful than saying nothing."

Aaron swatted at her. "Ease up! It's like getting pistol-whipped."

"I'll show you a pistol-whip!"

He rolled his eyes in response. "Yeah, maybe after you grow half a foot and can reach me. Ow! Stop it! We're already here."

Gavin whistled, lightly applying pressure to keep Durham from throwing out painful limbs. "Gotta say, this is a surprise. Didn't think you much of a holy man."

Aaron chuckled. "I have my moments. But if anyone knows about the Church's movements, it will be Leah."

Gavin nodded. "That's right, you mentioned you knew her. But she's not really with the Paradise Church, she's just a follower."

"Why does Lady Baal even allow it?" Durham asked. "Always seemed like asking for trouble."

Aaron shrugged. "To each her own. I think it's nice that she allows followers of the faith to practice in her own capital. And Leah was born in Paradise, so she knows all the ceremonies."

Durham grunted, unimpressed. "Ugly thing though."

Aaron looked at her, wondering if it was a joke. It wasn't worth the argument, but if she was serious, he couldn't imagine what she called beautiful. The church was at the center of its own small square. Its walls gleamed a marble white, dazzling in the midday sun, while its roof was shingled in polished red.

It didn't stand tall; that was not its nature, but instead loomed wide with a rear altar attached to a blooming garden that grew outward from the dome shape that allowed as many within as possible. Most catching, shaped above the doorway, was the insignia of the Paradise Church: a circle, divided horizontally and vertically, then framed by branches that crossed outward diagonally. Aaron figured it was supposed to represent the world divided as it was into frontiers. Nobody had ever remarked on it. It shone a blinding gold, simple yet such a splendor that it made his eyes ache.

It was crowded, with dozens of onlookers taking in the view and dozens more filtering through the large doors. Aaron scanned it, searching for Leah's distinctive attire. Noticing his searching, Durham ribbed him. "Ever been inside?"

Aaron adjusted his glasses to affix her with a withering stare. "What do you think? It's consecrated. I can't so much as touch the door unless I want to burst into flames."

She snorted. "Yeah, that's what I meant."

Before he could even realize the implications, they were interrupted. "Fear is a healthy thing, friend," a man called from behind them. "But remember, fire purifies."

"Spoken like someone who hasn't been burned," Durham laughed, though it died abruptly when she, like Aaron and Gavin, beheld who had spoken.

He stood at an average height, with a symmetrical, round face and neat blond hair cut short. He dressed in a white cassock wrapped in a black sash, and resting against his chest was the signet of the Paradise Church. On his right hand rested a silver ring, lined with several incisions that wrapped around the band like vines. He smiled slightly and inclined his head.

"I'm sorry to interrupt," he said, voice even and polite. "I just couldn't help but overhear your conversation. If any of you would like to enter, you're welcome to join us for a prayer. Once we're done, there will be a shared meal, too."

Durham laughed. "How do I put this politely? I'd rather get bent over and-"

"Enough of that!" Aaron cut in, glaring murder at her at an angle so as to not be seen by the man. He turned to the paladin, adjusting his glasses to briefly reveal his eyes. "I can't speak for them, but I'm afraid that prayer may be wasted on me."

He shuffled uncomfortably. Even then, he could feel the oppressive presence of the building, as if a mountain of silver had been laid at his feet.

Another voice spoke from behind the man. "Nonsense! There's no better soul to reach out to."

Behind him, they spotted the approaching form of a second paladin. He wore the same white cassock and black sash, and the twice-crossed sigil adorned his neck as well. He was a handsome man, tall with broad shoulders, cool brown skin, and a shaved head. He tilted his head three times, acknowledging Durham, Gavin, and then Aaron individually.

"You have a distance to go, to be sure, but none of us is any different. There's no need to hide it. We all have to struggle if we want to be saved."

Aaron blinked. That was a new one. "Still," I know when I'm not welcome. Better to keep this covered up and have the people be at ease."

The first paladin's head tilted slightly. "Admirable, sir. But have you considered that by taking too many measures to hide what you are, you might just lose track of it yourself?" He looked at Aaron's gloved hands.

"Human or nephilim, we shouldn't be afraid to feel the touch of another."

A chill racked him. Aaron shuddered, feeling the ghostly echo of the last silver that had touched his hand.

"Pretty words," Durham stated. "My favorite kind. But you've got a little bit of a reputation. Kind of like the one we have, where the real work is done with weapons, not words."

The paladin's lips drew into a too-wide smile. "You have half the mindset already. Holiness is found in eradicating evil, but there are two sides to that coin. We're vain creatures, and pleasant as it is to think we're the bringers of justice, that same fervor must be focused inward as well." He stared intently at Aaron. "Tell me, have you ever done so, sir nephilim?"

Aaron smiled tightly. This wasn't going to end well, and he knew it. "I wouldn't call what we do holy. It keeps the world spinning, makes sure that we're here to see tomorrow."

The fair-skinned man shook his head. "Close, so very close. Ah, where are my manners? I'm Brother Alexander. This is Brother Oris. It's a pleasure to meet some of the dogs of Sitri Baal. Though I don't recognize your uniform, you're her hunters, are you not? Those who deal with the inhuman...threats that face the city."

A silence took them. Aaron took note of those around them. People had begun to look their way. He did not like the direction of the conversation. He decided that excusing them was the safer bet.

"Our work is not your concern," he said simply.

"Of course," Oris said, stepping forward and affixing Alexander with a scolding look. "I'm sorry. We are guests here and should know better than to pry. This is a wonderful city, even if the people seem troubled."

"You think they're worried you might be here to kill them?" Durham offered.

Oris blinked, taken aback. Aaron drew in a breath, but before he could say anything, the paladin laughed. His smile that followed was bright and open, as if it were the natural state of his face.

"The thought crossed my mind, ma'am. But that's an oversimplification, I think. After all, there were plenty of people eager to talk to us. To some of the other *special* inhabitants, they appear less forthcoming."

A small crowd had begun to take shape around them. Aaron could hear Durham's blood pressure rising. He put a hand on her shoulder to gather her before she could snap.

"If you've been around the world, then you know how bad it can get," he said. "If they're worried, they have the freedom to speak it. We can't help what we are, but we can try to improve *who* we are. That's all any of us can do, isn't it? Try to be better?"

Alexander's grin was intense and unsettling, everything Oris's was not. If anything, Oris seemed invigorated. "Well said, sir. Very well said, in fact. You're a credit to nephilim everywhere! If only they all shared your consideration."

He offered his hand toward them; his right, which was conveniently bereft of the silver ring. "May I have your name?"

Aaron eyed the hand for a few moments, debating whether it would turn into a snake if he took it. He could feel eyes on him, Gavin, Durham, Alexander, and the bystanders. Oris examined him calmly, face not showing any signs of sarcasm, disgust, or duplicity. Resigning himself to what followed, he accepted the handshake. "Aaron White. Nice to meet you, Brother Oris."

Another warm smile, eyes turning upward with enthusiasm. "Pleasure to meet you as well, Mr. White. While I'm not sure entering the church would do well for your health, please feel free to stop by anytime. You're always welcome to listen."

He excused himself from them, beckoning Alexander to follow him to the entrance of the building. When they had opened the doors, he paused in consideration, instead taking a place at their side so that any could enter or exit while they spoke. The assembled citizenry gathered around them, but Aaron didn't need to approach to hear him begin to speak.

"Days such as these should never be wasted. You all have shown yourselves to be of open hearts and minds to my brother and I. May we show you the same care in turn. I understand that some of you feel abandoned, alone, and afraid. We feel these things too. It's a part of living. But we're together now, and we will hear those fears. We'll speak our own. We aren't omniscient and we aren't omnipotent, but we are the defenders of humanity, and so are all of you. If you would like to take the first step toward that destiny with us, then come, listen, and speak if you will. That is the first step toward finding and building Paradise."

The three of them watched for a bit longer as the crowd grew larger around the two. Oris spoke with engagement and passion, looking at individuals in the crowd with care. He told of the land of Paradise from which they'd come; of tall buildings and marvels of technology lost in the frontiers to the depredations of nightmares. He spoke of the order maintained through centuries and millennia by way of discipline and of grace. But mostly, he spoke of the responsibility for all people to better themselves and their place in the world, and the rewards that such a holy struggle would bring. He seemed to grow more engaged with each word, as did the onlookers.

As the speech went on, Aaron spoke quietly to Durham. "So, do you wake up escalated or do you build to it over the course of the day?"

She nudged him lightly. "Just looking out for you. Nothing comes of playing at their speed. So, tell me, smart guy, what do you think of them?"

He looked at Gavin, still staring at the impassioned Oris with concerning intensity, his eyebrows slowly drawing together in a rare display of quiet anger. "I think they have a lot to say," he answered. "And I think we'll be hearing more from them shortly."

It was a trivial answer: one that didn't truly address the nature of the question. But he didn't have a true thought to make, and so deflected the issue. All the while, he scanned the crowd, looking for auburn hair and a woman in black. Yet, the caretaker was nowhere to be found, and he bid them to leave, for the eyes that weren't on the agents of Paradise had long since been drawn to him.

–CHAPTER 8–

REPRIMAND

Aaron leaned against the cold wall, tapping at the hilt of his sword. Though it was not required for the debriefing, he found it helpful to hold something he couldn't break. He had been at the barracks, searching through archives for information on any nightmares with a resistance to silver, when Eric came to him.

The summons was immediate: He had only an hour to assemble his lieutenants. Thankfully, he was prepared for that. Durham and Dalton were ready and waiting, fully aware they could be called on at any time. They made their way to the castle gate as Aaron had before. The guard captain was the very same who had refused him, and when he saw them, he didn't even approach their vehicle, instead signaling to have the gate opened for them and not wasting a word as they passed.

After that, they navigated the necessary checkpoints that followed. Though guards were plentiful, they weren't delayed further. Some of the attendants of the castle were regulars, recognizable by face if not name, and none looked at them twice. They walked in silence. The trepidation of meeting with Lady Baal was one of the few things that could curb Durham's tongue.

They had spoken before, of course, but rarely. She was their ultimate benefactor, the one who provided them with targets and directed them. She was also a nephilim, and more nephilim than perhaps any other. She was highborn with a lady's courtesy, but the three of them had also seen her in states of less decorum. Considering the likely state of her mood following recent events, none of them were particularly excited.

From the second gate, they passed beneath the crossed spears of the Baal emblem to enter the courtyard. It was more open than the castle exterior would lead one to believe, and in the center of it was a rectangular atrium that let in the daylight. Within it, a single Atsali tree grew past the castle ceiling some two hundred feet above them, its bone-white leaves standing out starkly against the rest of the plants. A pair of willows framed a central path alongside a small pond, and as they walked beside it, Aaron made out the shapes of small, brightly colored fish darting beneath the surface. At the end of the path was a set of doors, above which were inscribed the words of House Baal: *Power Incarnate.*

Despite its austere exterior, Aaron found the castle welcoming. The hallways were lit by a series of evenly spaced lamps and accessible windows. There were a few pieces of decorative art hung on the walls, mostly pertaining to the Baal family and its symbolism crest and colors. Hanging beside those pieces were photographs taken of members of military staff, mayors, officials, and others with notable achievements of the house. The three of them climbed a set of stairs together, and he paused to take in the view from one of the corner windows.

It was a unique sight. From there, anyone could look out just as Lady Baal did and behold the vista beyond. The elevation and clear skies gave a pristine view of the empty horizon before them. It was a mark of despair that it held the nightmares they so despised, but also the hope of endless freedom.

"Captain White," came a voice measured and dispassionate.

Aaron did not need to turn to identify who called him, but did so out of custom, closing his eyes as he inclined his head to hold onto the view in his mind. When he opened them, he was met with Valentine, the unblinking assistant to Lady Baal.

He was dressed in an immaculate suit with shoes and gloves to match. His clothing, stance, and expression were out of a painting: a picture of unmoving and unflinching class. However, behind his circular spectacles, his eyes were dark and murky. His skin, perhaps even more than Aaron's, was nearly translucent. His suit fit tightly to his lean form, illustrating the movements of his limbs that were too smooth and even to be ordinary. He tilted his head once in greeting, his body staying perfectly still.

"Please, come with me. Forgive the delay."

"Gladly," he replied with a casual smile.

There weren't many nephilim with whom he could enjoy such an even conversation, which made it a shame that Valentine spoke so little. Then again, nephilim might not have been the proper term for him. The definition of the word varied from person to person. Strictly speaking, it was a far-reaching and inclusive term designed to contain every being with a mystical persuasion that was neither human nor nightmare.

Rare as it was, humans could practice magic, but that did not make them nephilim. People or animals that were enchanted with magic didn't fall under the umbrella, but those born with an inherent power or abnormality were generally included. All of that only made it harder to place Valentine, however, who had lived and died as a human but been reanimated as something new.

He had heard several terms describing Valentine: zombie, walking corpse, and living dead among them. Lady Baal herself had once referred to him as a "doll." Whatever the case, he was the product of sorcery, a soul possessing his own corpse. That didn't make him any less interesting to speak with. He was hardly unfriendly, simply quiet and a bit lacking in expressiveness.

While Valentine was more than capable of speaking with the rank and file, his unique situation made him utterly unflappable when dealing with the more unruly of Lady Baal's servants. Supposedly, he never tired, ate, or slept, and had been in the Baal family service for an indeterminate period. That would make him an ideal assistant, but it still left his true nature in a state of limbo.

Aaron seized the moment to start a conversation. "Do you have any updates for us?"

Valentine neither changed his pace nor turned his head. "Regarding what?"

"The Paradise Church," Aaron replied. "Two of them are in the city now. It looks like things are going to heat up."

"Are you inquiring as to my personal thoughts, or the thoughts of Lady Baal?" Valentine questioned. "I do not presume to know my mistress's intentions nor to share her tactics."

Aaron didn't laugh, though the robotic response made it tempting. "You've known her longer than most. But no, I wouldn't ask you to do that. I thought you'd have your own opinions on the matter, as someone with a unique perspective."

This did turn Valentine's head, though his pace remained brisk as ever. His unblinking, dull eyes stared into Aaron's. Durham shivered, letting out a muted sound of disgust at the look. Valentine returned his attention to the hallway before them, silent for another second before speaking again.

"I hadn't considered it. While there's no harm in contemplating the possibilities, I wouldn't concern myself with the actions of the two visitors. The Church as an organization is predictable, but its agents on their own are not. We may all find ourselves quite busy soon."

"Busy is rarely good," Dalton said, speaking for the first time.

"I have confidence you are all capable." They came to a stop at the end of the hall. It was not the entrance to Lady Baal's personal offices, but instead a conference room. He had sat in it before, but did find it curious that it was where she had chosen to receive them. Valentine knocked once on the door, then turned toward them.

"You'll find refreshment inside. The best to you all."

Aaron extended a hand toward him. "A pleasure as always. Thank you, Valentine."

The dead man looked at the hand curiously, as if it were something he'd never seen before. Then, taking it in a cold, stiff grip, he shook once. "You may call me Valen, Captain White."

With that, he opened the door, ushering them in with a bow and closing it behind them after they had stepped through. The conference room they entered was large, rectangular, and with high windows. It allowed daylight to stream in and fill the space with brightness and warmth. The walls were undecorated, leaving them decidedly plain but also drawing the eye to the center of the room.

A wooden table, simple but elegant, took up the majority of the floor space. Laid over it was a large map of the eastern frontier, alongside a more detailed map showing the center of the continent and the smaller domains that made up greater Paradise. Though the table could seat well over two dozen, it was occupied by only a single figure. He was tall, imposing, and decidedly not Sitri Baal.

"White," was the only greeting the man offered. His face, marked with lines of both age and battle, was angled downward but instantly recognizable. His brown hair had become stitched with silver, as had his beard. He was in uniform, the only thing Aaron had ever seen him wear. The heavy jacket was a featureless gray, save the green sigil of the House of Baal that adorned it.

"Colonel Constantine," he greeted.

Once upon a time, he had tried to salute the man. No longer. He was now acutely aware that monsters had no place imitating the respect of a human. Removing his sword from his belt, he laid it against the table before taking his seat opposite. Dalton and Durham followed suit.

Aaron assessed the situation. Constantine's expression was set in stone as he looked over the papers before him. He had next to no visible tics to discern his mood. It was fortunate then that he wore his distaste so plainly on his face, lest those around him be deprived of it.

After a short minute, he shuffled the pages together and looked toward Dalton, inclining his head lightly. "Deadeye, good to see you." That done, he turned back to Aaron, jaw squared, neck straight. "We will begin now."

"I was under the impression that Lady Baal would be directing this meeting," Aaron said.

"Lady Baal is otherwise occupied," Constantine declared. "As I would be, had your excursion not been such a mess. But what's done is done, so I'm here in her place."

Aaron kept his response measured by biting the inside of his cheek. "Excuse me?"

Constantine straightened a paper into place. "Was I unclear? Your orders were simple: search and destroy. What you did was—"

"Hunt down and exterminate a rogue nephilim roaming the wastelands?" Durham cut him off. "No man's land. Basic resources. No landmarks. What do you call that?"

Aaron's teeth came together on his cheek, drawing blood. He hadn't prepared for this. Not that he disagreed with Durham's opinion, but now that she knew that Lady Baal wasn't there, there was nothing to keep her mouth in check. And Constantine was the person he least wanted to have in a room with her. Or him, for that matter.

The colonel's eyes narrowed. He slid a marked map toward Aaron. "Those are the coordinates of the takedown; the coordinates you reported. That is the territory of Roman Sterling, lord of the noble House of Sterling. He's a shapeshifter and warden of the eastern frontier for nearly two centuries. You might have heard of him. What would I call it? Misleading, bordering on treasonous."

They stared at one another, the weight of the statement hanging in the air. Aaron struggled to formulate a response that captured his faith in their course of action as well as his outrage at the insinuation of dishonesty.

"You'd prefer I had let him go?" he asked. "Just pack everything up and head back to the city while a traitor roams free?"

Constantine's palm hit the table. "I'd have you not start another war." His eyes blazed with fury, but his heartbeat never sped up. "You lost seventy silver bullets out there. For seventy silvers, people would kill a dozen men. A hundred, a thousand. You think we're so well off that we need problems stirred up from within right now? Not bad enough to have you on the loose with this rabid dog, but now you've got Deadeye dragged into it trying to cover for your ass."

Durham simmered in her chair, and Aaron could feel the venom rising in her throat. Dalton stared calmly ahead, unbothered by the colonel's words.

"Respectfully, sir," he said, "I was upfront with my perspective, but I don't believe that Captain White in any way misconstrued the details of our operation in his report. Though you may disagree with his method, it's a serious accusation to question his honesty."

"You can call me a traitor some other time," Aaron said. "If you read the coordinates, then I hope you also read the rest of my report?"

"Oh, I did. Three times, just to be sure I didn't miss a word. *Talking nightmares*…Weeks in the wastes robbed you of what little sense you had. I thought I was having a stroke at the audacity of it."

"Audacity?!" Aaron exclaimed. "You're in charge of the borders. That includes the information that you gave me! Not only were your reports incorrect as to the pack that Silas was following, but they also neglected to mention the *five* aberrants in the area. They tracked us and broke into a reinforced bunker. Maybe you could have mentioned that Silas could turn invisible and Paradise knows what else!"

"You had all the information on the target that we did," Constantine countered. "And our reports have never been more reliable. Those numbers were within the expected margin for error. I might also add that it was not in *our* territory that it occurred. You are more than informed as to our network's effectiveness, and anyone with the common sense God gave a rat should know that it isn't infallible. But you, Captain White, failed to follow the simplest of parameters. You track the vampire, you kill the vampire. You failed to catch him before he made it to Sterling's land. Then you followed him into the wolf's jaws and exposed yourselves, wasting our resources to save the enemy."

This time, it was Aaron's hand that hit the table. It was a miracle it didn't shatter.

"Someone has to set an example!" he hissed. "Those people would have been massacred! I saved their lives! Do you not care at all?"

Constantine leaned forward, voice steady and even. "Don't you dare say that, you goddamned skeleton. Not to me. Nightmares attack. Nephilim attack. These are the facts. But there's a pile of dead civilians whose families saw Baal soldiers. If Sterling gets wind of this, it could be considered an act of war. What happens to all those lives you care about then, eh? All of them, up in smoke. You're lucky you have Lady Baal's crest written on your skin. If you didn't, I'd have had you gunned down at the gate."

Aaron stammered, eyes wide as he tried to formulate a response to the colonel's words. "I…" he began, but no retort followed.

Constantine was unfazed. "You have deceived yourself into thinking you can be something more. That pact with Lady Baal only holds while you serve. You will *serve*, White, or you will be disposed of with the rest of the monsters."

That word again. *Monster.* That was what he was. That was what all nephilim were. Without a name, there was no purpose. Animals, lost and damned. The familiar twinge in his heart. He had no reply and knew he had lost. Aaron looked away.

"We could all be more…"

In the quiet that followed, the only sound was Durham snickering. It began slowly, barely any louder or more distinct than a breath, but quickly picked up. It became a harsh, mean-spirited laugh, as utterly devoid of humor as the joyless grin on her face.

"Something funny, Durham?" Constantine asked.

"Alice, don't," Aaron began, but it was halfhearted at best, his spirit flayed away by uncaring reality.

"Oh, you know," she said, voice dripping with false courtesy. "Just didn't think you were a joker, Const. I mean, the ones that kill the monsters are *us*, you know?" She drummed a finger on the table. "You arrogant fuck. You think you can threaten him? Debts in this world are paid in money or blood. That freak that went out of control was on your watch. It killed our guys under *your* nose and scampered off without a care in the world. We cleaned it up because it's what we do. If you've got even a word of complaint about that, then you're not just stupid; you're a coward. And we don't take orders from a coward."

For the first time, the colonel's heart rate accelerated, blood running molten in his veins. "You stupid bitch. Do you have any idea what you put at risk when you and this thing do whatever you want?"

She smiled wider. "I don't care. We killed the vampire, and the nightmares for good measure. And like we said, which you've *conveniently* ignored, there were more."

She pulled out her silver knife, the very same one that had burned Aaron, and stuck it into the table. "How many lives is this worth? A million? A billion? To me, it's trash. We shot them with silver and they…didn't…die."

With each word, she twisted the knife on the table. "That's the message. Take it to Sitri, because you have no authority over us."

For a second, Aaron thought that Constantine would truly erupt. He inhaled, the tension in the air rising to a boil as he filled his lungs in preparation to respond with venom of his own. Then, something stopped him. He exhaled, relaxing in his seat and laying his palms flat on the table. When he opened his mouth again, his voice was calm, with only a hint of contempt in the echo of silence that they left.

"Don't worry. I'll investigate these aberrants, if only to prove you wrong. And if you pull a stunt like this again, not even Lady Baal will be able to save you from me." He shook his head. "Get up and get out. When I find nothing of note, I'll be sure to let you know."

He returned his attention to his papers. Aaron made to speak, but Constantine didn't acknowledge him. Aaron stood, his chair sliding outward across the length of the room. Constantine displayed a profound lack of interest, not further acknowledging either Durham or Dalton when they followed. Only as they made it to the exit did Aaron notice the three glasses Valentine had left on a table adjacent to the door. Two were filled with water, and the other, something darker for him. He took the glass and drained it in a single gulp, hoping it would irritate the colonel further. He broke the handle from the door as he flung it open, and they exited to the sight of Valentine, waiting behind it as if he hadn't moved.

"Mind the castle, please," the aide said politely. "Colonel Constantine, your next meeting is present."

The voice didn't acknowledge his provocation, despite the sound of the door handle rolling on the floor. "Send her in."

They exited through the same hallway they had arrived in, with Valentine following alongside them. They found their way to the staircase, at which point they drew to a stop. Valentine stepped past them, a minuscule crease forming around his eyes. Resting at the window, a pendant of Baal dangling from its neck, was a werewolf.

Like others of her kind, her body was not really like that of a wolf. The term was used interchangeably, but the most accurate description for the nephilim was "shapeshifter." In her true form, she had a body like a living shadow; a dark outline where no light could pass through, one that blurred the line between real and insubstantial. It had no effect on the world around it as it rose, but Aaron knew that could change in a moment.

He thought he could make out the shape of limbs resting against the floor, but it just as soon could have been a trick of the light. Her form shimmered, flickering and shifting at its edges like flame, or as was commonly perceived, like raised fur. Her long body warped and curled as she rose so that she was even with Aaron in height, lips parting to display teeth as long as knives.

"We discussed this," Valentine declared, producing a long cloak seemingly from thin air. He wrapped it around the approximate shape of the werewolf's indistinct body. "When in the castle, you wear your humanoid skin, Helena."

Helena's jaws snapped shut, and a sound halfway between a bark and a hiss followed as the shadows of her form coalesced into a solid shape. As they shrank into the size of an ordinary human, they peeled away, revealing her guise underneath. Wild black hair flowed down her back, not unlike her true form. She adjusted her provided clothing with a muscular arm decorated in scars. Bright, searching eyes slid over Valentine without pause and found their way to the members of S-0, and she walked past him to approach Aaron.

"Captain White," she greeted cordially, lingering just a touch too long on his title. "So good to see you. Still keeping up the good fight?"

Her lips twitched, and he shifted, not wanting to give her the satisfaction of whatever joke she was telling. "If you say so."

It didn't work, and she giggled, voice disarmingly light for her appearance. "Really, nothing? I'm hurt. You know, for a mutt, you have a high opinion of yourself. Little good it does you, though."

"I'd like nothing better than to put my feet up and rest," he told her. "But our brethren keep forcing my hand."

"So dear old Silas is dead?" She grinned. "Served him right. He was always a bore and pitifully weak besides. Could only get his kicks out of hunting the helpless. I'm all for a simple game, but make it too easy and you lose the satisfaction."

The implications were not something he wanted to hear. "Maybe you should find your thrills elsewhere."

"Maybe you should, too," she said with mock-sweetness. "Paradise knows you could use it. Maybe get some sun on that skin of yours."

Without warning, she reached out with preternatural speed, popping the buttons of his jacket and tearing his undershirt. Helena's face lit up as she saw what Aaron had hidden. His skin, like dented paper, clung to protruding bones on his emaciated frame, every joint and rib clearly defined. Black veins stood clearly visible against ghostly muscle. It was the body of a corpse. Aaron inhaled sharply and, too quickly, made to cover the sight.

"You're so cute when you're flustered," she whispered. "Oh, that's a scary face."

Durham took a step forward, affixing Helena with a hateful stare. "Watch your step, bitch," she threatened. "Silas lost his head. I won't kill you so quickly."

The situation might have escalated further had Valentine not intervened. He took Helena's hand like she was a disobedient child and led her down the hallway. Aaron stalked past her, going down the stairs as her laughter picked up.

"Oh, Captain White. You love it, I know!" she called out. "You just love taking a hit!"

–CHAPTER 9–

RE-HUMAN

The three of them returned to the barracks wordlessly. Eric saw them and made to speak, but noted their expressions and then thought otherwise. Aaron sent Durham and Dalton to join the rest as he changed into a new shirt, having held his jacket closed the entire way back.

When he climbed the stairs to the meeting room, S-0 was waiting for him; it was the first time they had assembled since their return to the city. Sif, Moore, and Lenz sat at a table. Before them was a deck of cards, but any game they were playing had been set aside. Brook sat apart from them, looking toward Aaron while her hands continued writing something he couldn't make out. Rista, still wearing the sling, gave him a casual wave. Gavin was laid back, feet kicked up on the center table.

"So," he asked with a smile. "How did it go?"

"He got his ass kicked," Durham answered before Aaron could. He glared at her, and she shrugged. "Well, you did."

"It wasn't like that," Aaron sighed as he took stock of those present in the room. Their eyes were on him. Brook never blinked when she was focused, and the detail distracted him. "I raised our concerns. They had their own and weren't pleased with my decision-making during the operation."

"It doesn't sound like Lady Baal was so interested," Brook commented, adjusting her position to sit even straighter. "Her priorities are different from ours, after all, but I can't imagine she'd disregard you entirely. This is a substantial find."

Moore nodded in agreement. "She has a lot to handle. Aberrant nightmares are a problem, but they still die. The Paradise Church is a different kind of threat."

"It wasn't like that," Aaron repeated, rubbing his eyes against the bright light streaming into the room. Durham drew the curtains for him, and he thanked her. "Sitri didn't conduct the meeting; it was Constantine."

Silence overtook the room. Durham took a seat. "Yeah, it was one of those."

Sif's palm landed flat on the table. Eyebrows furrowed, she brushed aside a curl of blonde hair. "I don't suppose you managed to keep from antagonizing him?"

She shrugged. "He was being an ass. I told him so. Clear?"

Brook's lip curled in anger. "So, the up-jumped thug spoke for us? Let me guess how that went…"

Durham grinned coldly and took a step toward her. "We can't all get by on our inbreeding, *milady*."

"Easy," Aaron interjected, speaking over the discussion before it could take a turn for the worse. He was only partially successful. Attentiveness had turned to accusation, and he couldn't hold it against them. Durham had only spoken out because he hadn't.

"Constantine wasn't receptive," their leader continued with what confidence he had. "But no matter what he thinks, he knows what we found, and what might still be out there."

Rista leaned forward. "He won't be having any of it, you know."

"He will," Aaron insisted. "And no matter what, he won't keep it from Lady Baal. After this mess with the Church is sorted out, she'll reach out to us. But," he added, "I wouldn't expect much freedom in the meantime."

"I'd call that a success," Gavin said lazily. "The wastes are treacherous and unpredictable. We never wanted to hunt them that far out of our turf in the first place. If Silas hadn't been such a messy eater, it might not have even landed at our feet."

"We only want to keep within city limits if it's by our choice," countered Brook. "This isn't that. This is a punishment for our performance, and a mark against all of us." Her eyes moved from Aaron to Durham. "So, now we wait."

"No," insisted Aaron. "Now we see what we can find about this new breed of nightmare, and we prepare for whatever Lady Baal has in store for us. If we're deployed again, we'll be ready, and we'll even make Constantine acknowledge that."

He looked at each of them, burning their faces, their eyes, into his mind. All save Durham and Gavin, who appeared wholly unconcerned with the affair. His hand twitched. He wanted to write them into his notebook to ingrain them into his memory. "Thank you for your time. Dismissed."

They filed out of the room until it was just him and Dalton. Aaron leaned against the table, exhaling. "That could have gone better."

"Which part?"

Aaron chuckled. "All of it."

"Never a dull moment with Durham," said Dalton.

Aaron agreed. "Lady Baal promoted her, but it's not like she wanted the rank. Tough enough to keep her civil with Brook, but her and Constantine in a room unsupervised..."

"Unfortunate," Dalton declared, accurately boiling down the entire situation into a single word.

"Unfortunate indeed," Aaron muttered. "I guess it's time for an 'I told you so.'"

"I didn't think you were so petty, but I understand."

Aaron turned his head. "What do you mean?"

His lieutenant was examining a small stack of papers provided by Eric, sorting through them dispassionately. He handed one off to Aaron, marked for him, and read through one with his own name on it. "I'm just saying that I wouldn't hold it against you if you wanted to tell me off."

Aaron blinked, adjusting his position as if the physical change would grant him perspective. "Yeah, that's what I don't understand. You should be the one telling me off. You told me it was a bad call to follow Silas."

Dalton set aside his paper, quickly turning through the others in his hands to organize them for his squad mates. "I did, at the time. The risk of war with Sterling is real and terrible. But if we hadn't pursued him as far as we did, then we wouldn't have encountered those aberrants. And if we didn't find them, someone else would have: someone not so well-equipped or experienced to deal with them.

"How many nightmares have you killed?" Dalton asked. "How many has Durham? Rista? It's what we do. And the first rule of battling nightmares is to control the engagement, but those things had control.

If you hadn't shown us what they were capable of and bought time when they attacked, we might not have made it out of that bunker. Whatever happened, it was…" He paused, squinting as he looked over a page. "For the best," he finished slowly.

"Ah," Aaron murmured, shifting from foot to foot as he struggled to find an appropriate response. "Well, thank you."

"You're welcome," Dalton replied, eyes still on the paper beneath him. "I still believe you should consider the consequences of your actions further. That goes double for Constantine. He may not like you, but he's our ally, and he takes his duties seriously."

Aaron took a seat, pushing back his hair. "You're right, as usual. But he's not exactly meeting me in the middle. Maybe you should be the only one to present our findings. The senior staff respect you more, not just for being human but for your experience and accomplishments."

But Dalton was not convinced. "All the more reason to take the stage. You have people against you for your attitude and your autonomy. If you want to be a lord, then you need to keep pushing. This is your team and your intent, not mine. Besides, I'm not much of a speaker. Unlike Durham."

Aaron winced, remembering her words again. "She's got a knack for it, that's for sure. No filter at all. But I…" He trailed off, trying to find the right words that would also fit his rank and position.

"She's your friend," remarked Dalton. "And she supports you, so you want to support her. All posturing aside, I disagreed with Colonel Constantine's focus. I think she managed to put his mind back on the issue, even if it pissed him off in the meantime. She's good at what she does, so as your second in command, I say best not to censure her, though maybe you should *censor* her."

At once, Aaron's head snapped toward Dalton, whose stony face relaxed slightly as his lip turned and his eyes creased with the hint of a smile, still looking down at the papers beneath him. Aaron tuned his trained hearing carefully, noting the unevenness of the man's breath. "What's happening here? Was that a joke? Are you trying not to laugh?"

Dalton coughed once, stroking his beard with a shake of the head. "I'm sorry. I know you expect me to be serious all the time, but I'm not heartless." He handed the papers he'd been looking over to Aaron. "This is the report we got back from Research and Development. The last one went directly to its recipient, so I guess this is the follow-up. They were happy with our work, but also a bit disappointed."

Aaron took it in uncertain hands, intrigued, enthused, and slightly scared at what could have broken through his lieutenant's composure. He scanned it, not finding anything odd until...

"Durham..." he growled, feeling something decidedly inhuman building in his chest. "Durham!" he yelled.

He stalked through the offices looking for her, calling her name all the while. He plowed through everything in his way, unintentionally breaking a door off its hinges in the process. The members of S-0 came quickly, drawn by the noise yet cowed by his change in demeanor. He moved past them all, tracking the one heartbeat that didn't react to the flurry of activity. It didn't take long, and he found her at what passed for her desk, reclining in a chair and balancing a switchblade against a pen. Grabbing her by the shoulders, he lifted her first from a slouching to a sitting position, and then to her feet.

"What?! What is it!?" she snapped, anger only restrained by her surprise at his own.

"Can you read?" he asked darkly. Durham squinted in response, confusion evident on her face. "Can you read?"

"What? I...Yes?" she stuttered, the hint of laughter only leaving him further incensed. "Is this a trick question?"

"Apparently so! Let me clarify. Apparently, this is a trick question because you cannot read! Behold!" he declared, brandishing the paper as his sword. "The egghead reported from Research and Development! Here you will find several comments, including a commendation for your maintenance of their experimental weapon, Re-Human. There's a note here about your thorough description of using the device, all very good. But wait! You can see an additional note here. It may grab your attention. It notes that for the *second* mission in a row, you neglected to activate the weapon! You failed to *turn on* the weapon! You've been swinging around a regular piece of metal, not even silver!"

Durham looked up at him, eyes wide. The scar across her face bent out of shape with how high her brows rose, and she uttered a single sound.

"What?"

Aaron clutched his head, aching for all the wrong reasons. "You dolt! Paradise be damned, you are so stupid...Would you forget to turn on the pact? Don't answer that. Give me the sword," he ordered. "Give me the sword! I want to see if I can figure it out in less than five minutes!"

"No, no, no!" Durham cried. "That's mine, give it back!"

But Aaron had already taken it. She had hung Re-Human on top of the desk like a mantelpiece, and he held it above her head with petty cruelty. She pushed and shoved him, but against his unnatural strength couldn't even make him budge. The rest were watching. Gavin was laughing so hard, he was holding his sides, with Moore and Lenz shaking their heads as if the sight was painful. Sif was incredulous but unable to mask her smile, while Brook hid her mouth behind her hand.

"Dalton, I hope you weep," Aaron muttered, pulling the blade from its sheath. It was a balanced weapon, with a slight curve like a saber, and a long hilt that let it be wielded in one hand or two. Along its spine was a series of geometric runes connected by what looked like wires. Etched in dyed green metal, it was elegant despite being a prototype. It felt perfectly smooth to his hand except for…

"Aha!" he called in victory. "A slot against the side of the hilt. What a novelty this is!" He pressed against it, and a small trigger extended from the weapon. "I wonder what this could possibly do," he called despite Durham's protests. "Could it, by any chance, activate the sword's enchantment as detailed in the instructions you were provided? Who'd like to bet? There are no wrong answers!"

Her words came out in a flurry, full of incriminating guilt but empty of remorse. "Okay maybe I didn't read the manual but I've seen magic weapons before and they gave me a whole blooded book and I figured it was all warnings and that's always just a load of shit so I just skimmed it and it all just came down to how to swing it *and don't use it before I do come on*!"

It was then that Aaron pulled the trigger, and a charge ran up his arm. In an instant, the weapon heated in his grasp, the sensation different from the burn of silver. It was extreme discomfort, bordering on pain, and made him shake and shudder like his bones were grinding within his body.

An invisible force tugged at the weapon. It twisted in his hand, dragging him downward, then up like it was swinging itself. It shook violently, only made worse when his free hand grabbed hold of it, and it pulled him. The members of S-0 moved backward in alarm. The heat ran upward, creeping past his shoulders toward his heart. Giving up trying to control it, he settled for the alternative, and it took all of his strength just to thrust the blade into the nearest wall. It buried itself halfway into the brick between a stunned Dalton and Brook.

Still, Aaron's hands shook, seized around the sword's hilt. It vibrated in his grasp, but he didn't dare pull away for fear of freeing the weapon. In the end, it took three pairs of hands to pull him free, and he fell backward to the ground, watching in awe as the weapon became still. The room was utterly silent, save the wild heartbeats around him. Durham whistled, leaning against his shoulder.

"So…" she drawled. "That's what they meant when they said for human use only. But hey, just imagine how much easier fighting will be— Ow!" she complained as Aaron slapped at her hands, his fury beyond restraint. "Hey, stop. Stop it!"

She tried to reach out to deflect and parry him, but he wouldn't allow it, targeting her wrist, forearm, bicep, shoulder, and then head.

"I am going to literally beat the stupid out of you!" he declared.

"Gonna be here a while," Gavin mused.

"Get me my sword," he ordered in response. "We're doing this right now."

Not ten minutes later, the entirety of S-0, including Eric, was gathered in the barracks training room. Durham stood opposite Aaron, examining Re-Human like she was seeing it for the first time. Aaron drew his sword. "Come at me," he commanded. "We're testing this for real."

"All right, all right," Durham said as she tied up her hair. "You know my head's gonna bruise. This is abuse."

"We just got practically demoted," Moore called. "Idiot abuse is sanctioned. Try not to knock out what little sense she has!"

"I know you've been through worse," Aaron said. "But I hope this makes a top ten."

Durham clicked her tongue, stretching her arms and legs, and then settled into a relaxed stance. "I feel like this is set up for me to fail."

She drew the weapon, slowly and carefully swinging it through the air in a series of practiced motions. Her eyes drifted around the dueling space as she did, barely focused, like she was waking up from a nap. Midway through, they snapped to him.

"Never been one to lie down and take it, though!"

She charged without further warning, closing the gap with the time her surprise attack bought. Without delay, she assaulted Aaron, delivering a series of high and low slashes in barely a second. She struck smoothly and fluidly, yet with ferocity far exceeding her frame. Each attack utilized the full range of her body's motion with no wasted movement.

It was an impressive assault. Pact or not, Durham was human, through and through. She couldn't shrug off gunfire, heal her wounds, or bring overwhelming strength and speed against her enemies. What she did have was an unyielding spirit and a desire to win that bordered on insanity.

Impressive as it was, it was not enough. Durham had the cleverness and skill to take more powerful opponents by surprise and hand them swift defeats; Aaron had seen it firsthand. It was no accident that she had wounded Silas not once, but twice on her own, and she had fought other nephilim besides. She was, as far as Aaron was concerned, the deadliest human combatant S-0 could offer. But he had practiced with her time and again. He knew what she was capable of and moved accordingly.

He met each strike with serenity, deflecting with enough strength to fully counter her movement and put her on the back foot. Widening his stance, he delivered a strong blow that shifted her whole body off balance.

"That's enough of that," he said. "I know what you can do on your own. Show me what that weapon is capable of."

Durham stumbled backward with a frustrated shout. Her shoulders shook from the force of his strike. He tilted his head, showing just enough smugness to ignite her anger. She brushed the lock on the weapon, resting her finger on the trigger.

"Just like the pact," she muttered, and pulled it.

A subtle hum permeated the room, felt more than it was heard. Aaron couldn't tell if the others perceived it. Re-Human rested in Durham's hands, now awash with light that danced on its tempered edges. It shimmered in iridescent hues that darkened and glowed from moment to moment. Runes glinted along its length so quickly that they might have been his imagination, and the branching lines that had caught his eye earlier stood out with greater definition. Durham's eyes were wide open. She drew in a deep breath. Aaron almost asked if she was all right, but then she engaged him again.

From the moment her body began to move, she was different. The way she drew in her arms when she ran, the motion of her heels digging into the ground, and the slightly loosened grip of her off hand were unmistakable. Nothing about her style had changed. However, she stood taller, as if the weight of the world had been taken off her shoulders, and when their blades met, Aaron nearly lost his grip.

The impact he had expected from Durham's full strength, the same he had experienced on innumerable occasions, came with a force behind it, like something far stronger was bearing down on the blade. Durham drew the weapon away, and the humming seemed to rise in intensity. Aaron's instincts bid him to meet the challenge, his blood running hotter at this strange development. Thrilled by the prospect despite his apprehension, he obeyed.

They struck in tandem, meeting each other's swings with fevered enthusiasm. It was different from fighting another nephilim: Durham had a sense for him, just as he did for her, only now it seemed like she could read him without effort. Her strength was still decidedly human, but where he could dance around her guard before and bully her with his physical power, she now moved in anticipation of his actions rather than around them, and when their blades met, every blow was masterfully parried, diverting his great strength without a hint of pause.

When she struck, there was an inexplicable force behind it that made every motion a threat. Aaron disengaged with a wide swing, taking two long strides to put distance between them. To his shock, he realized that his heart had sped up, and his breath came shorter. He looked down at his hand; his glove had been cut.

Durham took deep breaths, a toothy grin twisting her face. "You are so done…" she panted, before releasing a hysterical laugh. "This is something else!" She lifted Re-Human with a trembling hand. "I could paint the walls with the next hundred nightmares, turn Silas into—"

The trigger on Re-Human locked back into place, dropping from her hand as she swore.

"Perhaps you should read the instructions first," Dalton said, though even his eyes appeared wide. "That was…"

Gavin grinned, but his eyes were mirthless. "Good God, they gave Durham that thing?"

The laughter that followed was mostly genuine.

–CHAPTER 10–

EVIL, PAST AND PRESENT

Aaron adjusted his position to better read from the old report. "Paradise calendar, year thirty-five thirty-nine. That makes…fifteen years ago. Attack on the city of Griffin. The battle took place over three days. The swarm comprised over two hundred nightmares. Casualties…conclusive." He paused as he observed the numbers laid out before him. "Military: One hundred eighty-six. Civilian: One thousand nine hundred ninety-five."

"You know you don't have to read them out loud every time," Gavin said from behind a report of his own. "It's depressing."

"Sorry," Aaron said, glancing over the stack of books arrayed between them. "There's more than I thought, is all."

Gavin nodded, blinking alertness back into his eyes. "Scary thing too, it's not even all of them. Reporting was sketchy back then, as the territory was in decline."

That was news to Aaron. "Really? How'd you hear that?"

"I knew a guy who helped do some of it. I think his service is over now, though."

"Ah, I see."

They had been combing through records for most of the day, and the day before. Aaron had Eric requisition not only the history of their own dealings with abnormal nightmares, but also the castle records from other special forces and documented nightmare attacks. He gathered every incident, from small packs to horrendous swarms. By going through them, he hoped to find hints as to the creatures they had encountered, and learn from whether they had been vanquished before.

That was easier said than done. The unfortunate reality was that details of nightmares were not always noted. So varied were they in appearance and so homogenous in their desires, such a thing was often not even considered unless in the case of something truly outstanding. Moreover, if they were exterminated, then odds were even higher that they would be given little further thought.

Sitri Baal had made some changes to combat this. Her efforts included a number of addendums to the policy just for the sake of an encounter like theirs. Even so, many records were either old, damaged, or lost and rewritten a dozen times over, and so they were forced to examine each manually.

Aaron resumed his scanning of the report, trying to do so as quickly as possible without losing any important detail that might catch his eye. A wall of text followed that detailed the damage incurred to infrastructure and the reconstruction efforts that went into restoring order and the defenses of the city. After that, a brief summary of the powers involved.

> *Nightmares attacked in a single wave. Outer defenses breached at nightfall. The majority of casualties were incurred within the first night before a lengthy holdout. Defenses maintained by stationed Captain Patenaude with assistance from nephilim of House Bleakshroud.*

Aaron paused at the mention of the name. Silas had been of Bleakshroud, or a bastard of it. He pulled out his notebook and wrote down the name.

> *Relief delivered in the form of Lady Lilith Baal and capital forces. Nightmares gathered around a singular entity: one immense nightmare of many limbs and mouths. Split into multiple bodies upon sustaining significant damage in a combined attack by human and nephilim defenders. These 'children' spawned from this event did not divide further. According to eyewitness testimony, seven were birthed and all were destroyed.*

He sighed. What followed was a lengthy series of anecdotes on weaknesses in command structure and defenses that allowed the attack to take place and the changes that were made in response. All well and good, but not to his purposes. He pushed it aside, marking it yet another old story not relevant and not needed for their current mission. Aaron hadn't exactly thought it would be easy to sort through a history of violence, and he wasn't expecting a direct answer. He was in search of a ghost of a clue, but he'd at least hoped that something would stand out to him. S-0 was created to deal with rogue nephilim; they dealt with foes that could not be handled by conventional force.

When it came to nightmares, he'd seen many with abnormal behavior and some with unusual abilities, but they still followed certain rules. Silver was their greatest weapon against the ravenous, monstrous beings. Any that didn't suffer from such a weakness must be expunged at all costs, and any creature that had ever shown itself to have such a resistance would have surely been remembered. A complete and utter lack of evidence in the past would suggest one of two possibilities: Either anyone who had encountered them before had perished, or the creatures were something new. Aaron wasn't sure which was the more unsettling prospect.

The restless thoughts were interrupted by the sound of soft snoring. He looked to the corner of the room, already knowing the source. Durham had collapsed on the tabletop, pages still beneath her as she slept completely motionless, save for her breathing.

He didn't move to wake her. She'd earned the rest. Following their duel and the entirety of the squad witnessing what Re-Human was capable of, they had not wasted time. Twice more, she and Aaron had sparred, testing the limits of the power the strange weapon bestowed on her. As they had, she'd shown signs of tiring. They were fighting, of course; it was no cause for alarm, but Durham was one of the most capable fighters he'd ever seen, and he should have noticed something was wrong. When her fatigue grew rapidly worse and she nearly collapsed on her feet, it was already too late.

The weapon was the only possible cause, but contact with the department of Research and Development had provided little in the way of explanation, but that the weapon was working as intended. They specified only that the weapon was intended for Durham's testing exclusively, and that while others could utilize it, anything other than short exposure could be considered unsafe. The rest of the details were privy only to Lady Baal's explanation, and the limitations were clearly laid out in the instructions that they had provided.

When Durham had fully returned to her senses, Aaron had apologized for putting her in danger in his anger, only for her to spring to her feet and ask where her "new baby" was. She'd jealously cradled it, a wicked smile on her face as she described the many new ways she'd hack apart her foes. Her complete lack of urgency for the situation reminded Aaron why he was angry in the first place, and her reading had been assigned just as quickly. He'd ordered her expressly to not use the weapon's true power until she'd read the instructions cover to cover, and though he knew she would ignore him sooner or later, it was better than nothing.

He resolved to ask Lady Baal about the thing as soon as he was able. He had no mind for technology and a middling grasp of magic, but that all fell at the feet of a single fact: Whatever power Re-Human bestowed, it was fearsome indeed.

Aaron returned his attention to his work. They had only been allowed to take so many reports at once, and when he returned them, he would be given more to sort through. What he had finished was the last of the stack of mainline incidents in their current collection. That left the smaller, older set that was tied up next to Gavin. When Aaron reached for it, his friend tried to dissuade him. "I'll get to them next, don't worry," he said, not lifting his eyes from his current reading but laying a protective hand on the documents.

"It's fine," Aaron assured him, taking them away with a precise application of his monstrous strength. Gavin's hand remained clinging, and he chuckled. "I know they're old, but I'm not going to break them," he insisted.

Still, Gavin didn't turn his head. "Tell that to the doorknob."

Aaron's smile melted into a frown. He gently but firmly stole the stack away, undoing the tie that held it together and taking the first file from the top.

It was shorter than the rest he'd read, but had a seal stamped on it that brought it to attention in the bright green shade of the Baal family crest. It was not the insignia he was familiar with; instead of two spears crossed unevenly, it was a single vertical spear in front of the same beams of light. That was a sign of age. When Sitri came to power, she changed the Baal crest that had been their colors since time immemorial. The words at the top of the page denoted its author. *Lilith*.

He paused: not quite so old, perhaps. Lilith was the mother of Sitri and the former head of the house. He picked it up gingerly, almost in reverence of what her words might have been. He had never met her. She had met her end well over a decade ago when the Baal family had faced collapse at the hands of the ambitious wardens of House Nero. It was only several years after Sitri's own ascension that he had arrived in the East, and from what he could gather, the two were different as night and day.

Aaron slipped past the report's designation and identifiers, wondering what might have prompted the warden herself to comment, and reviewed the details with the curiosity of beholding a taboo. Rather than the curt, clipped descriptions of most of the other documents, it was written in elegant hand, more like a description of a story.

> *Summer of the Paradise calendar, year three-thousand five-hundred and thirty-seven since the pact of the nephilim. A trio of nightmares encroached from the farthest wastes. Sightings came in from across the northern borders and continued for several weeks. Each time, we were provided descriptions that were quickly determined to be stories of the same nightmares. They were always sighted as three, tall and thin, with wide mouths. Hairless and scaleless, the shape of their bodies bore a passing resemblance to starved dogs.*

The description was vague, but not that far removed from his own encounter. Aaron leaned in close and continued. Each time they appeared, they lingered at the edge of our outlying bases and towns, eventually spotted outside the city of Rymon. But every time, they did not attack. They watched and waited, once for as long as a day. But whenever forces would move to engage them, they would depart.

He drew his finger across the letters, underlined as they were. A paragraph broke off from the others, the weight of the pen strokes indicating more force behind the words.

> *Despite their monstrous appearance, it is common knowledge that nightmares possess some form of twisted cunning. However, self-preservation that drives them away from their primary desires is rare and*

uncharacteristic of those found in the frontiers. Though the priests of Paradise would have you believe that their realm is pure and safe, the paladins exist for a reason. The nightmares that come to be in their domain are fewer in number. Drastically so. But, close-kept a secret as it may be to them, those that do appear there are markedly more dangerous, with a sort of fiendish intelligence to match. I write this not for those ignorant of such things, but for those with knowledge of them, so that you may appreciate the significance of what occurred next.

At some point, this group of nightmares was able to infiltrate the capital city of Veridian. My own home played host to these creatures for three days and four nights. During this period, these nightmares killed twelve civilians and eight of the city's police force. They avoided my forces and slipped through cracks in formations as if they had a sixth sense for it. They seemed to have a taste for prey that couldn't fight back, as the guards who were discovered were always killed but never fed upon. Moreover, those armed were always killed while isolated, away from their respective groups of crowds that could alert others for help. In the end, I dispatched the monsters myself.

My personal guard and I found them near the edge of the city, their prey still in their arms. Each had one in hand, bludgeoned unconscious and cradled like newborns. They attempted to flee at first, rather than fight. When I was able to keep pace with them, they discarded the captives. One even threw theirs at me like a projectile. Only once I had caught up to them a third time did they deign to fight. I took no chances. I used my magic, and the power of Entropy saw the vile monsters destroyed.

What I write now, I write as mere speculation. They were oddly close to the city's walls, and they had taken no others far from their hunts. Perhaps they had meant to flee the city, taking their meals with them. But to me, it seemed strange that they would take them alive. Such behavior is reminiscent more of rogue nephilim. Though they were clearly abnormal, Nightmares eat the dead and the rotten with no distinction, unlike our kind, who find such things revolting.

Yet in the death throes of the final creature, I heard a strange sound. It was a haggard whistle as it breathed its last, but almost sounded like the murmured words of the delirious and the dying. Even to my ears, it was scant more than a whisper. "Run away," it said. Was it a trick? My imagination? Was the creature mimicking the speech of the dead? In my two centuries of life, I have encountered all manner of nightmares. I have heard beings that imitate sight and sound before. But this was different. There was a cadence to it, as if the faint ramblings were unprompted. I know not. I will consult my records, for the other wardens will no longer heed me. Should I find anything of significance, I shall update this record as well.

For our future, Lilith Baal.

Aaron closed the report, pulse audible in his ears. The story was disturbing enough, but that the warden herself had seemed so unsettled was even more chilling. That she had claimed to never have seen creatures like them was telling in and of itself.

They had supposedly spoken. The last wheezing breath of the nightmare that had attacked the bunker lingered in Aaron's mind. *Help.* That was a start. Unfortunately, the report went into little detail about their slaying, other than that she had used her own power. Entropy was the inherited magic of House Baal and the power that had elevated the vampires so highly for thousands of years. It was shield and sword both, the essence of chaos distilled. Aaron had only seen it a handful of times, and when Sitri had deigned to use it herself, nightmare and nephilim knew fear. All things that the light of Entropy shone on were reduced to dust. That Lilith had been able to destroy a handful of aberrant nightmares wasn't a surprise. But the story didn't say why she had taken the field to fight the beasts.

But then, the timing of the letter was important. It would have been when the Baal influence was rapidly waning. Lilith had died only a few years later.

He shifted his thoughts. Given the time she had taken to write the report, he was confident that Lilith would have noted it had they displayed a resistance to silver. Instead, he drew out his notebook and made a record of his thoughts once more.

"Aberrant nightmares encountered before have drawn the attention of the prior warden," he mouthed as he wrote, the better to ingrain it into his mind. "They didn't display the same ability, but their vocalizations are similar. Lilith Baal drew a comparison to the nightmares of Paradise."

Lilith had been true in her description. Those who resided there were a rarity, but they were also of particular viciousness. They often grew to be singular legends of folklore rather than the constant ravening threat of hordes that menaced the frontiers. It was the only means of maintaining their existence in a place so populated by paladins and high-class nephilim with little else to ease their boredom. Aaron's own household had been lax in that matter, so far as he could remember.

A familiar twinge in the back of his skull accompanied the thoughts. As always, memories of the time before his arrival on the frontier were hazy at best. Rather than a coherent stream of consciousness, he instead contended with scattered images and sounds that polluted the clarity of his mind, the more he tried to make sense of them. He saw a great serpentine abomination, cut open in a dozen places, and with each wound, bleeding skinless limbs. The cries of doomed citizens sharpened his hunting senses to their limit while the trail of destruction the enormous nightmare had left rent the very foundations of what had once been a temple.

His clenched hand folded the notebook it held, crushing the hard cover like an eggshell and leaving it bent uselessly out of shape. He sighed. Constantine's criticism had been demeaning and hurtful for no other reason than its accuracy. Whatever had passed for his youth was long gone, now, and all he had left to remember it by were these sad, incoherent kaleidoscopes of sensation.

The memories of the castle of his birth were fleeting and indistinct. The faces of his family were eroded beyond recognition. There was nothing truly there anymore. Black hair, sharp eyes, a superior smirk: These were the only things to fill the void. All that he truly remembered was the comfort of sleeping, and when he awoke, the despair that all was in ruin.

With nothing, he chased rumors of a queen rising in the East. A distance traveled that he couldn't comprehend. A desolate wasteland. Taking an oath of fealty. He arrived during Sitri's war with Roman Sterling. She recruited him herself. Everything since had been razor-sharp by comparison, as if forcefully shoving those dying memories into the abyss.

Aaron put the notebook away. Gavin's eyes hadn't moved to it, but he was ashamed to know that his friend had undoubtedly noticed. Instead of dwelling on it, he reached for the next report in the stack, only to find that the entire pile of paper had come with his hand. It had been bound together as one, which he found curious. No single incident would require so much paperwork to document. Then he took it and lifted the cover page, seeing once more the seal of Lilith Baal atop it. He moved aside the cover and read what followed.

The Hell Breach. The lettering was different from the first report. Unlike the neat, orderly writing prior, this was sharp, hasty, almost slovenly. The bunched, dense lettering spoke of a rushed work or exhaustion, as did the slight smearing of ink on several sentences.

Paradise Calendar year three-thousand five-hundred thirty, the twelfth day of the month of wrath. We don't often track dates anymore. The Paradise Church is rather meticulous, but we prideful "immortals" have never done so. Perhaps we haven't felt the need. Many live through events themselves, and the desire to set our lives above those of humans leads us to treat them differently.

It all feels like nonsense now. I'm rambling. This is because I do not have a date to provide now. Information is a rarity these days, so I will say only what I know. At some point in the final month of Paradise's calendar year of three-thousand five-hundred and twenty-nine since the first pact with the nephilim, the incident occurred.

I have seldom interacted with the wardens of the southern frontier. There is little need to. However, by mere coincidence, I did once meet the then-current leader of House Vulkan. He was a hulking creature, a minotaur, with a great, wide, horned head and a body of steely muscle. He spoke softly and jovially despite the way his mouth suffered difficulty pronouncing the common language. I'd heard only that he had a personable reputation, and never a word of hate for him.

That's a rarity in this world. I am saddened to see it gone. For one day in that month, a nightmare swarm of unprecedented size and ferocity attacked his domain. His cities were lost in days, along with him and his entire bloodline. What followed was true horror.

Without the warden as its shield, the southeast frontier collapsed, and the nightmares, whose numbers we cannot say but surely comprised many thousands, drove deeply into the domain farther and farther until they entered Paradise itself and scattered to the wind like poison.

The nephilim families of Paradise were roused. The paladins of the Church moved into action. Wardens from all frontiers were called for aid. It was not enough to triage the catastrophe taking place over such a wide area. The primary advantage of the wardens and their frontiers, a definite concentration of nightmares to direct our forces at, was lost, and we paid the price for it. Through the combined efforts of humanity and nephilim, the swarm was eventually destroyed, but not before wreaking a catastrophic toll. How many hundreds of thousands died? Who can even say? The humans will catalog their own losses. For us, we have lost something even more precious.

Many nephilim come to be because of the use or misuse of magic. Many are wholly unique within this world. Actual species are rare. Finding mates and reproducing has always been a slow and challenging affair, made easier by an abundance of time. But some were more populous than others, and so had a distinct advantage. The Baal family could be said to be one of those. That, too, was lost. Most of our supporting members perished. My sister and her husband died without children. My Lord Lucius, my mate, perished as well. Our minor nobility was decimated, as were those of the others. Sterling had siblings, too, lost to the swarm.

Who knows what we are to do now when the time comes to raise the next generation? My own children are near adulthood now, Sitri and Vergil. But neither is ready to rule. Vergil, the younger, is now destined for regency in Paradise with the loss of our supporters. His intelligence and personality are powerful tools, of which he is a master already, but he is too gentle. The world is crueler than he can reason with.

Sitri, my firstborn and heir, seems to think she can bend the whole world to her will. So strong, so willful... That arrogance now, more than ever, could cost us everything. But maybe that arrogance is needed. I cannot be certain anymore. I weep for the fates of those in the south. The following is a poor accounting, but it will serve as a reminder of why we fight and the cost of defeat.

For our future, Lilith Baal.

Aaron flipped through the following pages as quickly as he was able, for no other reason than a desire to stop seeing them. Page after page, report after report of cities and towns laid to waste. Names, endless names of the dead. The number was staggering. He could hardly bear to keep going, but he knew that if he didn't finish, he would be compelled to look again.

"Captain!"

The exclamation nearly made him jump from his seat, both from the interruption of his thoughts and from its urgency. He looked up at Eric, who was leaning against the doorway and his cane. His expression was solemn, and by the way he carried himself, he'd hurried his way there.

"Take a seat if you need to. What is it?" Aaron asked, disconcerted at what could have prompted the man to such haste.

Eric offered a polite thanks, pulling up a chair adjacent to him. He placed a paper on the table. "New orders from on high. You've been called for a case."

"A case, just like that?" he exclaimed. "We need more time to research those nightmares, and we've only scratched the surface of these reports. Lady Baal is busy with the Church. What could have happened?"

Eric tapped on the paper. "Constantine might have it out for you this time. His signature is on this."

"Constantine doesn't give us orders," Aaron replied.

Eric wiped a bead of sweat from his brow. "He has a pact, too, you know. He speaks with her voice, and the seal is still Baal."

Aaron bit his lip, wary of his clenching hands and what might be crushed in them.

The paper in front of him wasn't a proper report. It was a simple one-page document with an assignment number on it and his name.

"Nephilim attack," he read aloud so that Gavin and Durham could hear. "When did this happen?"

Eric's expression grew darker again. "Just a few hours ago. They want you on the scene."

"A few hours?" Gavin tilted his head thoughtfully. "You're telling us it got to Lady Baal and Constantine in just a few hours with an active threat by the Paradise Church in their hands?"

"Yes," said Eric. "I got my feelers out while I waited for confirmation. They want you now."

Aaron stood, Gavin and Durham rising with him. He looked at her, trying to gauge her state, and her eyes narrowed. "Don't you dare," she hissed. "We're not fighting the damn thing yet. I'm going."

He shrugged. "We'll finish this later. For now, get your gear. Eric, contact the rest of S-0. If this is really so bad, I want all eyes on it while it's still fresh."

They left in a hurry, as they were wont to do. For his part, Aaron was glad enough to leave the horrors of history behind, even if that meant confronting one that was new.

The attack had taken place in the north quadrant, along what many of the people called Oldtown. Before the city had been retaken, it was the skeleton of what had once been a staging ground for the castle. It was refurbished when Lady Baal reclaimed the territory, but it had received less attention than other districts. It also served as the primary connection to a large series of underground tunnels built for storage, now known as the undercity, and held a large volume of housing.

Aaron didn't enjoy navigating it. The buildings had a surprising amount of space between them, built without thought for the city that would come later. They also lacked the presentability and scale that came with modern architecture. Spearhead had been modeled as a recreation of the Baals' former capital and was built in its image.

The buildings were light stone, white or gray, and built close together to make the most efficient use of space. They made frequent use of symmetrical and geometrical structures, and had been built upward, with many attached columns and spires that reached toward the sky with the promise that they could be built upon and expanded even further in the future.

Unlike these newer constructions, the works of Oldtown were paltry in comparison. They stood apart from one another, with their color looking pale and sickly rather than bright. The buildings were squat and unremarkable, hardly different from the unnamed village that they had saved so recently. Plain as they were, they looked as if they could have been left alone for centuries. More than anything, though, the remnants served as a reminder. They had been held once and then abandoned, only to later be reclaimed. Those who lived in and around them could feel it. What was built could be lost, and what was lost was never the same.

S-0 drove through the wider, less-populated streets with ease. Those who saw them in their oversized transport quickly found a reason to make themselves scarce and parted before them quickly. It didn't take long for them to spot the location of the attack, surrounded as it was by members of the military police. Following the knot of personnel presiding over the cordoned-off alleyway, Aaron instructed them to pull over. They stepped out of the truck, boots rendering each step on the cobblestone with a distinct weight.

"This street sees plenty of use," Gavin remarked. "Not too far from public view."

Aaron didn't reply, making toward the scene with redoubled urgency. The police stiffened when they laid eyes on him, but that faded quickly enough when they noted his uniform. He singled out the man in charge, an officer with a heavy cap and heavier scowl.

"S-0," Aaron said, keeping his introduction simple.

The man nodded. It was always easier to start with his position. "Captain-Commander Sietz said you'd be here," he said, voice a low rumble. He regarded Aaron with the eyes of a veteran, cold and suspicious. "He also warned me what you were."

Aaron took a breath, smelled the overpowering scent of blood, and dread filled him. "I wish he really did know what I am."

The captain grunted. "He said to give you whatever you need. Right this way. Maybe you can make something of this horror show."

They walked into the alleyway between the buildings. Even in the afternoon, the shadows left it dark. Aaron had no trouble, of course, but in that moment, he wished that he did. Sif coughed.

"Cold damnation," she cursed.

"Dear God, there's nothing left," Moore breathed.

"What happened to his chest?"

"Do we even know the cause of death?"

Durham chuckled. "Just one? I can list like fifteen off the top of my head."

Aaron looked at the officer in charge. "We'd like to know which of those fatal wounds was the first. Once he's taken away, see if you can determine anything conclusive and let us know." He returned his attention to the body. "As for the chest, it was opened up, as were wrists and throat."

He withdrew his spare notebook, taking down the thoughts both for professional and personal recordkeeping. "Opened up is a bit delicate," he said as he wrote. "His throat was torn out, maybe with teeth. Chest is pried open with extraordinary strength. The ribs are snapped rather than sawed through, and the sternum is pulverized. Looks like the blood is drained. At a glance, I'd say heart, lungs, stomach, kidneys; all removed."

Aaron sighed. He'd have been driven to vomit by the sight before him if the vilest of his instincts didn't quiver at the thrill. The remains were little more than meat, and half of it looked to have been blended into the ground and walls, with a clear path showing how the scene had played out.

His mind worked rapidly and autonomously, the exquisite details carving themselves into his memory. A series of blood splatters on the nearest wall showed the transition. They were first in still, perfect circles, and then expanded into larger droplets. The man's thoughts as he had tried to run would surely have been nothing less than a hurricane of pain and fear. What had followed was nothing short of barbarism.

Aaron bit his tongue, the pain restoring clarity to his mind. "Have pictures been taken already?" he asked the officer.

"They have," the man replied. "We're developing them now. "We'll get them to you as soon as they're ready."

"Thank you," Aaron said. "I want to know who this man was. I want to know where he worked and where he lived. I want to know the exact last time he was seen alive."

The splatters of blood caught his attention again. Some of them were on the far side of the alley as well. Their pattern suggested that they'd been flung, like he might swing his blade to clean it. But even dried, he could see they ran heavily, as if little force had gone into scattering them. It was casual, almost thoughtless.

He ground his teeth. Dalton exhaled next to him. "What do you think, Captain?"

Aaron murmured the old rhyme of the Church before speaking. "I think that for all their misery, nightmares have their charms. They don't grow, they don't live; they simply exist. But cruelty is a cultivated evil."

–CHAPTER 11–

TO KNOW A MONSTER

Soft morning light was gentle against Aaron's eyes, though he still donned his glasses out of habit. It had been only a day since the murder, but he was eager to begin his work. Despite the horror of it, the city had a tranquil beauty. The pale blue cobblestone streets at the heart of Spearhead were carefully maintained to the point of gleaming in the morning light.

The sidewalks were dotted at regular intervals with trees that injected color into the city of stone. As with most things native to the frontier, they weren't particularly pretty, with sharp, angular leaves and irregular branches pruned to avoid those on the road. However, they played host to sparrows and other small birds that trilled and chirped.

The lightness of their songs was a comfort to Aaron, and he enjoyed listening for the subtle differences between them, even when they voiced their alarm at the circling of a hawk above. To each side of him were the housing blocks of the city. Each was a bright, multi-story building built into the shape of its neighbors like a row of puzzle pieces. They had little variation among them, but carved into the windowsills, he could frequently make out the spear emblem of the Baal house, as well as old glyphs of warding and protection.

They had little meaning, he was sure. The practice of magic was strictly policed. But it was a common custom in the frontiers to ward the windows in hopes of repelling the attention of nightmares and nephilim. The roofs of the buildings were nearly flat, some being actively worked on and built up further. This sight stretched into the distance until the houses ran up against the northern mountain of

Spearhead, where they were terraced against the incline. Despite the early hour, most had been emptied for their residents to go about their work already. This allowed him a measure of freedom to walk and discuss the matters of his grim quarry.

Rista squinted against the morning sun. He and Sif had been chosen as Aaron's company. Both were residents of the city since its rebuilding, and both were approachable enough when it came to civilians.

Where Sif maintained her usual two-step distance from Aaron, Rista was surprisingly talkative.

"Bit quiet for this time of morning," he remarked. "I hear more people are stopping by the church now. Do you think Lady Baal will step in if it continues?"

"I don't think she would do that," answered Aaron. "It was her choice to allow it in the first place. But I'd rather not talk about it too much. It feels like by doing so, we risk making it happen."

"I'm not sure why you worry. Even if there's conflict, you're durable."

"A rock is durable, but I've seen her break those, too." Rista chuckled at that. Even Sif's lip twitched, and Aaron smiled at the occasion, careful not to let it show.

"Well, there's always a scarier monster," Rista remarked. "Speaking of monsters, where's Durham?"

Sif gave him a pointed look. "Durham's a walking, talking hammer. You want her here for this?"

"You know we work well together," Aaron said. "To your point, she knows her strengths. She knows she's not suited for this."

"Not to be that girl, Captain, but you might not be either."

"Maybe I'm not," he replied, stopping to allow a small group of civilians to pass them by. Once they'd crossed the street, he continued. "But it helps me paint a profile. It's hard to explain, but I need to be there myself or I can't fully understand it. I'll trust you to step in if it looks to take a turn for the worse. I can always pivot to helping comb the streets. As for Durham… mission or no, she's on study time all day, every day. She's reading until she's memorized that manual."

"I don't know how fast you age, Captain," said Rista, "But that could be a while."

Aaron laughed, failing to convince even himself. "No better time to find out. The false exorcist was an easy job, but this last mission could have gone wrong very easily. She got hurt in the field, and so did you." He pointed to Rista's arm, which was still in a sling.

He rubbed the arm in question. "Well, it's not so bad. Gave me a couple of days off."

"You're in a good mood," Aaron said. "What for?"

"Not your concern."

Sif's words were immediate and biting, almost drawing him to a halt with their suddenness. Both he and Rista were put to silence by her affixed stare. Aaron bit his tongue, knowing he had overstepped in his eagerness. It wasn't the first time, but that didn't make it any less clear. "Sorry."

"It's nothing," Rista said quickly. "Nothing important."

Aaron shrugged in surrender, feigning nonchalance. "Your business, of course."

A crow flew into their path, settling on the stone to peck at something too small for them to see. It flew off just as fast, vanishing over the roof of one of the surrounding buildings. Sif continued, "Back to the matter at hand, do you have any thoughts as to what kind of nephilim we're dealing with?"

Aaron shook his head. "Your guess is as good as mine. The standard procedure is to see what was missing and work from there. Though we feed on…well, you know. Most nephilim are picky about what they eat, and prefer a particular…piece. The blood that wasn't painting the walls was drained, but that doesn't say much.

Vampires are always a possibility, with Lady Baal in power, there are plenty of them in the region, but that doesn't prove anything. Muscles seemed left alone, so any species that would eat indiscriminately wouldn't have left it that way. There are nephilim that don't need to kill, but that would make the death an accident, and I think we can agree that what happened was deliberate."

Rista considered it. "You could consider that it was a kill in error, and the body was mutilated as a cover-up."

"I hadn't considered that," Aaron answered. "Or I should say, it didn't feel that way to me." He thought of the state of the scene, more than just the corpse, and reaffirmed his belief. "That isn't to say there wasn't an intent. The throat was ripped out, so there's no way to check for bites. If it targeted a specific organ, it took more than it needed. Whatever this thing is, it dismembered its prey in such a way as to cover up its identity, and that means it's going to kill again."

On that sobering note, the conversation died. To catch a nephilim was no easy task, especially when that monster had already revealed that it was clever. The smart ones knew someone would come looking for them, and so they acted in anticipation of it. But even a cover-up provided information. A creature that killed so brutally could have taken steps to hide the body, but had instead left it to be discovered. That was important, and Aaron would use it to build a profile of the threat they were dealing with.

The profile was vital. Nephilim had access to incredible strength, intelligence, and unique abilities. Traditional investigation techniques were stunted at best. If Aaron were to describe the other "special powers," as they were referred to in the military, it would be "polarized." They felt as they acted, in extremes. Some were all fire, full of passion and fury in equal measure, who would laugh and rage far longer than an ordinary person. Others were cold and detached, so numbed by centuries of fighting that they were practically alien. The key to hunting a nephilim was to understand their personality in order to predict how and when they would choose their prey.

That was how he'd gotten the better of Silas. The vampire was a coward, one who had resorted to hiding in the shadows of nightmares to scavenge from their kills. That led Aaron to lie in wait for him by tracking the path of the nightmares he followed. Once he'd known the town was occupied, it had only made things easier. Though the operation had not been without flaw, the murderous traitor had played into his hands, cutting and running at the first chance he was able and choking on his own arrogance.

Aaron considered the state of the corpse again. There was no hair, nail, or skin left behind by the culprit, and no hint that the victim had even had a chance to struggle. The body was left as a message, brazenly. He could already tell that this one wouldn't be so simple. "You said he lived on Regis Street?" he asked.

"Yes, sir," Rista answered. "Roy Currie, age forty-five. Construction worker. Not pretty, not ugly. Not young, not old. Nothing outstanding to make him appeal to a monster."

"Or maybe nothing noteworthy is what made him appealing," Aaron said.

Sif pointed. "Up here, it's building number six, unit one."

They ascended the front steps with renewed speed, a pair of residents parting hastily before them. Inside, they were greeted immediately by the door marked as unit one. Before they could even knock twice, the woman answered the door. She had an angular face with deep-set eyes and braided blonde hair streaked with silver. She greeted them quickly and politely, bidding them to enter before Aaron could introduce himself. Still, he did anyway.

"Good morning, ma'am. My name is Aaron White. Are you Carmen?"

"Yes," she answered. "You haven't found…whatever did this yet?"

"I think you can help us on that front." He listened to her heartbeat as she led them inside; it was surprisingly even. "We were hoping you might provide us with some information."

"I've already spoken to the MPs," she said.

Aaron smiled as he had practiced, slight, without showing teeth. "I know. But I represent a group more specialized for cases such as these. We'd like to collect some additional information. First, I'd like to say that I'm very sorry for your loss. May we sit?"

Carmen regarded them for a moment, then nodded. They sat down quietly. Aaron noted the room: neat, orderly, and excessively clean. There were several picture frames scattered across tables and countertops, but all had been turned over. He felt his radio buzz, and muted it before gesturing for Sif and Rista to leave. They excused themselves quietly, leaving him alone with the widow. He cleared his throat and withdrew his notebook. "When did you meet Roy?"

The question seemed to surprise her. "Ten years ago, I think," she muttered. "Maybe it was eleven. Roy once worked for Eydis before the return of Lady Baal. We both moved out when Spearhead was retaken."

"How did that happen?"

She smiled slightly, and for a brief moment, her eyes shone. Just as quickly, however, they retreated into sorrow. "A fresh start, I think. We'd both already split up. We both had kids. It was nice to talk to someone who understood."

"Yes," Aaron agreed. "Being understood is important. Was he frequently home late?"

She shook her head profusely. "Hardly ever. Sometimes, he would go out with his coworkers, but even then, he was always back before midnight. It's how I knew something was wrong. It still doesn't feel real. Why not anyone else? Why him?" She twisted a ring on her finger. Aaron wanted to reach out, to put his hand on hers in comfort and security.

"Roy was found in Oldtown," he said. "He wasn't near a bar or a restaurant. Do you have any idea what he might have been doing there?"

"No, I don't think so. He would take walks, but not on nights before work. I don't know of anything but residences there. What could he have…" She trailed off before staring at Aaron through lidded eyes. He could see dark circles beneath them.

"Can you tell me more about him? What were his hobbies? His likes and dislikes?"

"What difference would it make?"

He paused, the turn in her tone not promising to his questioning. "I want to know everything about him, so that I can try to understand what could have been used to hunt him."

"Oh," she said softly. The grief in her eyes slowly cleared, replaced by realization. "You know what that's like, don't you? You cover it up, but you're one of them."

The words were pointed, accusatory. Aaron knew their direction, but let her speak her mind. "I am a nephilim, if that's what you mean."

She was no longer meeting his eyes, and her gaze fell to the ring on her finger. "I met them before, you know," she said softly. "I'll never forget them. Lady Lilith and Lord Lucius visited my town. There were others with them. Minor nobles or family, maybe. They were so different from what I expected. They had a shine, a feeling I couldn't put into words. Lucius died in the South, fighting against the hell breach. Lilith died defending us as well. Lady Sitri tells us to trust you, but I saw what they *did* to him. Tell me, have you hunted? Have you killed people before? Was it for food, or just for sport?"

Aaron wondered if there was a single answer that would satisfy her; maybe bring her some kind of comfort in his ability to bring the death of a loved one to justice.

"I can't remember the last time I killed a human," he said with his most practiced smile. "It's a badge of honor, you could say. I'm of the mind that humans should be the ones to pass judgment on themselves. As for nephilim, that's why I'm here."

"But why?" she pressed. "It isn't the same for you. You don't pass the judgment, Lady Baal does. You and the others just kill what you're pointed at. You don't have to worry about being weak. You don't live in fear with your home destroyed and your loved ones gone! So, what do you get out of it? Is it satisfying? Does it make you feel strong? If you weren't killing your own kind, would you just hunt us too? What does she have over you?"

Sif took a step around the corner, but Aaron stopped her with a look. He still believed the conversation could be salvaged. He saw the resentment in Carmen's eyes, the indignation. She was hurt, truly, but more than anything, she looked trapped by her anger and helplessness in the face of loss. It was a familiar look: so familiar in fact that he knew there was nothing to say to placate it. It was something he knew he would be helpless in the face of, and so the words that followed did so without care. He brushed a strand of deathly white hair from his face and smiled at the silliness. *Aaron White.*

"I was promised…a name."

The mask of grief cracked, momentarily repressed. "Maybe you guessed it already; White isn't an alias, it's just what people called me. I have no family name of my own. I was nothing before I came to the East. Nothing.

"I can't even remember it now. I was put to sleep; that much I know. Why? How long? I can't say, but I woke up in a coffin. No family, no friends, just an empty shell, like me. Whatever that was is lost to me now, and a nephilim without a house is a dog, to be put to work or put down."

The words were melancholic, as if spoken by a stranger, but they were unstoppable in that moment, fed by the fear he faced in the nightmares and saw in the eyes of every person he tried to save.

"Others can't tell what I am. I can't either. Oh, there are possibilities. A mutant? A slave? A bastard, hidden away? I came to the East because I heard whispers of somewhere that a thing like me could belong. It's the only thing I remember, really. I do what I do for a future, Carmen; a house to call my own."

Realization bloomed in her features, though he couldn't tell whether she was shocked, horrified, or both. "You want to become a noble."

Aaron tugged at his collar, careful not to reveal much. He resented the starved, deathly state of his body, but he only needed to show his collarbone where his pact was.

"You know what this is," he said. "Humans offer their loyalty to highborn nephilim and receive power in return. But I am not human. Instead, I give my service for a chance at something better. To be a noble, yes, but it's more than that. I'd like to make a place for myself and those like me who believe in something better than our natures. I don't know if I can change the others," he admitted. "But I think…Yes, I'd settle for a world where we only have to face nightmares. That would be enough for me."

Behind Carmen, Rista took a step closer. His hand closed into a fist over his head, his expression one of deadly seriousness. The signal was one of urgency, used only in the field for cases that were extreme or life-threatening. That alone brought Aaron's self-awareness back to the forefront. He shifted, suddenly acutely aware of how much he had overstepped.

Carmen Currie looked at him as if she were seeing him for the first time. Her face made her unease clear, but the resentment was gone from her eyes. He bit his tongue, looking down at her, trying to find more fitting words to end their conversation. Instead, he let out a breath he didn't realize he'd been holding. "Please excuse me. Roy's belongings will be returned to you soon. I've provided you with the line to my office. If anything comes to mind, or even if you need something, please let me know. I'll see to it."

He left in a hurry, passing the downturned picture frames as if they were looking at him. Only when He had exited the housing unit did he address his teammates. "What is it?"

Sif stared at him, and he realized that he'd taken a step closer without realizing it. Retreating, he smoothed over his appearance. "Sorry," he said. "That was uncalled for."

Rista appeared unperturbed by his outburst, but his expression was still darkly serious. "I got word from Dalton. There's been another attack."

The words ran over him like a chill. "Already? How can we know it's the same creature?"

"I asked the same thing. He just said, 'We know.'" Aaron didn't question it further. The three of them left the apartment and made their way out onto the street, which had grown busier in the short time they'd spent inside. As they moved, Sif kept the same usual distance, eyes focused firmly ahead of her and face set in grim determination as if their goal were already in front of them. Rista, however, took a half step closer, thin face tilted as if to get a better look at him.

His expression was curious, but surprisingly open, the usual focused passivity uncharacteristically absent. He looked far more at ease than even when he had approached them at Dominic's Cafe. Aaron didn't acknowledge it, still uncomfortable from his own lapse of self-control in the interview. He wouldn't have spoken at all if the man hadn't asked him a question.

"Captain, did you really mean all that?"

Aaron smiled sadly. "Would it change anything if I said yes?" Neither Rista nor Sif replied, though, so instead of waiting for them, he quickened his pace. "I hope so."

–CHAPTER 12–

A PRAYER TO NOBODY

Aaron waited patiently at the corner of the street, reclining in the shadow of the Spearhead Mountains. They'd left hastily, moving to get to the site of the second murder while it was still fresh.

The body was found on the west side of the city this time, in one of the lots that hosted the buses used for public transportation. The victim was identified immediately this time, but only because she was in uniform, as the body had been sliced nearly in half from shoulder to hip. Liesel Borro was her name. She was thirty-five years old, an employee of the city. No doubt she was doing her rounds of the lot when she was attacked. From what he could tell, it was only after she was dead that the creature carved her up for her organs.

He hoped so, at least.

Aaron spent an hour inspecting the scene for clues as to the identity and movements of her attacker, only to come up with a frustrating lack of information. Solid pavement left no footprints, and there was no hint of blood aside from that of Liesel. Once more, there were no hints of skin or hair under the victim's nails, and no trail had been left to follow. Given the nature of the damage to her body, it seemed like an attack Aaron himself might perform, using a bladed weapon with strength far exceeding a normal human. It was a quick kill, he deduced. Brutal, but efficient.

Dalton conferred with him at the scene. "Two victims in nearly as many days. Do you think there's more than one of them?"

"It's possible," Aaron conceded, mulling over the thought. "But I feel like that would just make it harder to move without being detected.

This isn't an alley in Oldtown. The killer had to sneak through public streets to get here without anyone batting an eye. Nighttime or no, that's not easy."

The cover of darkness would provide some advantage, he supposed, but it wasn't absolute. The night was often busy in the city, its residents taking after their nocturnal mistress. He considered the routes that a nephilim could take to get to the location of the lot without being detected. The buildings were denser there. There were fewer alleys to move through, and around the bus stations in particular, the buildings were lower. There was hardly space for a single nephilim to move unimpeded, let alone a group. And yet this one had done so, out of the sight of anyone who should have seen it.

"I'll say this," he had said as the city guards took the remains away. "I almost hope it is. If that's the case and they're sated, then it will at least delay the next attack."

The monster had thrown him off, attacking so brutally twice in quick succession. More than that, the nature of the two killings was disturbing. They were horrific but controlled. The sheer lack of any evidence left behind indicated professionalism and intellect, while the degree of spectacle in the treatment of the bodies spoke of a twisted sense of showmanship. Most rogue nephilim were either looking to eke out an existence in any way they could or viewed humans as little more than meat to be consumed.

However, both archetypes took appropriate measures when hunting, especially in the city of a warden like Lady Baal. Once more, their target had been killed in such a way as to leave a gruesome scene to be discovered. It was telling them it had no shame, no fear. Aaron worried about the implications. Nephilim like that were rare. They knew their place in the world and had just enough control to conceal their urges, making them exceedingly difficult to track while also capable of turning the tables on their pursuers. In Aaron's experience, they were by far the most dangerous to hunt.

That was why he decided to look for help, and he knew exactly who could be of service. He went to the only place he knew Leah could be found, and the place he had tried to find her at just a few days earlier for a brighter purpose. But when he arrived at the church with the scent of the murders still haunting him, Leah was absent once again.

He stood uneasily, considering where, or even if, he should search for her. The first time he'd come looking, it was for work on another case. It had been some time since they'd spoken, but he knew of no other place she might be. While he could never enter the church himself, she'd always noticed his presence within seconds. Now she was missing, but the church was far from quiet. The paladins were there, and they were speaking.

It was Alexander who held them at attention, his eyes wide and intense. "Strength swings our sword, but temperance is our shield. It is not enough to simply slay the evil that surrounds us. No, we must kill the evil within ourselves! If we do not, then the death we deal with will simply return to us: Such tragedies will play out over and over again. These truths have been proven by our struggle; a struggle that will not end so long as we remain slaves to our own vices.

"Remember when Saint Jeremiah triumphed over the devouring plague and the tyrant Lord Selry of the Bastille. He had no great army. He had no blessed silver. He had only determination and holy wrath for his treacherous foe. His efforts, and those of the ordinary people he led, saw a land untouched by nightmares for decades!"

One of the onlookers audibly gasped. Aaron couldn't see who it was; the crowd was too thick to tell, and the air was still with so many holding bated breaths.

"But the light of such a miracle inevitably fades," Alexander continued. "Eventually, the nightmares returned, as they always have. They are a vile power, and drawn to power they are! It is that very ambition that damned Selry, driving him to the darkest of sorceries. He pursued perfection, heedless of the teachings of his faith. We are all imperfect, my friends, but there is grace in that. The great sin is to believe otherwise, for it is to reject what is human! It is easier said than done. We are surrounded by frightful monsters. Some come to us in pursuit of our flesh. Some wear a more pleasant face."

His eyes flickered in the direction of Lady Baal's castle. "But we must not forget what we are. So, friends, I ask that you embrace it. Let none forget what it means to be a human being. We cannot look to salvation in our neighbors, our guardians, or even in what we call God! God is the totality of humanity. It is our successes and failures together. It is unstoppable, absolute truth, and that truth is this, my friends: Only we can save ourselves."

After that, the crowd was silent, though Aaron suspected they might have applauded were it appropriate. Instead, they bowed their heads in silent reverence for the words. He, himself, did not; there was no point in doing so. Oh, he could think about God, the same as anyone else. He could believe all he wanted, and he did, but it was a performance: shouting into a void. He didn't feel what the others felt when they prayed to their idea of divinity. The act of prayer was one that only ever filled him with emptiness. Still, he tried his best to listen, to learn, and to better understand the people he wanted to be.

Aaron looked up; some time had passed without him realizing it, and the crowd had begun to disperse. On a second glance, they were not leaving, but parting for Oris to walk toward him. He stood from the corner he had leaned against, taking a step forward to greet the paladin.

"Good to see you again," Oris greeted with a slight bow of his head. "I was worried Alexander might have scared you off. Between you and me, you wouldn't be the first. He has a certain candor."

"Well," Aaron acknowledged the gathered crowd who had come to listen to the sermon. "I guess it's a bit easier to convince those who can be saved."

"You don't think you can be saved?"

The question caught him off guard, not for how it was worded but the tone with which Oris spoke. It was one of surprise and genuine sincerity. It gave him pause before his next words. But the words came; in his time with the caretaker, he'd learned a thing or two about the scriptures of Paradise. "I'm no expert, of course. But I've read a bit about Saint Jeremiah. Brother Alexander was all too keen to mention his triumph over his fallen brother. Didn't he also say that all nephilim were monsters, cursed to damnation and evil? He used the power of the faith to kill many of them."

Oris laughed heartily. "You're well-read, Mr. White! Well-played, well-played! You're right, of course, about Jeremiah's words, but he was a warrior. Due to his blessings, it's sometimes understated that he could be a bit of a dunce."

At Aaron's expression, he laughed once more, taking a friendly step closer, the smell of incense heavy on him.

"Does it surprise you to hear me say such things? It shouldn't. We should venerate our heroes, but to do so without considering their vices is a stain on history. Those saints were as flawed as any of us. Remember Alexander's words. They were human, remember? It was by accepting those flaws that they became what they did. Those were their strengths, and they could be anyone's."

"A nice thought; something attainable by anyone," Aaron replied, trying to read the priest's expression. "But what about something like me?"

The paladin gave a sheepish smile. "That's where it gets a bit tricky."

He brushed at his cassock before taking a place next to Aaron, leaning up against the wall. Together, they looked out at the people around. Some of them were still kneeling in prayer. Some went about their day through the streets, and some stared at them, the odd duo that they were.

"It's difficult," Oris said after a pause. "The Church was created to save humanity, and none other. Your kind are as alien to us as we are to you, but we are inextricably linked. To be a nephilim, as we understand it, is to be at least partially human. And though ostensibly, the workings of the nephilim are their own business, it is a fundamental commandment that so long as that spark exists within, anyone can find Paradise. And I don't mean that sham that we call the land far from the frontiers, either. The paradise of the soul, eternal and everlasting. That can be available to anyone. It must be."

His words, spoken softly and carefully, were stunning to Aaron. They were the second time he'd ever heard something like them. The first was by the very person he had come to the church seeking. He looked around for her again, all the while remembering the expressions of the people of Sterling when they'd realized what he was and trying to keep the bitterness from his face.

"I've seen some people who would disagree. I wonder, does that really apply to all of us? For as long as I can remember, all I've wanted was to find a place for myself in this world. But is that something I can have, or does it belong only to the wardens and the nephilim who are tied to Paradise?"

Oris caressed the ring on his finger. "Well, that's just a matter of faith. Many hold no love for your kind. It's not hard to see why. Even amongst the wardens, there exists corruption and vice. The pursuit of power is a temptation that we of the faith have tried to stamp out for that very reason. However, for a nephilim, power is inherent to their nature, not something learned." He smiled. "Listen to me ramble…some do genuinely realize the best of their nature. There are those who dedicate themselves to not just the protection of humanity but to its uplifting, and no true believer would ever question them. Fighting against the evil inside is the making of a saint."

There was an edge to his voice, a sharpness punctuating his belief. "And do you know any nephilim that have done this?" Aaron asked.

Oris stood, exhaling slowly, eyes closed. "Maybe there were others in history, but I know of just one. He was a nephilim with the drive to uplift both his kind and humanity at once, pure of heart and determination. A living spark for all the world. The dragon, Lord Marcus Talos. You said you wanted to make the world less frightening… Now that I think about it, you remind me a bit of him yourself."

He considered the reverence with which the name was uttered. It was a strange one to hear. It was common knowledge, of course. Marcus Talos had ruled the territory North of Lady Baal for a long time. By all accounts, even hers, he was a figure respected and admired. Unfortunately, it was undercut by the present truth.

"He died, though, didn't he?"

The paladin's expression was stony and solemn. "Yes, he did. A shame that the only Talos the people will remember is his tyrannical son, Ethan. Well, I seem to have spoiled the mood. I apologize for that. It was a pleasure speaking with you again, Mr. White."

The paladin returned to the church, politely addressing the many people who wanted his attention. As he left the corner, Aaron noticed that for a few fleeting seconds, the people did not regard him with the same initial hostility, as if he had been touched by a spark of the man's divinity. But for all that the conversation had proved engaging, it had left him with more questions than answers, and even with the church doors open, there was no sign of her.

Still, she was nowhere to be found. The dismay of the citizens returned to its usual indifference, and Aaron made a silent prayer to the nothing that listened. *Be safe, Leah, wherever you are.*

–Chapter 13–

Method of Terror

Aaron sat in near-complete darkness. It was comfortable for him; his shades existed not just to hide his eyes from others, but from the brightness of the day. So, with no one else present, he enjoyed his element.

Before him was a carefully maintained encyclopedia. It was his idea, approved of and even contributed to by Lady Baal herself: a catalog of known nephilim. Within it, he'd included origins, characteristics, and natural abilities with which the different species were endowed, as well as the powers unique to any major or minor houses. He provided detailed accounts of those encountered by S-0, and then Lady Baal supplemented it with her family's knowledge of the different mystical creatures that roamed the world. It was a valuable treasure, and one that he hoped to utilize to help categorize the creature that now hunted the streets.

Another day of no leads had been frustrating. The being was leaving no flesh, blood, or hair behind. It hadn't been spotted, and there were no credible claims of a nephilim being seen elsewhere. There was no discernable weapon that it was using, and nothing concrete to connect the victims. The crimes were so perfectly executed that Aaron was considering magic.

Contrary to what a civilian might believe, not all of their kind were skilled in it. Few at all, in fact. Magic was rare for nephilim, just as it was for humans. He was no exception. Though Aaron did have a vague sense of its presence, it could be unreliable with clever or subtle enchantments. Just as the eye could miss a well-hidden detail, so could his own sixth sense.

But then, who could hide it from him? Magic was unreliable and dangerous, more likely to consume your soul and collapse your mind than to create a miracle. That was why both the Church and Lady Baal dealt with it so severely. Avoiding such consequences required intense control and careful restrictions. The Paradise Church avoided this through the discipline of its priests, while noble nephilim tended to inherit their affinities. Even more perplexing, as such a being wouldn't just appear from nowhere without anybody having heard of them.

Silas returned to his mind. The vampire had shown the ability to hide his appearance and mask the sounds of his presence, if only momentarily. He bore at least some relation to House Bleakshroud, who were rumored to be able to transform their bodies into mist. Such a trait would be the ultimate tool for a predator of the night to escape notice. But the Bleakshrouds were loyalists and located at Sitri's western border, keeping rule closer to Paradise. Lady Baal's entry concerning them had been short and conclusive.

"The only house to stand with me against the forces of Nero and all odds. The loyalty of the Bleakshroud is beyond all reproach."

Which meant he would have to look elsewhere.

Aaron tapped on the next entry in the book that marked his thought. *Ghasts* – a rare breed. The first were thought to have been created through an attempt to extend mortal lives, though that was mere conjecture after centuries of superstitious rumors. Whatever the case, the result was a vile perversion of the sort of thing that Valentine was: a body unnaturally fused with a soul, each tainting the other and torn between spiritual and corporeal.

They appeared as horrific, rotted versions of what they had been in life, but were able to meld with shadows and temporarily restore a human appearance to lure in victims. According to Lady Baal, the creatures had a preference for flaying their victims. They did not have an established hierarchy or houses. They were not the sort to ally with humanity.

Aaron frowned. That wasn't good enough. Ghasts were known only to attack with teeth and claws, a wild and messy affair. Liesel Borro's death had been brutal, but there had been an efficiency to it, and in both attacks, there had been no tooth or claw marks to be found on or around the bodies. If nothing else, he doubted the attacks would have been executed with enough precision and silence to remain undiscovered for any amount of time.

The next entry that he landed on was a familiar one; he had entered it himself. *Satyr.* There was a reclusive warden family of them on the western frontier, but only a single one was known to be in the east. They had the natural ability to release an aura of intoxication, depriving those around them of their senses. The one that Aaron had encountered possessed an additional ability, an inherited magic that allowed them to manipulate, travel within, and hide in the earth beneath their feet.

They were "of the earth" and so held some of it in dominion. But that Satyr had only come to the East to gain Lady Baal's attention, and she'd wasted no time in recruiting him to her cause when he revealed himself to be little more than an admirer. Supposedly, they drank blood, but also fed on the revelry of the people around them. They were more inclined to make mischief for fun than to terrorize. That this could be another creature of the same kind would beggar belief.

It was only a few pages later that another option presented itself. *Shapeshifter.* The very same nephilim as the House of Sterling. Some nephilim skilled in magic could use glamours to hide their more evident traits. It was incredibly rare and difficult to do so. Supposedly, even the prodigious Lady Baal would find herself incapable. Only one in several generations had the sheer skill in spellcraft needed to accomplish the feat.

Shapeshifters, however, didn't merely hide their nephilim traits with an illusion. They had an abundant mastery of their bodies, able to mold their forms into a near-perfect guise. That form was not an illusion, but their own "self" in human form, as it was understood. They could not change their appearance; it was merely how they appeared when they walked as physical beings. The concept was headache-inducing, but the result was the same. They could hide amongst humans with ease. Moreover, once returned to their true forms, they were possessed of boundless strength, among the highest of any nephilim.

Those were two traits that, together, painted a very real picture of what could have infiltrated Spearhead, and his recent excursion into Sterling territory had not helped his unease. He couldn't push the thought from his mind. No matter what horror presented itself before him, the idea that they could go to war all over again assaulted his conscience. *Could it be one of his? Did the town report it to Lord Sterling? There's no way he could have acted so quickly unless the killer was already here.*

Once again, he wished he could have spoken with Leah. The first time he'd been sent to her, he'd dreaded what the caretaker of the church would say or do to him, but she'd instead listened, learned, and let him learn from her in return. She had seemed invigorated by his curiosity about the scriptures and his desire to understand their history. Her insight and experience had been instrumental to their success, and he needed it again, if only to comfort himself.

But he could understand why she had left her post. For someone like her, who no longer had an official connection to the Church, the appearance of the paladins could spell trouble.

"Paladins, nightmares, nephilim…" he muttered. "How many threats can we face at once and survive?"

His radio buzzed, startling him to attention. He reached for it hastily, the reinforced case creaking as his finger closed around it just a bit too hard. He took a calming breath, relaxing before speaking into it.

"This is White, go ahead."

But he only heard some of the words that followed because when he did, anger surged through him, and his fingers closed shut into a fist, crushing the device. He stormed out of the study room. Eric was already waiting at the exit with his sword and a replacement.

"Where?!" he demanded as he walked.

Eric, unable to keep up with him due to his leg, merely called back, "The park!"

By the time he arrived, the military police had already quarantined the area. A small crowd had gathered at the perimeter despite the officers' warnings, and Aaron could see even from a distance that the zone they had created stretched out and around the park. He quickly tired of trying to maneuver his way through the crowd and removed his shades with visible frustration. The citizenry parted quickly after that, allowing him to approach unbothered. The reality of the situation began to dawn on him when he saw Noah Sietz at the scene.

The captain-commander of Spearhead's domestic security was a short but powerfully built man. One wouldn't assume his youth, weathered away as it was by duty. His hair was already lined with silver despite barely pushing thirty. He spoke with two of his officers in hushed tones, not acknowledging Aaron's presence until he was standing directly next to him. Only when he had finished addressing his men did he turn his head. "White, good. About time you showed up."

The words were clipped, but they skipped over insults, and that was to be thankful for. Aaron didn't have the mindset for it himself. Business was the best tool for interacting with the commander. Though he'd at one time hoped that the two could bond over a shared desire to protect lives rather than merely exterminate foes, Aaron at least accepted that they could work together efficiently.

"What's the situation?"

Sietz's eyes, so dark brown they were nearly black, darted off in the direction of the park for a split second, then returned to him. "Messy. What have you heard?"

"I can smell it," he answered, taking a deep breath. Stone, sweat, grass, trees, flowers…and then blood. "Where's Dalton?"

Sietz gestured to one of his subordinates behind Aaron, his grimace briefly twisting further. "Deadeye is by the bridge with one of yours. I suggest you get to him."

Needing no further prompting, Aaron strode past the guards and deeper into the park without another word. It was a beautiful place, as pretty as anything that could be found in the East. A small series of rolling green hills and trees was carefully cultivated to bloom against the combination of hot days, cold nights, and dry wind that made the region so uncomfortable.

A pond was fed by a small stream, itself an offshoot of the nearby Ironblood River that provided the city with the bulk of its water. Flowers bloomed alongside the stone path he took through the greenery, almost uncomfortably bright yellow and deep shades of purple splashing in colors rarely seen anywhere else in such a rugged part of the world.

It was a glimpse at something better, and it was dashed into oblivion by the sight beyond it. In the park center, a small wooden bridge crossed over the stream, right where it bent and curved around an apple tree. It was morbidly appropriate then that the bodies had been strewn about like windfallen fruit.

The first was slumped up against the tree. He might have been peacefully resting, were it not for his head in his lap. Where his neck had been torn was linear but jagged, as if a rusted saw had been used to sever his life. Dried blood clung to the trunk of the tree, perhaps from spurting out even as the man had fallen against it.

The second corpse was that of a woman disemboweled. She had been split at the waist, nearly in half. A burgundy arc splattered the ground around her, darkening the vibrant grass around where she lay in a tangled heap.

The final victim was draped over the edge of the bridge guardrail. Dalton stood over her, examining the massive hole that had been punched through her chest. Rista was beside him, examining where the blood had pooled beneath her. Aaron took a place behind them, assessing the wound. It was almost perfectly circular, perhaps the size and shape of a fist, but subtly different. Aaron pulled out his notepad, scratching down his thoughts before speaking.

"How long have they been here?"

"A couple of hours, I'd say," his lieutenant sighed. "The pond was closed off. Fountain's always having issues, but some folks just sneak in anyway."

Aaron found the comment oddly specific. "Where'd you hear that?"

"I come here with my family, sir." Dalton's hand clenched. He shook his head, looking at the other corpses in sequence before meeting Aaron's eyes once more. "We'll have their names shortly. How long would it take you to do something like this, if you really meant to?"

It was an uncomfortable question. Aaron hated asking himself what he could really do if he gave in to those base, spiteful impulses. But he knew why Dalton asked it, and respected him enough to do so. He chewed the inside of his cheek, biting into it as quickly as it would heal.

He imagined how he would take each of them. A single strike apiece if he was feeling generous, or a more deliberate pace if he wasn't. He imagined the way their bodies would cave beneath his strength, and the rush of heat and exhilaration that would follow.

"No time at all," he concluded. "If I put my mind to it. That's assuming I'm doing so quickly, and there was a threat of them making a scene."

"Do you think they were drugged?"

"No, I think they were killed," he retorted. "Quickly and brutally. Maybe they were taken by surprise."

"I agree," stated Rista. "I believe that, given what we know so far, it's safe to assume that our target is a shapeshifter performing these murders in its transformed state. While in its human guise, it has a high capacity to move through the city unhindered. That would also explain how it's gotten into public spaces twice already without being discovered. Once it's in position, it shifts to its real form and does the rest."

It wasn't a bad analysis. It echoed half of Aaron's own thoughts on the matter. But it didn't feel right. He looked at the corpses one after another, each more fantastically brutalized than the last.

"Premature. Still premature."

Dalton didn't respond. Rista cocked an eyebrow and continued his line of thought. "Captain, be reasonable. There are plenty of nephilim with raw strength to pull this sort of thing off, but far fewer who could do so without getting caught. I'm not familiar with every species, but I can't imagine one we know nothing about showing up out of nowhere with this kind of power and capacity for stealth. If we had records of one, you'd have found it by now. The narrative fits."

Narrative…a word was too clinical for what their investigation was trying to create.

"That's exactly why I don't believe it," Aaron countered. "If we make a mistake here and start making assumptions, we risk losing control of the situation even further. We can't start making decisions on a theory for which we have no definitive evidence. You know as well as I do, so why are you so hasty to classify it?"

A set of even footsteps from behind called his attention. Dalton spoke low and quietly so that only he could hear. "He has a point. It's a step forward. It will help."

"And I won't take that step if it's just for appearances," Aaron rebuffed. As the footsteps drew closer to his back, he raised his voice to a normal speaking volume. "We have no conclusive proof that it's a shapeshifter. We won't give a statement as such, even as a presumption."

"You've got to be kidding," Sietz stated, voice raised just a fraction above what was normal. "It hasn't been a week yet, and we're looking at five bodies. You're telling me you can't even guess at what this thing is?"

Aaron turned toward the commander, acutely aware of Rista's stare at the back of his head. "Of course I can guess, but you said it yourself: It hasn't even been a week. The number of victims aside, this creature does not wish to be identified. The methods by which the victims are killed are a deliberate choice to make identifying the species more difficult. With no wounds that we can definitively say are inflicted by a shapeshifter's teeth, we'd just be taking the easiest option presented to us."

Sietz's jaw squared, teeth clenched, but he didn't change the tone of his voice. "So, you're telling me we are five lives deep and you've learned nothing?"

"We've learned," Aaron responded earnestly, trying to communicate his feelings with as much sincerity as he could. "I wish that it didn't have to come at this price, but it has. I'm not going to squander it."

"I'll mark your wishes for posterity, White. I'd prefer some progress."

Aaron drew in a breath, not sure what he would say but certain it would be emphatic. As he did, though, he noticed Sietz's eyebrows drawn together, and his hand twitching, as if to reach for his waist. It was a familiar gesture. He stopped himself, exhaling the breath.

"Unfortunately, some nephilim don't make progress cheap. You've come here for a reason, I assume."

The commander paused, taking a breath of his own. "Actually, I thought I'd offer you some help. I know you've had your people combing the streets, but I also know you don't have many. I'd like to see where you've hit. I can get two hundred people onto this case. They'll do the groundwork and sweep every dark corner of the city while you do what you need to."

Aaron looked at Dalton, who returned his stare with a remarkably visible look of surprise. It hadn't been what either of them was expecting, clearly, and there was some comfort in that. But when that faded, and his lieutenant's shock was gone, Aaron beheld the sad look of certainty that told him they agreed on the answer. He sighed and returned his gaze to Sietz, anguish in his heart. "I'm sorry, but no, I can't accept that."

The captain-commander's expression immediately darkened. "No? Are you out of your mind?! This thing just painted our park. We have to do something!"

"We *are* doing something," Aaron responded. "This isn't the first nephilim we've exterminated, and it won't be the last."

Rista took a step forward and interjected. "Captain, at least hear him out."

"Even your man agrees with me!" Sietz snapped. "This is the most prolific killer we've had in the last three years. I have the obligation and the authority to act on that!"

"And in my capacity as the captain of S-0, I have the authority to veto you," Aaron intoned with a pointed look. He took a slow step closer. "But I'd rather you not make me. I appreciate the offer. I do. But this isn't your area of expertise, Noah. It's ours, and we will deal with it in our way, on our terms. It's for the best, for everyone. You do this, you're putting the public at risk."

Sietz grabbed him by the collar, pushing him back up against the guardrail. The touch was so foreign that he froze up, completely unsure of how to respond. "How much more *at risk* do you want them to be? We've got the threat of war in the air, and there's a monster *eating* them! This is the way we keep it from ending in a massacre!"

"If we do it your way, it's guaranteed to be a massacre!" Aaron snapped back. "Look at them!" He pointed to the bodies strewn around them. "They weren't fed on. This thing didn't do it to eat; it killed them because it served its purposes. You of all people should know that with nephilim, it's never as simple as it appears!"

The man's blood pressure rose, and he pressed harder. "That's exactly why we are acting now! But you knew that. You don't fool me for a second! You're in this for your own kind. This isn't about saving lives; all that concern is just self-serving tripe!"

"Easy!" Dalton hissed. He pulled Sietz off and shoved him back, careful to keep him from the corpse on the opposite guardrail. The commander looked at him with a mixture of shock, anger, and subtle betrayal.

"You too, then, Deadeye?"

Dalton betrayed no emotion, the moment of exertion quickly leaving him his usual stoic self. "You forget our training, Noah. Let the captain speak."

Aaron took a half step forward, simmering but holding tightly to his calm. He knew well what losing his cool with Constantine got him, and bit his tongue to keep it in control.

"I'll forget that," he said slowly. "These deaths weren't predatory. They were a statement, and so I see two possibilities: Either the monster is looking to provoke us, or it's just doing it because it can. I don't like to play to my enemy's intent, and if it's just so unfeeling that it finds amusement in displays like this one, then you're going to be throwing those lives away for nothing. How long do you think until one of your people finds it, sees their comrade's entrails ripped out, and sounds an alarm? What happens then? You think this thing will go quietly? If panic takes, it'll be carnage. Maybe you remember last time?"

He saw Sietz's resolve falter, his expression cracking as if the memory caused him pain. Aaron continued, seizing the moment.

"Three years ago, the red street? Sixty dead in an hour to a two-bit ghoul on the run. I remember you getting promoted after it. It was well-deserved: You were one of the only people to keep your cool when things turned to chaos. This will be even worse if you mobilize two hundred warm bodies into the dark places in this city. So, if you want to go over my head, you'd best go to Lady Baal herself! I won't let you cause that again!"

Sietz stared at him, face blossoming with a dozen different shades of anger. He readied himself for the rebuke that would follow, but it never came. Instead, Sietz exhaled through gritted teeth before nodding once, turning on his heel, and marching away.

"Come to me if you need anything," he growled. "The watch will support you in any way you need. But remember, you aren't a lord just yet. You and Lady Baal aren't the same. You can't use her name to get whatever you want, and I won't let my people die for this…whatever this is. Put this animal down, Captain White, and don't think you're irreplaceable. We survived without you, and we'll endure after you're gone."

Then, there was quiet. Aaron, Dalton, and Rista walked away from the bodies, taking grateful breaths of cleaner air while officers took their own account of the scene. Dalton looked unbothered by the confrontation, calmly adjusting his collar as if they were in a meeting.

"He's a passionate man, but I've never seen him so shaken. You argued your point well."

Aaron's fingers dug through the bark of the tree he had leaned on. "Self-serving…Is that what you think this is?" When he didn't hear a reply, his shoulders shook, and he exhaled slowly, desperate to vent the rage. "I'm asking you a question. Both of you," he hissed. "Do you all really think that I don't feel anything? That this is all some *performance?*"

"We're not the ones you need to convince, Captain—" Rista began, but Aaron cut him off, whirling to face him so quickly that his hand clawed grooves into the tree trunk.

"Is that right!?"

Rista took a step backward, eyes wide with shock. His good hand had moved out of sight behind him. It was a trained gesture, as familiar as it was painful to watch.

"No," Aaron continued. "I don't think it is. How many times do I have to put my life at risk? How many nightmares do I have to cut down? Tell me, Rista, did you know I've never killed a human being? Or if I did, it's been so long that I can't even remember it anymore, but not once since coming to this wasteland have I ever taken a human life! How many soldiers can claim that? Can you?! Or maybe that isn't it. Is it just that you don't like what you see? Is the idea that I'm not so different from you *insulting?!*"

His clenched hand turned shards of bark into dust. When he turned to look at the damage he had inflicted, shame filled him. A hand fell on his shoulder, stopping him in his tracks. It was Dalton, face still neutral.

"That's enough for now," he said. "Even if it doesn't look like much, you've made a difference. Now do it again and again until you see it. That's the only way anything truly changes."

His lieutenant nodded once, formally, then clapped him on the shoulder once more. He turned toward Rista.

"Your thoughts are your own, Anthony, but do not undermine the captain and the unit in front of outsiders again. We will discuss this later."

Dalton and Rista left the scene, and Aaron was left behind. Pulling out his notebook, he tried to gather his thoughts. But he discarded it just as quickly, deeming his feelings unfit to record. Garbled memories of a far-distant castle played in his mind, laced with the same impotent rage he felt, surrounded by those he couldn't save. He looked to the East, to Sitri Baal's castle, and the rage was soothed by the memory of a gentler voice. *"The path to Paradise is a thorny one, and we often lose our way. To fight is natural, but it will never end if we pursue only our own salvation. Remember, Aaron, that only through the salvation of others do we save ourselves."*

-Chapter 14-

Scent of Blood

Days later, at the S-0 barracks, Aaron was doing his best to relax. It was a difficult process. His body reacted to rest with the disappointed resignation of a man watching his roof cave in. He was more than happy to enjoy peace when it came to him, but amid an investigation, the ability to distance himself from his hunt seemed practically immoral. He would never have done so unprompted, of course. It was Gavin who convinced him, snatching the records of the police reports from his hands in a lazy gesture that hid the dexterity needed to achieve it.

"That's enough of that," he told Aaron with a note of paternal disappointment. "You're cut off."

He hadn't immediately acknowledged the jest. "Give it back, Jaycen; we have work to do."

Gavin replied by pulling back the nearby curtain and letting in the light through the windows. "Look around. It's morning. We already worked through the night."

Aaron winced, eyes stung by the abrupt brightness. "You're welcome to take a break. I don't expect you, either of you, to follow my lead." He acknowledged Durham, slumped over her own reading but still awake.

"We will be taking a break," Gavin declared. "And so will you. Don't look at me like that. We aren't meant to spend days at a time reading, and neither are you. Take your mind off it for a few minutes. It'll help, I promise."

It had taken some more convincing, but the two of them were able to separate him from the endless work. Not content with simply standing him up, they marched him out of the study and into one of the adjacent rooms to better distract his mind. There they stayed, preoccupying themselves with benign conversation that was of no importance but a welcome change of pace. Durham pulled up a target, and they idly tossed darts when not speaking.

For his part, Aaron was skilled enough with his hands. His ponderous strength meant he was no stranger to improvising a thrown weapon. However, his idea of a projectile was a bit more variable, and while he enjoyed the ease with which the darts flew, he wasn't quite accustomed to the feel. Durham was a ringer, of course, hitting her marks with frustrating ease that only compounded with her smug grin that followed each bullseye. Gavin hadn't seemed as interested in traditional accuracy, happy to put his feet up and recline in a chair rather than rise to the game. Instead, he amused himself by hitting increasingly improbable throws from his precarious position.

It ended with Durham declaring her victory, though they had never established that it was a competition. Then the three took more comfortable seating while Durham regaled them with tales of her indoctrination into the Baal armed forces.

"They like rats with a record," she explained. "Shows you can keep yourself alive. But rats are stubborn, you clear? They gotta whip out the free spirit, so they give us to this crusty old bastard to break us. He went by Bruise, because that's what he gave you. And he didn't care if you were a woman or a kid or missing your legs. He just loved to hit. First day with him, there's no training. He has us dig ditches. It's winter, and the ground is as solid as rock. Twelve hours straight. One word out of turn, and he punched you in the mouth. Day two, we're filling the ditches in and digging more."

"How are you even alive?" Gavin asked, incredulous. "Not for the digging, but the punishment for talking back."

She grinned. "Always had a strong jaw. But that's not all he got up to. Everyone had a number for when it was time to eat, and if you stepped up before your time, he'd beat the shit outta you. The only way to improve your number was to challenge whoever was ahead in line. I managed to move up quick, only got stopped at two by some seven-foot-tall freak who looked like every bar fight rolled into one asshole. I cracked his nose, and he just choked me out with a hand."

Aaron struggled to contain his laughter. "Let me guess, Bruise took a shine to you after that?"

"Not even a little," Durham answered. "Remember, he didn't care if some gutter trash made it as soldiers. He knew the meanest would survive no matter what. He just hated anyone not being miserable. I remember one time he had us climbing while carrying weights. I'm getting to the top of the wall with a bag of rocks in each hand, and he just starts poking me in the chest, trying to get me to fall off! *It's an obstacle,* he said. I just thought the old prick was gettin' handsy."

Aaron leaned in, knowing that no story of hers that started that way ended cleanly. "And what did you do?"

She brushed at one of the many scars around her eye with wild glee. "Fell back, and took him with me. *Removing the obstacle,* I told him. I think it was the only time he ever liked me. Not that I'd go back to that dump and ask him."

"Wait, wait," said Aaron. "He's still active?"

"Active might be the wrong term," Gavin interjected. "I think you mean 'at large.'"

They all laughed at the absurdity of it, and when Aaron realized that he'd nearly forgotten their circumstances completely, he acknowledged that the diversion had been helpful. "Of course it was," Gavin said with a smile. "You should really trust us more."

Aaron raised an eyebrow. "Are you sure you're not just avoiding work?"

A wry smile before Gavin replied, "Not this time. Too much focus can narrow your perspective. A little adjustment can be just the thing you need."

Aaron inclined his head, accepting the defeat, such as it was, with grace in order to preserve his dignity. "Well, you're not wrong."

Durham whistled a tune, fingers drumming against the arm of her chair. "Speaking of perspective, you've been getting awfully chummy with the paladins, haven't you? I didn't think they made a good impression."

Aaron opened his mouth to answer casually, only to take a second to collect himself when he saw the looks from the two of them.

"They…" He stopped and corrected his phrasing. "One of them at least isn't what I was expecting."

She shrugged. "Well, they haven't lit you on fire yet, so that's not what I was expecting either."

He laughed in return. "It's not like I haven't heard the stories. Actually, I think I might have heard worse than most. But I've been surprised before. It just feels like they want to understand the people. I can sympathize with that, and I feel like learning about them could be helpful too."

"Sure, sure," Durham said with a wave. "Just be careful with them."

"I won't let it go too far," he assured her. "Let's just say I've enjoyed Oris's company for now. Your pact hasn't activated either, has it?"

She frowned, her hand moving to where it rested on her arm. "No, not yet, but it won't light up until you're in real danger. They'd have to be actually trying to hurt you."

"If it makes you feel better, it's not them I'm really looking to talk to."

"Leah, right? That caretaker friend of yours?" Gavin pondered. "We never did meet her."

"Shouldn't she be wetting herself with those paladins here?" added Durham.

Aaron spared her a disapproving look, which she ignored. "She has her reasons for avoiding them. But I find it hard to believe she'd just leave the church to them."

"Maybe Lady Baal summoned her," said Gavin after a moment of thought.

This gave Aaron pause. "I hadn't considered that. I certainly hope so. But I haven't heard from either of them since we got back to the city. For now, we're on our own."

"The usual, then."

Aaron twitched as he picked up the sound of distant footsteps. Though Gavin and Durham lacked his acute hearing, both picked up on the tic and straightened themselves. The steps grew closer, accompanied by two more pairs. After just a minute, the door opened, and Dalton walked in, followed closely by Rista and Brook.

"Captain," greeted Dalton. "Good morning."

"Good morning," he greeted in turn. "What news?"

Brook stepped forward at attention. "We've combed the list of entrances to the undercity that Sietz provided us. Unfortunately, they see semi-regular use. Not legal, but not our jurisdiction. Nothing for us to do about it."

He rubbed his neck. "That's a shame. The fact that they see regular use is a damning mark against the idea that this nephilim is using them. At least we've narrowed it down. Good work."

Brook nodded, accepting the praise with grace. "And yourself? How goes your investigation?" she asked, eyes sliding toward Durham and Gavin, who answered on their behalf. "We've gone through sixteen volumes and counting. If you have a problem with it, you're welcome to switch."

She looked at him with the cold composure of a painting. "I think you're right where you need to be, thank you."

The silence that followed was uncomfortable, and so Aaron cut through it to address Dalton. "What's happened?"

His lieutenant, who hadn't acknowledged the tension, answered directly. "Another attack, sir. Eric just got the notice as we walked in. He wanted me to deliver the news."

Aaron bit his tongue. "It's only been two days since the park…why did he want you to tell me?"

"Good news, if you can believe it. He says your request was answered. He's calling them over right now." He exhaled. "Small miracles, but we'll take what we can get, isn't that right?"

"That's right," Aaron agreed, standing up. "With me then."

He looked over at Durham and Gavin. Both made to rise, but he couldn't help but hesitate. On closer inspection, he could see the exhaustion on their faces. They were no stranger to sleepless nights, but they didn't have his unnatural body. Given what they hunted, it was both dangerous and cruel to press them. "You two stay here," he ordered. "Get some sleep."

Though she hadn't spoken since the others entered, Durham objected. "Going to keep me out of the action again? I'm going insane reading this manual."

"No action to be had today," he assured. "Unless we get very lucky. When the time comes, I know where to find you, and I want you ready to swing that thing."

He thought she might argue, but after a moment's consideration, she relented. Smirking, she tapped at the mark of Baal on her arm. "I think it's the other way around, monster man." They waved him off, and he returned his attention to the three who had brought him the news. "Let's hurry then. Who knows how long Eric will hold their attention?"

The four of them departed immediately after gearing up. Unfortunately, they were immediately met with an obstacle. "I really have been too focused," Aaron commented, taking in the sight. "How long has it been happening?"

Rista, who had been silent until then, answered. "A few hours. All under control, but still a hassle."

Aaron took in the sight, then looked at Brook. "You inspected the Undercity entrances like this? Very well done." She didn't reply.

The streets were packed past the realm of comfort, people standing shoulder to shoulder on sidewalks who were moved only to accommodate the public transport that was their only reliable way of traveling. They continued as ordinarily as they could, and Aaron watched them do so. He could tell apart the locals from the visitors: the tradesmen and the merchants had come from the relative safety farther inland. The difference was to be found in the tension in their faces and the way they winced when they heard the crack of distant gunfire.

Nightmares had been spotted outside the city, and so the alarm had been raised. There were differing tiers of emergency for such cases and different restrictions that were to be followed in accordance. As Dalton informed him, the day's incursion was classified as tier two. That generally meant a group of several dozen to a hundred of the creatures. It was a size that could easily wipe out a small town, and should they enter the city, the death toll they would wreak in a short period was immense. But they were spotted a few hours before they came within city limits, and there were no aberrants. As such, he and S-0 were not to involve themselves.

This was just the sort of threat that Spearhead was designed to deal with. Lady Baal was adamant that order be maintained, especially in emergencies. Chaos could cause just as much damage as nightmares, and when such attacks were expected, diligent planning and the compliance of the population were essential.

As soon as the alarm sounded, trained responder groups went into action. The gates of the city were manned for just such a purpose, and the activity that took place outside the boundaries of the walls ceased. The ever-growing factories built along the Ironblood River went into lockdown. Any action that could be safely abandoned was left and discarded, and any essential tasks were addressed by the military police. The nightmares would seek the people, not their belongings, and so those belongings were left behind until such a time as they could be retrieved. Vehicles were pulled to the sides of the road, and all personal traffic was stopped. Officers took up pre-planned posts throughout the city to direct and maintain the flow of civilians, and dedicated centers were prepared to house them until the crisis was over.

He had seen it plenty of times, but with each, Aaron grew more impressed with the city's population. Those who could went about their day with as much normalcy as they were able. The event closed down most businesses, but some made room for those citizens who had difficulty returning to their homes. Though they were packed, Aaron could already make out the signs of the traffic clearing as the police directed them to designated shelters or to less-crowded streets, where they could be more comfortably housed.

It was a miracle of cooperation, one that recognized the great threat that the city faced by its very existence. Such was Lady Baal's vision. Nightmares would be attracted to humanity no matter what they did, and so by creating a beacon to attract them, she could also ensure that the beacon was prepared to deal with the consequences of the horrors' attention. Every monster that was drawn to Spearhead was one that didn't attack locations more poorly defended, and with every attack, the city grew more efficient at protecting itself.

That left only the nightmares themselves to deal with. Though easier said than done, when Aaron listened carefully, he could make out the pitched shrieks of the creatures. The full might of the city was prepared to slaughter them, and he was sure that they would soon be vanquished.

Or would they? Would they fall as so many others had, or would they rise, unharmed by the precious silver that should have destroyed them? He shivered, pushing the thought aside. The image of the smiling nightmares still haunted his mind, but he couldn't dwell on it, not yet.

The incident was being handled well, but it still took them longer than it should have to get to their destination. The block in the residential district was cordoned off, only exacerbating the traffic. Still, that made it easier for them to find the site.

When they finally broke through the crowd, they found a group of Sietz's officers holding the many people back. The man in charge saluted them, though his eyes were on Dalton and not Aaron as he did so. He didn't say much, merely regarding Aaron warily before directing him forward and taking his place at the barricade.

As one, they examined the bodies. Rista pulled a piece of paper from his jacket and read from it in a measured tone. "Reginald and Elia Sol, better known as Reggie and Ellie. Married two years ago, her twenty-four, him twenty-five. She was a teacher at the new school on the south side. He just finished his term of service. Apparently, he was also interested in teaching."

Aaron gritted his teeth. "And their residence?"

Rista pointed to the second building on their right, taller than the other apartments and undoubtedly more recently built. Its stone walls were a light cream color, a shade brighter than the others it was built between, while the carvings around its windowsills were a higher quality of newer constructions, wrought with designs like extending beams of light.

"Right here. Died about twenty feet from their home. They were churchgoers by the looks of it, and there was a late ceremony last night. I guess they were taken on the way home. Then the alarm went off not long after the MPs arrived to look at the scene."

The narrative fit neatly into place. Those with military service were entitled to higher-quality housing. The nightmare attack was nothing more than unlucky timing, as the alarm would have taken priority and police attention, preventing a timely reporting. Or was it? Could the creature have known the nightmares were coming and taken the opportunity to attack?

"Do we have any witnesses?"

"No," Rista answered. "It would've been the middle of the night. The thing probably waited until the street was empty to make its move. We have some testimony reporting the sight of a cloaked and hooded figure, but that's after the fact."

"So, after they heard about the bodies?" Brook clarified. "Could be reactive, could be hearsay. But if more than one person reported it, then it's something we should investigate further."

"I agree," said Aaron. "Get their names and we'll set up some meetings. If we can connect their stories, we might even be able to figure out exactly how the creature is killing."

Brook's noble features creased briefly. "Respectfully, sir, let one of us do the interviews. With the current state of things, you might create more trouble than progress."

Aaron sighed. She wasn't one to hold back when she made up her mind on something. "You think so?"

"Let me do it, Captain," Rista chimed in. "I've got some experience, and I can work with the police. If there's a truth, I'll find it."

His voice was unusually eager, despite a measured expression. The two had hardly spoken since the incident in the park. Deciding against trying to learn more, Aaron accepted his offer. "Thank you, that would be helpful. Then, before we proceed, we'll just need-"

"Right here!" the husky voice interrupted him.

She weaved her way through the crowd with ease, avoiding those she could with light steps and callously shoving aside those who were in her way with precocious strength. Those she sent reeling looked at her in shock, clearly not realizing what she was at a glance. Then they noticed the insignia of the Baal House wrapped around her neck and paled as they scrambled from the nephilim. She ignored them all, smiling at Aaron with far too many visible teeth.

"Pleasure to see you again so soon, *Captain* White."

"Helena," he greeted curtly. She had traded her black cloak for a low-cut dress embroidered with white at the hem, as mis-suited for the situation as her attitude. She gave him a teasing look that lingered just for a second at his throat before turning her attention to the others.

"Ah, you brought your friends!" she called out. "Even better!" She took a step forward, as if she might embrace them, but Aaron made a point of stopping the gesture by placing a foot between her and them.

"That's enough of that," he said.

She batted her eyes as if offended, only to shift into a sly smile. "It's enough when I say so. What's the matter, don't want to share your toys? You're a bit bratty when it comes down to it. They're just humans, you know."

Brook shifted in place, tilting her head to look down on the shapeshifter, despite being only slightly taller. "Is this thing going to do its job, or are we going to have to hurt it?"

The smile didn't leave, but any illusion of warmth behind it vanished. Helena took a slow, deliberate step past Aaron to better observe the other woman. Brook met her eyes with a stare like the barrel of a gun, but this only seemed to amuse the shapeshifter further.

With a half shrug, she moved on, her attention fleeting and dismissive. She didn't acknowledge Brook's readiness to spring into motion, and instead spoke to Aaron as if she weren't there.

"I didn't realize they grew so tall here. A noble scion? Humans have gotten awfully brave lately. They forget who really protects them."

Contempt turned to hatred in Brook's words. "My family has guarded this frontier for hundreds of years. Don't mistake your leash for status just because it suits you."

"Where are the others?" Aaron asked, diverting the conversation. "I requested at least two, and one with a taste for magic."

Helena rolled her eyes and gestured to the mountainside, where the faint sounds of battle could still be heard by the trained ear. "My dear Captain, where do you think? When the opportunity for amusement presents itself, how many would choose to be here instead of on the front lines? Even if the alarm hadn't sounded, I doubt any of them would have actually shown up. You can be so very silly sometimes."

The truth of the statement was the most frustrating thing of all. "Then why are you here?" he challenged.

Her lip curled in a smile. "Amusement." She turned her head to the sight behind them. "And this promises to be amusing indeed. I could scarcely believe it when I also heard you were stumped, but then I suppose enemies that actually think from time to time are a bit tricky. Although I won't deny your foe is clever. Moving so swiftly and discreetly is impressive, and to make such a mess…"

She giggled, walking around the radius of the crime. "Marvelous."

She drank in the sight of the bodies like it was artwork. They had been moved out of the way of the street, but only slightly, tucked behind a small outcrop from the wall that lined the buildings. Both had been dismembered, their limbs and torsos sliced through, and their heads removed. The angles of the wounds implied that whatever had struck them and gone clean through, such as a diagonal blow that had severed the husband's forearm and seemingly kept going to bisect him at the chest.

"Those are cleaner than a fang or claw, Captain," Rista noted. "It's closer to what your sword might do."

Aaron considered it, resting a hand on the hilt of his blade. He looked at the bodies, noting their orientation on the street. "You said they were on their way back, right by their home?"

Rista nodded, and he pointed to the stains on the sidewalk. "Look at the blood splatter. It seems like they were taken from behind."

Helena laughed, flitting between them with glee. Her pattern of movement changed from moment to moment, glimpses of her true self apparent as she strained the limit of her human form.

"What a tragedy," she cooed. "What a farce. The poor darlings! But we'll bring this beast to justice, won't we, White Knight? I know we will!"

She leaped up onto the wall, bending and twisting as if to get a better look at the scene beneath her and the disfigured remains that had been people. Shaking her head in disappointment, she clicked her tongue. "It truly is sad. So much effort just to waste the meat."

His frustration turning to anger, Aaron fixed her with a solemn stare, tempering his response with what self-control he had. "I didn't ask you here to make jokes. People are watching. They don't need to see this."

"Oh, you prefer the blood, isn't that right?" She recoiled in mock horror, raising her voice further. "Oh, Captain, that would be a crime! We couldn't possibly partake in such a feast as their remains! What are we, animals?!"

"Enough," Dalton intoned. "Shapeshifter Helena, your immunity has limits. If we suspect you of trying to start a panic, you will be sanctioned. Choose your words carefully. We're not in the mood for games, and killing nephilim is our specialty."

Helena's expression returned to a relaxed neutrality, and she shrugged. "No fun, no fun at all. Well, except for you, Captain White. Aye, aye and understood; whatever it is you people say."

She pushed through them without care, taking her place before the remnants of the murders. Turning to them, she unclasped her dress, grinning as she made a show of disrobing. The change took her. Her hair and skin shimmered before darkening into black smoke. Her form elongated, stretching and curling into a thick serpentine coil. Her eyes narrowed, then vanished into darkness while limbs flickered in and out of sight like a mirage. The substance that made up her body curled away, drifting in the still wind to form an impression of fur. When the transformation was complete, the only truly physical part of her that remained was a wide mouth of serrated teeth.

It didn't take her long to inspect the scene. She ran herself over and around the abundant bloodstains with apparent relish. As ever, her demeanor was as quick to shift as she was. Smooth, sinuous motions became halting and twitchy between passing seconds. She settled on the spot stained the deepest, finding focus with the scent.

Aaron knew it to be strong. Even to him, the remnants of the killings were an aroma that stirred his basest urges. His fingers twitched involuntarily, and he pulled a perfumed cloth from his pocket, but it was too late to stop the itching in his throat. Helena's form shivered, and he involuntarily mirrored the gesture. All the while, Brook, Rista, and Dalton looked on silently, only occasionally glancing at some detail of the scene that caught their eyes.

Something triggered Helena, and she shook her head like a dog might. Fangs parted to let out a frenzied growl, the sound raising a clamor in the civilians who were kept away by the police. Her body contorted to an upright position, and she returned to a more human shape. Dressing herself once more, she turned up her nose in disdain.

"Fools. Maybe if they'd chosen better company in life, we'd make some meaning of their death."

Aaron resisted the growing urge to scream. "You're telling me there's no foreign scent? You can't smell anything?!"

She rolled her eyes, the accusation finally giving way to genuine annoyance. "What exactly is that supposed to mean? They reek of piety and holy oils. Everything else gets drowned out. I'm surprised our friend even wanted them. They must have a poor sense of smell. Damn Paradisers ruin everything."

"The gathering at the church was well-known," said Rista. "Could the nephilim have been waiting for them to leave?"

"Who knows? Act like cattle, be slaughtered like cattle. I know I like predictable prey." She shook her head in a gesture of genuine mourning, then shook the expression off, patting Aaron on the shoulder. "Well, my part's done. Let me know the next time someone is butchered. I'll swing by if it's convenient. Maybe the next ones won't be so stupid, but I doubt it."

That was how she left them, strutting off and whistling while he fumed. "Not a word of help," he muttered. "We're no closer than we were before, and she seemed to enjoy it."

"I'm really not sure what you expected," said Brook. "That's about in character for one of hers."

His anger rose, threatening to ignite. His hand shot out, grabbing the adjacent brick wall and holding it tightly enough that he felt it crack. "Helena might not have had the answers, but I at least expected her to take it seriously!"

"They're not all as invested as you are," Rista remarked.

It was spoken casually, but the truth of it was undeniable. The nephilim, barring the nobles, weren't as concerned with the lives of the citizens as he was. As long as they continued in aggregate, he was certain most of them couldn't care less. He was an exception, not the rule, and the sadness at that truth doused the fire in his chest.

Dalton stared at the bodies in contemplation. "She wasn't totally unhelpful. Helena has no reason to lie, and if she had a lead, she'd have held it over you. This nephilim is doing what it does with pure brute strength, no damage to the surrounding area, no witnesses, and now it's targeting those who mask its scent."

Rista grunted in affirmation. "I'm starting to think we're hunting an actual ghost. Wait, no; we killed a ghost last year."

"Categorically, I don't think that's the case," said Brook. He shrugged. "This thing, whatever it is, has a taste for blood not easily sated."

"Only metaphorically," said Aaron. "You've noticed, haven't you? The pieces are all here, just like the last ones. If it's drinking their blood, it's doing it in tiny amounts. These two weren't killed for food either. It's done feeding. Now it's killing for sport."

"Maybe that's its cover, so we don't know what exactly it's eating from them. Not all nephilim feed on specific parts, so this keeps us from finding out more about it. You don't need to eat much to keep going either." Brook sighed. "So, Rista, you're on the interviews? Dalton, you mentioned going through the records to try to identify a pattern in the victims. Do you need company?"

"That would help move things along."

"I'll join you then. The captain can finish his research in the meantime." She looked at Aaron, officially needing his permission but appearing in no mood to be refused. "Does that work?"

Still taking in the sight beneath him, and with little else to say, he nodded. Brook briskly saluted him and dismissed herself, as casually as if he'd asked her to pull together a report. After a moment, Dalton did the same, expression neutral and courteous.

It was just him and Rista then, who watched him just as he did the remains of the scene. Aaron reached for his radio to inform Eric of his return, only for it to crack in his grip. He swore to himself, releasing a quiet, hissing breath. Rista offered his own radio without a word, and he accepted it gratefully. After he had used it, he returned it gingerly with thanks.

"Sietz would have had us send his people after this creature."

Rista pursed his lips, pausing for a moment before replying. "I suppose it's for the best that you refused him. I'm sure he's got a handful of competent investigators, but that's not enough. Dealing with a nephilim is even more dangerous than nightmares. You need people with a strong mind that won't give in to fear, but also the smarts to deal with a creature that's faster, stronger, older, and crueler."

"And those are in short supply," Aaron finished. "There are other special forces, but they're scattered through the frontier and our other outlying towns. I thought that the nephilim might help us bridge the gap."

Pocketing his radio, Rista paused before speaking. "Do you hate them, Captain?" he asked. "Other nephilim, I mean. Seems like if they weren't around, people would be a lot more willing to hear you out."

"I…" Aaron forced himself to stop speaking without thinking. He didn't want to do so. The question meant more to him than that. "No, I don't think I do. Certainly not all of them. Before Lady Baal appointed me to S-0, I met…*saved*…those who just wanted to live their lives peacefully. Life is hard, especially when you've only ever been able to rely on yourself. I know there's more to our kind than *this*."

He took the moments of silence that followed as a reply, but before he could open his mouth again, Rista spoke. "That's a good thought to have. For what it's worth, I think it's the right idea."

Aaron looked at the man questioningly, but he continued without pause, "You shouldn't take it to heart. We're as capable of cruelty as you are."

"I know that," Aaron answered, an edge to his tone that he wished he could restrain. "We stand guard over the people, and we strike down the monsters that threaten them. It's good. It's noble. We do this to protect others so they might not have to risk their lives themselves. But we're not just weapons," he continued, remembering Constantine's words. "We need to aspire to more because, without that purpose, all we have is violence. If that's all we're good for, and all that we can see for ourselves, then we'll remain monsters forever."

He'd said more than he wanted, not for the first time since the investigation began. Unsure of how to follow it, he made to excuse himself, only to be stopped when Rista smiled at him. "You sound like a noble already, Captain. I think I get why Lady Baal likes you so much. Just be careful. It's a big dream, and in this world, there's nothing more dangerous."

–CHAPTER 15–

PARASITES

The first hints of dawn's light were beginning to brighten the sky. The brightness crept at the edges of the buildings as figures ran between them. Aaron ducked and weaved between pipes and debris scattered by his target in haste, focusing only on keeping the figure in his line of sight. His hunch had been correct, and he wasn't going to lose the lead now.

The figure he pursued moved at a desperate sprint, though hampered by the oversized cloak and cowl that covered it. It reached out an arm, tearing a section of ladder from the nearby scaffolding and hurling it at Aaron in an attempt to slow him down. He struck it aside, though it bent around his arm and still managed a glancing blow at his ribs.

When he returned his attention forward, he saw the figure scaling the vertical stone wall. If there were any remaining doubts as to whether it was a human, the strength and athleticism the creature displayed quashed them at that moment. Drawing his pistol, Aaron tracked the figure's motion, took aim, and fired.

The nephilim didn't see him, vision obscured by its own cloak, and the bullet struck. It let out a scream of pain as the silver bullet burned it on contact. It fell from the wall, landing hard on the alleyway stone and writhing in a bundle of its own heavy clothing.

Aaron breathed a sigh of relief. Now that the creature was struck with silver, it was unlikely to come to a duel. He almost felt sympathy for the target, and then he remembered what it had done, and Aaron hardened his heart to it. He grabbed his radio and reported into it. "It's down. Still alive. Sif and Lenz, work your way around the long way. Dalton, stay put. I'm moving in to capture."

The reply was immediate. "Understood. I've notified our contact with Sietz. The police are keeping the public at bay and are on their way to assist."

Holstering his pistol, he responded, "Remind them that the one in the uniform is me."

"Yes, sir."

Aaron hung up the radio, not wanting to take his eyes off the creature again. The murder of the couple had proven to have even worse repercussions than those in the park. With people gathered up and the police response delayed because of the alarm, the bodies had time in the daylight, in plain view for anyone to see. It was public and ugly. The tension that had been building in the air was rapidly giving way to fear, and for the fourth time, there was no evidence that they could use to pin the nephilim's identity.

Following his dead end with Helena, Aaron had assigned Eric to assist Dalton and Brook to try to find a pattern in the victims. He ordered Sif, Lenz, and Moore to retrace the steps of everyone who had died in the predations in hopes of mapping a hunting ground where the killer might be selecting them. Since they weren't being killed in the same location, it was possible they were being tracked from a common area.

The inspiration for his next step came when he noted just how many of the victims were living close to the northwest wall that marked the edge of the city proper. He considered the old records and the encounter of the nightmares with Lilith Baal. Seizing the chance to move forward on the case and foster relations with Sietz, he requested the captain-commander set up discreet monitors for activity near the major and minor chokepoints that led to the guard towers there.

His intention was to scout for any locations that may go unnoticed by the day-to-day guardsmen, as the interior of the safer end of the city was not so carefully watched. More importantly, he wanted to cut off any potential avenues the creature could have to escape them.

It had been a fair compromise, using the military police as eyes and ears while they reported to Aaron to follow up on leads. It hadn't been long before a figure had been spotted, totally covered and hiding in the shadows as if probing the defenses themselves. It skulked about for hours, but Sietz's people had been discreet, and they hadn't lost track of it by the time S-0 went into action and moved to surround the creature. By the time it took notice of them, they were already closing in for the kill.

The thought of the deaths still fresh in his mind, he stalked toward the downed nephilim, carefully observing the flickering of light where the burning bullet had caught its clothing.

"That looks like it hurts," he remarked coldly.

One hand rested on his sword while the other felt his side where the metal had struck him. All appeared in order, with the throbbing of the wound fading as his body unnaturally healed itself. It must have hit him harder than he thought, for the fading pain ran deeper than skin. But as with any superficial harm, it didn't last. For his target, the damage would be considerably worse.

"Are you done?" he asked, trying to get a better look at its face. He still hadn't identified any features beneath its heavy clothing. If it wanted to go unrecognized, the attire served its purpose. However, he'd already chased it down, so it seemed pointless to keep the obstructing cloth on…

It hissed, and the plink of metal on stone followed. From the layers of cloth that obscured its body, a bloodied, steaming silver bullet rolled at Aaron's feet. Eyes widening, he drew his pistol yet again.

"Stop it!" the voice rang out, a melodious tenor but cracked and colored by desperation. It drowned out all other sounds from the earth around them. At its command, Aaron's buzzing radio was respectfully taciturn. The birds and rats and distant sounds of the city's life drew to an abrupt halt, and even the wind died out as the air around them stood still.

The only noise that remained was a faint and unnatural ringing in the ears. Aaron was frozen, not by surprise but by an invisible force. He stood, locked in a position halfway to action. Tension seized every muscle in his body, and even his eyes were unable to waver from their target. All the while, the figure beneath him struggled to its feet.

Aaron fought against the force holding him within the prison of his own body. Anger ran through his veins, feeding him strength. The hooded figure panted, blood trickling from the gunshot wound somewhere near its right shoulder. The ringing began to fade from the air, and sensing the change, Aaron struggled against it. His finger twitched. The nephilim's head snapped to him, revealing the face of a man and the flash of shining scales.

"Away!" he screamed, and the word became reality. Aaron was sent flying backward, wind whipping against his skin until he collided heavily with the nearest wall.

Aaron fell to the ground, even more disconcerted than he was hurt. His vision blurred and sharpened back into focus as his body righted itself, and he looked up just in time to see the figure vanish around the nearest corner. He grabbed his radio, issuing orders immediately.

"He's moving southeast! Cut him off before he gets to Oldtown. Target is a siren!"

He took off in pursuit once more, fallen behind but now able to easily follow the trail of blood left by the creature. He heard another gunshot, followed by the scream and gust of wind indicating yet another use of the nephilim's strange magic. Aaron rounded corner after corner in pursuit of the creature until he came to the site of the damage, a wall leading to the main street that was cracked and chipped, and taking cover behind it was Sif. She moved out to join him.

"It's deflected north," she called to him. Take the second right!"

He took the lead, following her instructions. The turn in question took him past the street she had been guarding, a thinner alley but one that allowed him to swing farther ahead of the path their target had taken. Emerging from it, he spotted Rista gesturing to him, flanked by a pair of military police officers.

"We've got the area contained!" he said with a nod. "Keep going!"

Following their lead, he spotted the blood trail on the ground again and heard the sound of a frenzied heart beating frantically across the intersecting street. He charged at it full speed, only stopping when he nearly collided with Durham.

She was geared for combat, with her mask drawn over her head, obscuring her hair and face. Despite that, he knew her well enough to recognize her smirk beneath it. She took a playful step back and gestured to the next alley.

"What do you say, herd the prey? We've got him now; this one's a dead end."

The siren was backed up against the alley wall, cloak fallen at his feet. Beneath was little more than ratty pants and a torn brown vest over a wiry frame. His bare arms were covered with oily scales the color of brass. Hanging from his arms, he had a bizarre appearance between that of a bird and a fish. His right shoulder was seared and burned from the silver bullet that had struck him and still bled profusely.

Whether due to the aftereffects of the purifying metal or the creature's own weakness, the wound hadn't healed. He leaned on the brick wall for support, breath uneven and labored. Dark pupil-less eyes looked out at them, alien but with a clear sense of panic. About his head, the air shimmered with the faint remnant of the magic his commands had wrought on the world around him. Aaron measured the gap between them; about twenty feet. He leveled his pistol at the creature.

"I'm giving you one chance," he said slowly. "Lie down on the ground. Do it now, or I will shoot you again."

The siren flinched, and Aaron didn't give him a breath before continuing, "If you so much as open your mouth again, I will shoot you. If you don't decide in the next five seconds, I will shoot you anyway. On the ground. Now." He spoke each word with finality, taking a single step forward. Durham rested her hand on the hilt of Re-Human, finger tapping against it.

"I'd do it," she warned. "I never see him this pissed off."

The creature looked at her, momentarily caught off guard. In the moment of hesitation, she whispered low enough that she knew only Aaron would hear, "Dalton's in the building directly behind us. He has a bead on it."

He tapped his foot on the ground once, a gesture of acknowledgment.

"Make your choice," he said to the nephilim.

The siren was shaking, clearly in pain, but all the more dangerous for it. He looked at his injured arm, bleeding and burned, then at his pursuers. Behind them, Aaron heard footsteps. Sif and a pair of Sietz's agents were now standing with them. His lips parted, revealing sharpened teeth, but his mouth didn't open.

Resignation flushed his pale face, and he nodded, slowly dropping to a knee. Aaron took note of the slow caution with which the nephilim moved, careful not to injure himself further or, worse, provoke their attack. Recognizing the concession in its gesture, Aaron relaxed his grip on his pistol but didn't lower it completely.

"Ah, that's boring," a bemused voice called out, drawing them all to attention. Atop the adjacent building, Helena hung, overlooking the alley. She showed her teeth in a wide grin, her hair whipped about by a sudden breeze. "We were hoping for a bit more blood."

"You'll have to settle for disappointment," Aaron muttered, relieved that it hadn't been yet another foe. "Wait, 'we?'"

Alongside the shapeshifter, a pair of hulking forms made their appearance. Around both their necks hung the crest of the Baal house, twin spears gleaming with their own unnatural light. That was where their similarities ended. The first was dressed in only a heavy black kilt wrapped around its waist and doing little to cover its unnaturally tall, leonine form. The other was large, but with skin that looked closer to pale stone than flesh and blood. An ugly, mangled face drew around oversized tusks that shifted as it uttered a deep, guttural chuckle.

"Took a bit," Helena remarked. "But you finally provided something entertaining enough to get your audience. A shame we missed the chase, but it's not so bad. At least we get to be here for the aftermath." She sneered down at the kneeling man. "You're in for it now, corpse-feeder. You'll wish he killed you with that bullet."

The siren stiffened, and Aaron tensed at the pressure. "Be quiet," he ordered. "He's surrendered."

Helena waved it off. "Oh, please, after what he's done? I know you're keen to offer everyone the same collar, but these broken things don't have the sense to take it." Her eyes shone brightly as she looked down at them lightly, whimsically, as if she didn't have a care in the world. "He'll refuse, of course, and then we'll pull him apart and eat or burn what's left. Am I wrong? I think that's pretty accurate—"

"Shut up!" Aaron shouted, his grip on his pistol tightening. "One more word and I'll consider you an obstacle to this mission!"

Helena tilted her head, lips slightly parted, still amused but given a momentary pause. For a second, he held hope that he had salvaged the situation, but quickly noted her eyes weren't on him, and that hope was dashed. The siren had risen from his knee, face drawn tight in fear and defiance. He took a stumbling step back as Aaron tried to speak.

"Surrender peacefully!" he urged. "I promise you fair treatment!" He lowered his gun, but the siren was taking a breath. "Stop!" Aaron commanded.

The siren's mouth opened, but it was not to be. It did not curse or yell or command them. Whatever words of power that would have struck out at them went unspoken, and any sound that would have been made was replaced by the singular crack of Dalton's rifle. His preferred weapon against nephilim was designed to take down larger classes of nightmares, and had all the force behind it that could fit into a silver weapon.

The bullet struck the nephilim square in the throat, with the high-powered shot punching through the creature's body and spattering the wall behind it with blood. The siren's body was limp before he even realized he was shot, and he fell backward into the wall before he could regain control of himself.

The silver pierced the body, and so he didn't immediately die. A noble might have even been able to survive it, but that was plainly not to be. Blood poured from his throat; his head was nearly struck from his shoulders.

Unfortunately, the nephilim's constitution was too resilient for its own good, and instead, the siren looked up in horror as Helena fell on it, transforming with a cackle as she did. Her cloak fell away as her body melded into its true form. Even had the siren been whole and healthy, Aaron doubted he would have been able to fight her off. As he was, he couldn't even scream as her teeth closed around him.

The carnage lasted only a handful of seconds. The gargoyle and manticore descended from the wall at a leisurely pace, but kept their distance, knowing it was pointless to contribute. Helena's monstrous growls mixed with the snapping of bones, saturating the air as she tore the siren into pieces.

The officers watched with expressions of stunned silence, and Durham wrinkled her nose in mild distaste. Aaron closed his eyes in a moment of sorrow, putting his weapons away. Helena's long body contorted and twisted as it smothered bloody twitching limbs and flung flecks of blood and scale. Ordinarily, Aaron would confirm the demise, but even as a matter of procedure, he didn't have the stomach for it. Instead, he picked up his radio and spoke into it.

"Target has been eliminated."

Dalton replied emotionlessly, "Confirmed, withdrawing."

Aaron put the radio aside. He drew his flask and took a sip of the cursed contents, strength and energy flowing through him the instant it passed his lips. Shaking his head to clear the taste and accompanying rush, he summoned the attention of the military police.

"Have this disposed of properly," he ordered, wincing as he heard the sound of dripping death. "When she's done," he added. "And I want to know who authorized *those* three to move."

The officer was still shaken by the ordeal, partly why he'd given the command. As such, she complied, nodding reluctantly. "When you say properly…"

"I mean, don't just throw what's left of him in a ditch!" he snapped. "Examine him, give him to research; just make something of his death!"

The outburst again startled her, almost as much as it did him. "Captain White, this nephilim…"

"He was surrendering," he said quietly. "He was scared. For God's sake, this isn't the monster doing the killings. It's not even close…"

–CHAPTER 16–

INSCRIPTION

Aaron walked the streets alone, having discarded an escort to simmer in his thoughts without interruption. Alien as he was, he had realized as soon as he looked into the creature's face that he wasn't the culprit. Nephilim were proud, vain creatures. The siren had been looking to escape the city, had fled their attempts, and only dared to fight when left with no alternative.

He was dressed in rags and looked half-starved already. The difference between the dead nephilim and what Aaron hunted was the difference between a street rat and a trained killer. The kind of being that could commit the atrocities he had seen wouldn't run from him, and would never even dream of surrendering. If the siren was their killer, then he was born a human, and while both things would have made Aaron rejoice, both were impossible fantasies.

Where did that leave him then? It left him with nothing. His latest hunch had been a waste, and one dead nephilim was far from appeasing Constantine and his own guilty conscience.

He walked to Dominic's Café, unmoved by the wide eyes that fell on him as he entered and picked a seat far from others. There he rested his head in his hands and emptied his mind, for he'd run out of constructive things on which to think.

He sat as such for an indeterminate time before being roused by the slight groan of Dominic taking a seat opposite him. "You really are bad for business," the older man laughed, scratching at his shaved head.

Aaron winced. "I'm sorry. That is something I don't think I can change."

Dominic turned to observe them. "Strange thing, though, no matter how many times you scare 'em away, they always come back. Not sure if it's curiosity or my excellent service."

Aaron looked at the eyes on him, an ugly voice in his head telling him it was the former. "Well, I'd like to be polite and say it's your food, but I can't really eat it to say."

"Well, maybe someday. And someday people won't be so scared of you either, eh?" He received a knowing smile. Dominic passed a glass to Aaron, its contents a pale gold and bubbling.

He accepted it with thanks. "Maybe someday," he said softly, taking a sip. It was ice-cold, light, and fruity but also sharp enough to sting. "What is this?"

The smile turned into a grin. "A new one; made it myself. We're expanding into beer, and I know you're picky, so I tried for something you'd go for. You like it?"

"It's good," Aaron said, breathing in the scent of the drink. "Great, actually. You made this yourself? What are you calling it?"

"Hell if I know," Dominic shrugs. "My wife named the kids." The two chuckled, and Aaron reclined, tension momentarily forgotten. "There he is," Dominic jabbed. "Sometimes you get so wound up, it's like I don't recognize you. Just takes a laugh to get you going again."

Aaron ran a hand through his hair, doing his best not to meet Dominic's eyes. "If I'm so easy to figure out, Dom, why does it feel like I can't make anyone understand me?"

"No clue," Dominic answered, taking a sip of his own beverage. "I always said you were an open book. Maya felt the same. But then, Sitri's nephilim saved my life from the Nero goons. Fact is, most people look at someone and see what they want to see. They'll think it's what they've already seen before, even if it's brand new. That's all they know, and humans are slow learners."

Aaron peered pensively into the contents of his glass. "Maybe it takes a certain kind of person to learn…"

"Hey, don't say that. You'll lump me in with Alice and Jaycen, and those two are as crazy as paladins in Sitri's own city!"

They laughed again, Dominic's joviality putting the rest of his customers at ease. He stole a glance at them, then gestured to Aaron subtly, mirth never quite fading from his face.

"Maybe it just takes a certain kind of person to show them. Those two make poor ambassadors, that's for sure. They're loyal as they come, but they don't exactly have the same goal you do; the whole noble lordship ambassador bit."

"Maybe not," Aaron admitted. "But being true friends doesn't mean sharing everything. Theirs might not be the same, but they'll always have a place in my dream."

At that, Dominic knocked his glass against Aaron's in an impromptu toast. "To dreams then." He took a drink. "Even if you chose the hardest one."

Aaron took a sip himself, not looking to finish hastily. "It was the only one that made sense. You know, when I arrived here, I was barely alive. I couldn't think. I can barely remember it. I was feral. Hardly more than an animal."

Dominic's expression sobered. "I know."

"I think about what I could have done. What I might have done without knowing. It makes me sick. Sitri should have killed me. Instead, she gave me a life. At first, it was just work under guard, fighting nightmares like the other nephilim. Sitri liked that I showed restraint. She gave me freedom for more complex assignments, things she couldn't afford to give to the others for fear of what they would do without supervision. Then one day, I'm told to meet with a man."

He frowned, remembering his face. He was old, with sharp, hawk-like features and a full head of silver hair. He never blinked once in all the time they were in a room together.

"A widower. His wife had collapsed on the street. Supposedly, her heart gave out, but he was certain she'd been murdered. I thought it was nonsense until he started showing me proof. He mapped it himself; three other people in the last month dropped dead in the same area."

"Sounds spooky," Dominic responded casually, but his eyes didn't leave Aaron's. "What'd you find?"

"Not much of anything, if I'm being honest." Aaron chuckled evilly at having taken Dominic off guard before continuing. "I couldn't find any signs of struggle. I checked every corpse for possible drugs, poison, and illness. The bodies weren't fed on, and nothing was missing. I was stumped, just like..."

He trailed off, not wanting to finish the obvious thought *like I am now.*

"They were near the church, though. That's when I met the caretaker, Leah."

"A Paradise churchgoer meeting a nephilim. Not a great mix."

"I thought so too," admitted Aaron. "But she heard me out, helped me understand. She was the first person to suggest that maybe the bodies *had* been fed on." He shook his head, remembering the time together. He'd had to knock on the chapel doors with the hilt of his sword to avoid catching fire. "It was a dragon."

Dominic's mouth actually opened. "A real dragon? Like Talos?"

"A bit smaller," Aaron replied. "According to Sitri, there are only a few in the whole world, and they're the most magically powerful nephilim there is. Sophia; she was just a child. Dragons feed on souls directly. There's no physical injury, and it's not fatal, not normally at least. But she was too young and too powerful to feed properly. She was killing them by accident and starving herself.

"And we saved her," he said with a smile. "Gave her a chance for life instead of death in a gutter somewhere. Sitri herself sponsored it. And she was so impressed that she allowed me to create a team. Most nephilim don't receive a pact. They're too proud to offer any part of their immortal lives, no matter what you put in front of them. I didn't do it because I didn't have anything I wanted. Not until I saw what I could have. A place for a nameless nephilim. A home for the orphaned and abandoned. It might be the thorniest path there is, Dom, but I'll walk it if it keeps us from something worse."

Dominic's expression was somber, all joviality gone. In his friend's face, he saw acknowledgment and the weight of memories.

"Worse always exists. We've done well for ourselves these past few years, but that just makes people more afraid now that they have the luxury to worry about losing something. The nephilim Lady Baal recruited do more good than harm, but they're not exactly saints, and that makes them easy to blame. Ah, you know what I'm trying to say. Maya's always telling me I chew on my words." He reached out and rapped Aaron on the shoulder. "I'm trying to say I'll be there too. And once you're a lord, you're gonna be the one treating me."

A voice called from behind the counter with a string of profanity. Dominic smiled broadly once more, all else forgotten. "Sounds like I've gotta tend to the missus."

He excused himself to return to his work. Aaron finished his drink in silence, considering his next move. He didn't have long to wait, though, because soon after, his radio buzzed. He lowered the volume, then answered it quietly.

"This is White, go ahead."

"This is Eric," the device replied. "Captain, there's been another. It's a child this time. They want you there now."

Aaron's palm fell on the tabletop, gathering the attention of customers and serving staff alike as he rose. "Send Dalton and Durham. I'm on my way."

He made his way across the city as fast as he was able. He made his presence clear and present, moving the military and civilians out of his way by sheer force of intimidation. For all that, his travel was surprisingly slow, with people not parting for him as they normally would. They looked at him, of course. They always looked at him, but the expressions he saw were not those of nervousness that day but of suspicion. Passing by, his acute hearing clearly picked out words muttered under people's breath or into crowds. *Feral. Killer. Monster.*

Following Eric's instruction, he navigated to the edge of Oldtown. He knew he was in the right place when he spotted a crowd of onlookers being pushed back by the police. Some were trying to get a view. Some were shouting angrily, and some looked like they were going to vomit. Though he did his best to circumvent them, the single utterance of "Evil" followed his steps.

The scene was a small alcove, not ten yards away from the road. They couldn't even be called alleys; they were just a convenient place to put barrels of trash. As such, it was perfectly visible to the public. Aaron was the last one to arrive. Durham was arguing with a pair of MPs, but that was normal. Rather than trying to rein her in, he instead confronted the two officers. They had the same vitriol as Sietz, but not his nerve.

"We will investigate from here. Leave us."

They exchanged glances, then begrudgingly left to assist in deterring the citizenry, though not without one of them muttering, "Maybe you'll find something before another kid gets killed."

"Maybe you'll be lucky and it'll be you next," Durham replied.

Aaron paid it no mind, moving straight to the scene of the crime. The MPs had cordoned off the zone, and thankfully, with his arrival, could devote their full attention to removing the distractions of onlookers. That didn't make it any less awful. The boy couldn't have been older than thirteen, with a mop of brown hair and a skinny build.

He was a late bloomer, it seemed. Across his throat was a deep gash that reached from one corner of his jaw to the other, and blood had sheeted down his body, seeping into his clothes. A pool had formed at his feet, but it was mostly dry by that point. His face was frozen in a look of shock, color already drained from him. He was slumped against the nearest wall behind one of the barrels, half-fallen over as if he'd simply been left there like the rest of the garbage.

Dalton was making a note to himself, and Aaron turned to him for guidance. However, his chest tightened as he saw the look on his face. "You're kidding me."

His lieutenant shook his head. "You're telling me that you've found nothing."

"They've given us nothing, Captain," Dalton stated. "Nothing we can use. We don't have blood, skin, or a weapon of choice beyond 'sharp.' No bullets, obviously. He's surrounded by refuse; I doubt any nephilim is catching a scent, and it will hide anything dropped or left behind, even if there were something to find. We have no footprints and no eyewitness testimony. Curfew is in place, and Sietz's people are on high alert. No sightings of anyone suspicious. The kid was out for a walk before sunrise, and he never made it home. That's all the story we've got. We can't pretend this is another run-of-the-mill monster, especially in plain sight of half the city now. This is turning into theater."

Aaron shook his head. "Well, I guess that makes us clowns. But it doesn't change that whatever is doing this doesn't just vanish in a puff of smoke. It's choosing its victims, Dalton, and it's making a show out of killing them in increasingly public ways. That means it's getting close to being discovered each time, but it persists regardless, and we can't find it!"

He longed to pull his sword from its sheath and bury it into the wall. He wanted to punch and kick and reduce it to rubble to satisfy his body's urge for violence. Instead, he checked himself and paced back and forth, avoiding touching anything he could crush in his hands.

"Brook checked with the wall; no activity moving in and out could do so consistently without being noticed. This thing is inside the city," Dalton reiterated. "And we need to think outside the box if we want to catch it in hiding."

"It's a big city for us to manage alone," Aaron muttered. "Sitri moved her other elite units west in case of activity by the Paradise Church. The average MP is more likely to get torn in half than stand against whatever this thing is, and the other nephilim aren't any damn help at all. I know what we told him, but I also know Sietz hasn't been idle. I'm sure he's investigating it discreetly and would act if he had something to go on. If this thing hasn't been found yet, then it won't be discovered in hiding. We have to predict its next move and catch it in the act!"

Dalton didn't respond immediately. He drew and lit a cigarette, face chiseled in concentrated thought as he stared at the glow. After a few moments of consideration, he put it out.

"More urgent and more obstacles than ever. Does this change your profile for our subject?"

Aaron sighed. "These spectacles have a purpose. They may be a means, but they're not the end. They're...directed. Deliberate. It's inciting terror, not in its victims, but in the city populace. Maybe that makes the killing easier for it, somehow? By now, it knows that it's being hunted. It might have experience using chaos to its advantage. I already tried seeing if any towns between here and Paradise have had killings like it, though, and no luck. It knows what it's doing; this one isn't young or reckless. The brutality is measured. Every death is calculated violence."

Dalton reached into his jacket and withdrew a bundle of notes. "I gathered the data. Eight murders now across age, sex, skin color, occupation, and social standing. No visible pattern. Even their residences are varied."

"No pattern," Aaron muttered. "But that's a pattern itself..." He took note of the alcove. "No blood or skin left behind by the culprit thus far. Its..."

Whatever he was leading to was silenced as he instead watched Durham. She had been silent since their arrival; uncharacteristically so. At first, she simply appeared bored, as she tended to when not fighting or consuming something. Her eyes wandered, while her face remained relaxed. She idly fiddled with one of her many knives, occasionally tapping it against the back of her hand.

However, as Aaron and Dalton were speaking, a change had overtaken her. Her eyes sharpened, a scowl darkening and twisting her face. She walked past the two of them, eyeing the dried blood before kneeling, fixated on a particularly large stain. She stared at it for nearly a minute as they watched, silent. "Alice?"

She didn't immediately react to him. After a few moments, she rose, breathing, "It's too clean. It isn't enough."

"What do you mean by that?" Dalton asked.

"Not enough for this monster," she answered. "Look at this. The blood looks positively ordinary."

"The boy's throat was torn open."

Durham wasn't fazed. "That's all? I saw worse in the undercity before I got my first scar. No, that's too simple. It doesn't fit. The others were split open, decapitated, chopped into pieces." Her eyes looked past the two of them, then sharpened, and her lip twitched. "So easy...but this one was different. If you were trying to make a statement, you'd leave him in the middle of the street or the park, like the others. He was thrown away with the trash, but at the same time, he was hidden by it. It took time for him to be found despite how easy it should have been. It was rushed," she declared.

Dalton blinked, his surprise quickly tempered by unyielding discipline. "Wait, are you saying that the boy *saw* it?"

She toyed with the hilt of Re-Human at her waist. "I think so. The thing kills him quick and easy, and once it was done, it dumped him here to make it look like he belonged and to buy time so that it couldn't be tracked. Keep it random, keep the authorities guessing."

Aaron agreed. "The pattern is that there is none. Rather, it's deliberately targeting with as much variation as possible. But even if it wanted them for food, this is far too many. The monster isn't eating them, so it begs the question: are these deaths a cover-up for other activity, or do they somehow further its goal? It's spreading fear, that much is obvious, but if it didn't mean to kill this boy, then that means it had another reason for being here." He cocked his head. "Tell me, Dalton, what is significant about this location? What makes it special?"

Dalton scratched his head. "This is a poor place to hide. It's near the north end of the inner city, but it's also in Oldtown. Maybe it isn't this place specifically. Maybe it's just close enough to..." His eyes snapped open. "I'm a fool. Roy Currie was murdered not two blocks away. He was also the only other body that wasn't in a public location. But that doesn't make sense..."

"It does if the location was special," Durham said with a grin. "Let's take a look."

They moved from the scene, and Aaron put the looks of the city watch out of mind as they returned to the site of the first killing. It was blocked off, but not guarded. They worked their way to the back of the alley. Aaron looked out at the street, partially hidden by the outstretched wall of the adjacent building. "Why would it return to the scene of its first crime? What could make this place important?"

"Nothing comes to mind from an infrastructure standpoint," Dalton said. "Aside from housing, I know there are a few storage units nearby. Smaller machinery used to be worked on there, radios and the like. But they're being repurposed right now, and people are there constantly. You couldn't hide in one."

Durham yawned. "It's only a few blocks away from the red street, for whatever that's worth."

Aaron scanned the walls as they closed in on one another. "Our monster's been making a scene with every kill. But this one took longer to discover. It was more out of the way than the rest. A message, do you think?"

Durham's finger twitched. "This was a hell of a scene, but not exposed to the public. It was just...close."

"So, the first kill is different?" Dalton pondered. The lines of his face hardened. "No, you two are right. It is different, isn't it? He was so mutilated; he didn't even look human anymore. Every kill after was brutal but efficient, single deathblows. Could it have been anger?"

Aaron made his way to the marked location. "This was the end of the line for him. This is where Roy Currie died. Why?" he asked, more to himself than to anyone else.

His head hurt remembering the scene; the mangled body surrounded by blood, spilled in any manner of ways. The body was gone, of course, but several stains lingered around where it had been. He took a step backward, following the remnants of the blood that had led a trail to the man. Aaron examined the wall. A slight crack split the segment to his right, like where a blade or talon might have scraped.

"It was made so hideous, so obvious. Maybe that kept us from seeing something more." He traced it with his finger, the echoes of the scene that had surrounded it still half-visible to him, and was stopped.

He hadn't noticed it before, covered as the scene had been in the fresh and overwhelming remains of the carnage. Even with the repulsively intoxicating scent of death absent, he nearly overlooked it again.

On the wall was a small series of marks, barely more than indentations. He did not recognize them as words or sentences, but they ran together as characters would in a script. He had seen stone carved, engraved, and drilled into, but this was subtler, as if someone had drawn in the brick and mortar like one might with sand or wet cement. No ridges or valleys stood out to help identify the barely noticeable characters.

But when he looked at the markings carefully, he noticed that the color of the stone was stained at the edges of the indents, as if a slight burn had accompanied whatever had left them there. There was little bright light in the alley, but when Aaron angled his head just right, the markings had a faint iridescence to them.

Durham leaned on his shoulder. "What…is that?"

"I don't know," he breathed. "I've never seen anything like it. But whatever it is, I don't think it's new." He waited for disagreement, but it did not come. "We're right next to the red street. The worst public massacre in the city's history. You don't think it's related, do you?"

Durham cursed. "Captain, that blood doesn't look a week old."

"What did you just say?" But he could already see it. He had been so focused on the inscription that he had not noticed the stains beneath it. There were seven in total, each more solid than the ones before.

Aaron spoke slowly and deliberately. "This isn't just predation anymore. This is a ritual. Dalton, I want this site watched at all hours of the day. Get pictures of these markings and send them to Eric. Tell him to make sense of them even if he has to go to Lady Baal herself."

He removed his glove, reaching to touch the symbols on the wall. His finger met the cold, smooth stone.

I hate you all.

The thought echoed in his mind with all-consuming purpose. He leaped backward into the opposite wall, his hand slamming into it with enough force to crack the stone, his heart thundering in his ears while his chest heaved. Durham called out to him, but he couldn't hear over the ringing in his ears and the tremors of his limbs. His vision flickered, and the city was gone.

Immediately, his senses were under assault. He saw piles of bodies, picked at by carrion birds. Distant wailing clawed at his eardrums. Acrid smoke and sweet blood mingled in the air, enticing and revolting in equal measure. The sun traced a path across the sky far too quickly. Time was indistinct. Ashes fell like rain.

Then he was rising, cold and alone. He was dragging his feet, pulling himself into the light of the sun. Surrounding him were the crumbling remains of a castle and the overgrown ruin that had once been his home. He called out for someone, anyone, but nobody answered. He was alone. *"Where is everyone? Where am I? Who am I?"* He shook his head. Only one name came to mind.

The world rushed back into focus as Durham shook him. Dalton pulled her away, his gun drawn. "Captain, answer me!" he ordered. "I demand you identify yourself!"

Aaron stared; limbs seized so tightly he could hardly move. Slowly, he forced himself to relax, and his jaw unclenched itself. He reached slowly into his pocket and caressed his notebook.

"My name is Aaron White. I just need a second..."

He slumped, bits of broken wall crumbling in his fingers. He calmed his body, but not his mind.

"What the fuck was that?" Durham spat, looking between him and the wall. Re-Human was drawn in her hand, and her arm trembled where he knew her pact was inscribed. She noticed his glance and flexed her wrist. "Caught me off guard, it's not hot like when we're fighting, but it gave me a jolt. Is that magic?"

Aaron tried to nod between breaths. "Different from the pact. From the others. Let me just..." He inhaled, desperately drinking in the present to avoid slipping back into what he had seen. He shook his head. "Was that the past, or is it happening right now?"

"Past?" Durham said, scar creasing around her nose. She looked at the wall, which shimmered with a haze like smoke. "For just a second, it glowed bright red."

Dalton cautiously placed his hand on the wall, looking between Aaron and it. "No reaction to me, and no residual heat. None of our pacts reacted until you made contact. If it's magic, it's clearly a subtler sort, and like Re-Human, it doesn't look too pleasant if a nephilim touches it. Maybe that's what our monster is trying to figure out."

He paused as a new thought occurred to him. His lip twitched, more emotional than usual. "But if we have Sietz circling the place, I don't think it will come back. It's smarter than that. For now, at least, it's progress. Captain, you should get looked at."

"To hell with that," Aaron muttered, standing with Durham's assistance. "We have to move before this thing strikes again. The two of you will meet with Sietz and explain the situation. Send a report to the senior staff as well. If this creature is using these deaths to work magic, then the entire city could be at risk. There's something I have to do."

His gaze was drawn to the bottom of the symbols. Carved into the wall, separate from the inscription, was a small pair of horizontally and diagonally crossed lines. He knew that handiwork. He had seen it several times in the past. It was the mark left in recognition of a death by a caretaker of the Paradise Church. "We're a step closer," he said, making for the main road. "But there's still more we need to know."

And something I need to confirm, he thought as he left them. I'm not just going to let this thing have its way, and I'm done waiting for answers. Leah, you know something about this madness, and you're going to tell me.

–Chapter 17–

Behind the Mask

"Without farmers to till the fields, we might starve. Without tailors to stitch our clothes, we might freeze. Without craftsmen to build our homes, we might be lost. Without family and friends to love us, we might falter. But without us to stand vigil, they would all die." A crowd surrounded the church. Aaron scanned the assembled faces, looking for Leah, but she was nowhere to be found. The telltale auburn hair and black cassock that made her so identifiable were absent as they had been since the paladins' arrival.

He visited each of the crime scenes in sequence, searching them high and low for any similarities. The strange symbols that marked the sight of Roy Currie's death were absent from all of them, but a different identifier was not. At each scene, hidden somewhere amongst the scenery was the same twice-crossed carving that he knew to be her calling card.

The entire time, Aaron hoped against hope that she would reveal herself to him, but with no luck. That was expected in its own way, and so he returned to the only place he could think she would be: the chapel. He made it as far as the doors before the ringing in his ears grew unbearable and the blessed building began to heat his extremities. On second look, his outstretched hand was showing the slightest signs of smoking, and he took a frustrated step back. The doors to the church were open, but he couldn't see her inside. When he questioned the guards stationed nearby, they hadn't seen her either.

That was a disturbing omen. There hadn't needed to be guards in the past. Aaron pushed the thought aside, focusing on the task at hand. Once more, she eluded him. He knew she had reason to avoid the paladins, but he wasn't convinced that was the whole story. And so, he watched, observing the goings-on of the church for nearly an hour, looking for a sign of her. But neither her face, voice, nor scent was there to guide him. What he did find was the ever-growing crowd that waited on the words of Brother Oris.

His voice carried on the wind, moving in and out of the open chapel doors as he spoke, gesturing vividly with each change in pitch. He spoke of blood and life, self-respect, and reliance. Aaron found himself moved. Unlike the grandiose Alexander, who whipped up anticipation and energy with his stories taken from the scriptures of the church, Oris was more direct. He appealed to each listener individually, encouraging them to pursue their own betterment, and there was something less practiced to his words that gave them authenticity that his companion lacked.

During his oration, Aaron heard many things he agreed with: the importance of love and of discipline, the willingness to help one another, and even accepting those who have wronged. However, beneath it, Aaron couldn't help but hear an edge. For all that Oris enraptured his listeners, there was a tightness in his gestures, one that spoke of a well-contained but very real wrath held beneath the amiability he presented.

"You look to the Church and see warriors," he declared, gesturing to some of the listeners in sequence. "You see blessings and ceremonies and divinity. You look at my brother and me and see paladins, templars, maybe even killers. We are all of those things, and none of them, but we are no different than you. This thing called holiness is something simpler. What do you see here?" he asked, holding up the sigil of Paradise at his neck. He waited for a reply, and a few tenuous voices spoke up.

"The Church?"

"Authority?"

"Silver?"

That was the word he was waiting for. "Silver!" he declared. "And what makes it special?"

"It burns nightmares?" another voice questioned.

Oris nodded. "It burns nightmares. Not just them. Silver is by its nature consecrated: a shard of purity, and it is anathema to any with a sickness of the soul. Nightmares are soulless beings. They are smitten the worst. Nephilim, who must feed on the souls of others to replenish their own, fare little better. Even humans may be harmed when they have fallen especially far and lost to their dark magics that their truest selves become blotted out. It is the most precious thing in this world." He plucked it from his neck and tossed it to the ground in front of the crowd. "And it's also worthless."

The crowd watched in confused awe, as did Aaron. Oris smiled gently, picking up the signet and brushing it off. "We must respect it. That is true. But it is a thing, in the end. Disposable, replaceable. Why do you think the nightmares and nephilim cannot cross the threshold of this chapel? Is it silver? No. It is consecrated in faith, my friends; protected by something special but common. Silver is a crutch: good to have, but best if not needed for what you can do yourself. You need but accept it in your heart, and you'll find a power even greater."

He closed his eyes, lips moving in a silent prayer, and as he did, the emblem shimmered just a bit more brightly in the light, just enough that Aaron knew it was more than a trick of the light.

When at last Oris had finished, the crowd began to disperse. Aaron was just beginning to reconsider his course of action when a woman approached him. She had short, blonde hair and a signet of Paradise hanging from her neck.

"You're Aaron White," she stated.

"Yes, I am," he replied. "Thank you for not calling me a monster again."

"I don't need to repeat myself," she snapped.

He didn't rise to the heightened state of emotion. "I don't recognize you, but it looks like you're here frequently. Have you seen the caretaker? The woman in black?"

"Not here," the woman responded flippantly. "Not much of a caretaker either. Is that why you're always lurking? Shouldn't you be busy killing nightmares?"

Aaron measured her up, taking note of the scar tissue around her knuckles as she stared daggers at him. "If I can," he answered. "May I have your name?"

"I don't have to tell you anything."

"If I choose to demand it, you do, in fact," he said, putting an edge into his voice. "But I won't make you. I was just hoping to get some information, but it seems like she's still gone. I'll be on my way."

If that made her happy, she didn't show it, instead turning away until a voice called out, "Eva! Please, I asked you to invite him, not send him off!"

The woman, Eva, looked at Oris, abashed, as he approached.

"Please, Mr. White, I implore you to stay," he intoned, his voice showing no sign of strain from his preaching. "I noticed you've been here for a while. Come to chat again?"

Aaron eyed him. He thought he'd imagined it while he was preaching, but now he more clearly saw the first hint of stubble on Oris's face; the first sign of anything but immaculate presentation that the paladin had shown him.

"Why not?" he said. "As long as it's not a bother."

Oris smiled, easy as ever. "Of course not. Would you like to join me in the garden? We've done some work on it, and we can speak there in privacy. I promise to show you a way that won't get you burned." Taking the invitation, Aaron allowed Oris to lead him, though he already knew the way. Leah had shown him herself when they had last spoken. But it would have been rude to point it out, so he followed the paladin's direction.

At the rear of the church, behind the dome of the structure, a high wall of brick formed a small enclosure hidden from the public eye. It was attached to the building, but a single obscured entrance remained that didn't force one to walk through the consecrated threshold. Once he had done so, he was surrounded and enclosed by diligently pruned bushes and stacked terraces built into the walls, within which were planted flowers of all shapes and colors.

It wasn't large, with only a few feet of room to move about a single central table, but that was a charm of sorts. It was a sight of beauty, more carefully and personally cultivated than the works of a park.

"Forgive Evangeline," Oris said, bidding him to sit. "She has lost much. First, to the war with the Neros when Lady Baal came to power, and just recently, her lover was killed in the line of duty by a rogue vampire."

The detail stuck in Aaron's mind, only one such vampire coming to mind.

"She puts a great deal of faith in you," he remarked, his sword aside and avoiding the details of the topic. "Even more than she has disdain for me."

"We're working on her," said Oris. "As we keep saying, we are not worthy of such faith."

"Faith is a beautiful thing," said Aaron as he sat down. "But it's different for everyone." He listened to Oris's heartbeat, in tune with his steps as he pulled up his own chair. "You seem different today."

Oris's head tilted toward him just a bit faster than before, only to turn away, as if scolding himself. "Maybe I am."

"Is the city not to your liking?" Aaron asked.

"Actually, I find it quite charming. Strong walls, architecture refreshingly new but not gaudy like the temples of Paradise. The people are diligent and ordered. There is a real sense of purpose, and yet I still see the signs. The fear remains. Have you ever been to one of the other frontiers, Mr. White?"

The question caught Aaron off guard. He did not know how to answer at first, primarily due to his fragmented memories. He thought of the visions that assaulted him as he recalled his distant past, and the crushing loneliness that it brought with it.

"No, just Paradise."

"Then you don't know the whole truth. It takes seeing the other frontiers to truly understand. The South is beset by plague. It's even worse than it is here. They were hit the hardest by the Hell Breach decades ago. Neither the Church nor the nephilim of the great houses have truly recovered, but there it's at its worst. Pestilence and disease run rampant. Technological regression occurred as its artisans were killed off. Normally, Nephilim houses that maintain such knowledge might step in to help, but they were so decimated that their own knowledge was lost. It's all the Church can do to hold it together."

"The North holds the steadiest, having been the farthest from the breach in the first place, but it was never a great place to begin with. It's a frozen waste cut off by mountains and treacherous terrain that makes safe travel at any speed or in any numbers nearly impossible. The people there are superstitious and cowed by cruel noble houses that hold them in body and mind.

"The West is overgrown with living weeds that tear apart infrastructure like it were so many pieces of a puzzle board. Wild magic is strong there, and while this does make nightmares less of a threat, it does just as fine a job at checking civilization. It's difficult to explain to a poor farmer that being eaten by a carnivorous tree is somehow better than having a nightmare do him in. You see, it doesn't get better." Oris shot him a slight grin, white teeth startlingly bright. "There's no need for pretension here, Captain. We are tools, and we serve our purpose. Now, how would you like me to prepare some tea? I promise not to lace it with silver."

Aaron accepted, eyes drawn to a brightly colored songbird that flitted amongst the rainbow of blooming flowers around them. He had never asked Leah how the plants were maintained, but there was almost certainly some miracle to it. The bird itself was a different breed than any he had seen; small enough to fit in a hand but with the sharp features of a raptor.

Its feathers were a pale gray similar to his jacket, but with its head and tail feathers a darker slate blue. When it moved, it spread four overlapping wings. This almost brought a smile to his face until it flew off, and Aaron saw the other paladin. He sat amongst the assorted flowers, watching silently with a grin like a slit throat.

"Brother Alexander," Aaron greeted, removing his glasses. "It's good to see you."

"And you as well, dear friend," Alexander replied with a tilt of his head. "Please, brother, don't exert yourself. I'll take care of it for you."

Oris thanked him, and Alexander vanished into the heart of the church. "You look like you've been through quite a bit, Aaron," he remarked. "Are you unwell?"

"Well enough," Aaron answered, enjoying a light breeze that washed over them. "You clearly don't have any problems gathering information, though, so I doubt I need to go into detail."

Oris almost appeared bashful. "If it makes you feel better, please know that I wouldn't dare ask. But, no, you don't. The people tell us many things. They want to know our thoughts on them: they want to feel comforted that someone is listening. The latest deaths have unsettled them, and fear loosens their tongues. When they don't feel safe in the system they know, they turn to one that they hadn't considered before."

"I've noticed," said Aaron. "The crowd has grown quite large quickly. But it looks like it's taken a toll on you as well."

Even as he said it, he began to notice flaws in the man's appearance. Wrinkles beneath eyes that were slightly bloodshot made him seem as if he hadn't slept. His posture suffered as well, with his knees locked and his shoulders drawn inward. He looked like he'd aged a few years in the days Aaron had known him.

"Well," Oris said, shifting as he made note of Aaron's attention. "I'm only human. Staying true to our nature is a sign of faith. We do as our natural function guides us. Respectfully, I think you might benefit from following that example."

The thought was not amusing to Aaron. "What are you saying? That I should revert to a feral and stalk the night like the nephilim of old?"

"I'm saying that you are deceiving yourself," Oris answered. "I see the distrust, the disconnect between you and them. You are the Other. Nothing can change that, and they expect things from you. Sitri Baal is respected as much as she is feared, not because she tries to imitate us, but because she doesn't. Power, ego, the surety of the self: these are the traits of the nephilim. They need not be used for evil, but to deny them you lessen yourself, and people are repulsed by it even if they don't know why."

Oris smiled gently. "You want something more. Something better. I see that. But you cannot realize those ambitions by acting as something you aren't. Your desire to improve your life and the lives of others may be genuine, but it will never be realized if you say what you think people want to hear instead of what you truly believe, and it will lead only to ruin. How much more could you accomplish if you simply acted on your wishes instead of enslaving yourself to them?"

He paused, considering his words carefully and speaking them even more so, as if each were fragile and precious. "I once struggled with who and what I was. It took a great deal of time for me to come to terms with it. But if you do, I promise you'll be stronger for it. It's not exactly a word of scripture, but I've found it more than worthy to live by."

Aaron exhaled, his eye caught by the fluttering of the four-winged bird that landed on one of the surrounding alcoves. "I won't ask what made you come to terms with it, but tell me this, did you feel like you were putting on an act before?"

The paladin drummed a gloved hand on the table. "Some days more than others, but the mania only grew with time. Knowledge of the world only takes you so far without answers to the questions of your own nature."

"And the Church helped you find your answer?" questioned Aaron.

"Maybe not in the way it was intended, but yes."

Aaron did smile slightly at that. It gave him the clarity to stop wasting time and ask what he intended. "You know, there was a caretaker to this church before you two arrived."

Oris nodded. "Of course. Leah, I believe it was. The place was in excellent condition; fine work by her. Why do you ask?"

"Where is she?"

He wasn't sure what he truly expected from the answer. Despite Oris's affable demeanor with him, the reputation of the paladins of Paradise was fearsome, and he was prepared for the worst. He expected hesitation, or at least consideration before an answer, but Oris responded immediately.

"Not the faintest idea. I don't think I've even laid eyes on her. Descriptions were clear enough, and it sounds like she'd be hard to miss, but we never spoke. Odd for a woman so devout that she held together the practices alone to avoid us, but not terribly unexpected."

The earnestness of the answer again put him off. "You weren't surprised?"

Oris gave him a knowing look. "It's not our first time on a mission, Aaron. Many fear the arm of Paradise, even if they are faithful themselves. She's not wronged us, so we have no business chasing her down. But you, Aaron," he said as he leaned forward. "Why might you be interested?"

"I'm looking for her myself," he answered. "I hope she can provide me with some information."

Oris acknowledged him, eyes glancing up and down as if reevaluating his character. "Well, if I do find her, I'll be sure to let her know your intentions. Though if you want to speak with her, I'd guess it's on matters of the Church. I have no small insight myself on those matters, and would be happy to answer any questions you may have."

"No, thanks," Aaron said. "This is a question for her. Unless you've been at the sites of the recent killings."

Oris gave a slight, muted laugh. "Well, on that front, I must disappoint you. I think Lady Baal would take exception to such things."

Aaron stared down at the table. Yet another potential lead dashed. But even if Oris hadn't seen Leah, he'd been more than willing to listen up to that point. Maybe the paladin *could* help him, in a way. He was certainly a fresh perspective. Pondering it, Aaron realized that he cared what the man thought. If for no other reason than because he had entertained his own judgments about the agents of Paradise, he found that Oris's analysis had left him unnerved.

"You say it doesn't get better elsewhere. I'm not sure I believe it. Tell me, Brother Oris. You say I should be truer to my nature; that I'm enslaved to my dream. Does that include me coming to you for help? It sounds like you believe I'd be better served simply exerting my will on the people around me. A child died today; should I just arrogantly disregard it as beneath me and hammer the world into a shape I prefer?"

"Of course not!" Oris said quickly. "I'm sorry if it came off that way. No, that's not what I meant. There's nothing wrong with having feelings. He was a kind young man; his death was a tragedy. I'm just saying that this world has moved past altruism, especially for nephilim. People won't accept it so easily. They'll be wary."

"I guess you're right," Aaron said. "But it feels like no matter how I behave, the result is the..." He stopped, thoughts interrupted by another.

"Kind young man?"

The question hung in the air for several seconds, absolute silence overtaking as the regular sounds of the city muted themselves. Oris tilted his head. "Yes, Henry. He visited us several times. Word travels quickly amongst our little circle, I'm afraid. We'll do his recitation this evening."

His words were even as ever, laced with profound sorrow. Aaron acknowledged them, and an easier silence returned, but something didn't sit right. He hadn't realized it himself, but in his haste approaching the crime scene, he had neglected to gather details on the boy's identity. Dalton hadn't provided him with any documentation, and a child wouldn't have needed to carry any, so it didn't immediately come up in their conversation.

He'd never even gathered the name. The murder was fresh, less than a day old. It may have even happened while they were pursuing the siren. The officers would have kept the scene as clear as possible, leaving little time for any word of mouth to spread unless the one who discovered the boy had been a member of the church. It was coincidental, but not immediately alarming.

His eyes were drawn to Oris's chest. The signet of Paradise rested in his gloved hand. The glove dredged up his memory of their first meeting and what Alexander had said to him. *None should be afraid to touch another.* Yet the black leather gloves were mismatched to his white cassock.

What was he even thinking? Aaron wondered that to himself. Whatever it was, it was circumstantial at best; a series of insignificant details ranging from the timing of the deaths to the scent left on their corpses. He had no proof for the wild accusation that had formed in his mind. In fact, the very thought of it was so absurd, he wondered how he hadn't thought of it before or heard Durham tell it as a joke.

But all of that inconclusive reasoning, fueled by instinct and emotion in lieu of logic, was insignificant in the face of one fact. For the first time since meeting him, Oris's heart had started beating faster.

Aaron's senses were weapons to him, just as his sword or his pistol was. His sight was impeccable, but it was suited for darkness. His nose was better than average, but mostly in response to certain stimuli. He couldn't track just anything like some other nephilim could, but blood left him an easy trail.

His hearing was his greatest asset. Though not well-suited for the sounds of gunfire, it lent him a great degree of awareness for the movements of others around him. Even blind, he could passably navigate in a pinch. The hearts of others acted as beacons for him; a distinct sound for each individual that he could separate from the rest of the world. When they picked up speed, he noticed.

Average humans didn't give too much away when they lied. In Aaron's experience, it was more common for people's bodies to betray them when omitting a key detail than outright speaking fiction. But even for a practiced cutthroat, it was nearly impossible to stop their pulse from picking up when they were caught in the act. It was an awful thought, almost treasonous, but it festered and grew until he met the man's eyes, and understanding passed between them, prompting the words that came next.

"What's written on that wall, Oris?"

Oris's heart thundered, and his hand clenched around the signet at his neck. For just a second, his face showed fear. Then, like a change in the wind, it was replaced by solemn sadness. "Damn it all. I really enjoyed speaking with you."

They stood at once, the chairs sliding out and tipping over behind them. "Don't be rash, Aaron," said Oris. "We don't need to be enemies."

Aaron's hand twitched, unsure whether to go for his radio or his pistol. "You bastard," he said. "What did you do to Leah?"

His foe retained his composure, assuring him calmly. "I told the truth; we've not even met her since arriving in the city."

"She'd see right through you," Aaron growled. "I was just too trusting; too stupid!"

Oris's voice rang a pitch louder. "I meant every word I said, Aaron. Your convictions are hollow. You follow them only because you feel you should, and you don't even know why. We could find a different path together if you make the right choices now."

Each utterance sounded so sincere, so sweet. Each brought to mind another corpse left to rot. "You've just been spreading terror, from the very first moment. Tell me, is it even your work? Do you even understand what it is you're sacrificing to?"

Oris's calm demeanor was replaced by blatant shock. "You activated it," he murmured. "Then a nephilim truly is the key. Then Aaron- No, Captain White, I'm sorry to inconvenience you, but you'll be coming with us. The tea will have to wait."

The heartbeat that had been slowly moving into position behind him spoke. "That's twice the shame," said Alexander. "I just finished making it, and you were fast friends besides. Your intuition is impressive, Captain White. But I wonder, did you consider what would happen after you outed your suspects?"

Damnit, he's right, Aaron thought, shifting his posture to keep the other man in view. There's too many civilians nearby, and in this garden, I can't move freely. Then my only choice is-

Alexander rushed him, drawing a knife from his sleeve. Aaron leaped sideward, grabbing his sword and rolling into a standing position. But as he came to the wall, a barrier of heat threatened to sear his skin. An uncomfortable sound ripped through his throat. He might have been able to enter the garden freely, but if he tried touching the walls, the results would be ugly. Oris drew a small metal cylinder from his cassock, and without visible prompting, it expanded, extending until it was the length of his arm with a conical tip.

The nail was a simple but deadly implement used for lethal thrusts in close combat. Sleek and silent, it was a preferred weapon of the paladins, and its tip would be silver to deal a killing blow to even Aaron. Oris moved with frightening speed, but Aaron was able to draw his sword and deflect it. Alexander threw his knife, forcing Aaron away, and then drew a nail of his own. The paladins closed in on him. Before they could attack, though, their eyes widened and they ducked backward.

In the second that followed, the air was split by the crack of gunshots. The sudden sound was especially painful to Aaron, driving his eyes shut in a wince, but his body meant that his ears readjusted in only a second. A panicked scream carried on the wind around them. The pair didn't waste the chance; they scaled the garden wall in an instant, and though Aaron reflexively moved to pursue them, reason drove him to slide to a stop.

Sure enough, as his hand reached the threshold, his glove ignited. He pulled it from his hand, swearing as the holy fire sprang from the scripture pages nailed to the ground. He struck the paper with his sword, pulling it free and preparing to move, but a hand on his shoulder held him back. He turned to the grimacing face of Durham, who shook her head.

"Not now," she cautioned. "That's just what they want. If we walk out after shooting at them, we'll only get mobbed."

"They'll get away!" he growled.

A third voice joined in. Dalton rounded the corner, tearing pages from the ground. "Even if we catch them, remember what we're dealing with!" he said. "These are paladins of Paradise. They won't hesitate to kill everyone here. We start a fight in a crowded street, and just like you warned Sietz, there'll be another massacre!"

Aaron sheathed his sword, picking up the discarded nail. He bent it in his hands, anger fueling his strength until the steel cracked and shattered.

"Thanks for the help," he muttered. "But why are you here?"

Durham pulled up her sleeve, revealing her pact of Baal, the tattoo glowing against her skin. "Call it a woman's intuition. Figured something was wrong. Then the mark got angry. I'd talk some shit about your choice of friends again, but at least we found the bad guys."

"Those killers are now loose," said Aaron.

"True," Dalton said. "But Rista tipped off the guards Sietz stationed nearby before we went in. They'll go into hiding, sure. But now we know their faces, and they can't escape a city-wide manhunt."

Aaron sighed. "Fine, you're right, as usual." He donned his glasses, stepping on one of the papers beneath his feet and tearing it with a twist of his heel. "Dalton."

"Sir?"

"I want you to gear up. I'm giving you Brook, Lenz, Moore, and Sif. Durham, you and Gavin come with me. We may have missed them here, but we're not losing them, and we're *certainly* not letting the watch find them first."

Durham grinned wide while Dalton blinked in acknowledgment. "Understood, sir. If I may, why only two groups?"

"Because I won't risk running into them with teams smaller than that. And one more thing…" Aaron's fist shot out, smashing the table they had sat in out of shape. Not even close to satisfied, he flexed his wrist. "This is our chance. I want this done cleanly, by the numbers. We take them in and we take them alive. They owe us an explanation, and I won't let Sietz or some petty nephilim kill them before we get it!"

—Chapter 18—

Less and More

"That's two more injured, one critically," said Eric. "He's cutting through the south side using the undercity. No idea how he knows them so well after just a few days."

"That's a hell of a thing for a paladin to be capable of," Sif replied. "The city gates are shut. We should be able to catch him the next time he surfaces."

Dalton's voice cut through the static. "Narrow it down. There are a dozen places he could show, but only one best option. He's smart enough to know it, so we just have to be ready to intercept. Brook, you scouted the entrances. Where would he try?"

Aaron turned the volume of the radio down. "That's enough of that. It's time to go. You two ready?"

"Ready," Gavin said as he loaded his rifle. "Did he specify which one we're hunting?"

Durham pulled her mask over her head. "Does it matter?"

Aaron tightened the belt that held his sword in place and thought of Oris. "Not particularly."

The city was on high alert; citizens had begun evacuating the streets under the eyes of the military police. Still, Aaron thought there were far too many out and about as they left the barracks. "What's the plan then?" Gavin asked. "They split like you thought, but just one of them is making noise."

Aaron had already considered it, and their next move. "That one's no longer our concern. We make for the site. If we bide our time, he'll come to us."

His radio went off, and he grabbed it. "Go ahead."

"Captain, we've got eyes on him, but there's a complication, a riot on the south side. Sietz's man reports that there are some other unruly elements to track. Bear it in mind as you proceed."

Gavin's expression soured. "They convinced ordinary citizens to turn on the police? What the hell have those two been doing since they got here?"

"Just what we need…" Aaron muttered. "But it doesn't change our plans."

"Hold on there, Captain!" a voice called from behind. "Don't tell me you forgot me?"

Aaron turned to acknowledge him. He had almost managed to sneak up on them, befitting his skills. Rista greeted the three with a nod. He was geared for combat, with his arm no longer in a sling. Aaron's eyes narrowed, a feeling gnawing at him that was more primal than conscious thought. His predatory instincts sensed weakness. Rista was stiff. The injury may have been healed with medical attention and a touch of magic, but like a lingering ache, it hadn't left him entirely.

"You said you had a fracture."

"I'm good enough," Rista replied. "Doc gave me the all-clear."

Aaron was unconvinced. "Did he know you wanted to hunt a paladin of the Paradise Church?"

"We'll burn that bridge, something something- You know how it goes." Rista moved forward, a half step closer than he normally would. "You've got a plan, right?"

Aaron said nothing for a moment. He could feel Durham's eyes on his back. "Rista, I don't know what you're trying to do here, but you don't need to do it. I understand what this is."

Rista's mouth tightened. "No, Captain, respectfully…Look, I didn't say this the right way before, and I wasn't ready to." He glanced at Durham, then Gavin. "The truth is, I never trusted you. My family has supported the Baals for generations, and I've lost more than a few people I care about to nephilim. I worked with you because I believed in the job, and…I wanted to prove to Lady Baal that you didn't deserve her support. You were a problem to be solved, and nothing you said or did mattered because I didn't want to hear it. It took a kick in the ass for me to actually try to understand. Human or not, you're a teammate, and that wasn't fair to you. So, let's start over. Give me a chance now, and I promise I won't let you down."

Aaron examined him, trying to determine exactly how to interpret the words. He could think of no real gain for Rista by saying them, and the slight smile that tugged at his determined face spoke of nothing but embarrassed honesty. More than that, he wanted to believe. So, instead of asking another question, he reached out his hand, placing it on the man's shoulder.

Rista didn't flinch. His expression didn't change, but he relaxed a degree, and his heart that had sped up in the moment of vulnerability slowed at the contact. Aaron sighed, but couldn't help a smile.

"For what it's worth, I think you're acting like a fool, but I do trust you, Rista. I always have."

Something moved across those determined features. "I know you do. Captain, when this is done, I'd like to have a long talk."

"You know I'm happy to hear it."

Rista clapped him on the arm, and the four of them turned in the direction of their destination. "You may not be, but it's something I want to say," he said as they made to move. "And just call me Tony!"

Durham turned her head. "Tony?"

"Don't ruin it for him," Gavin said. "He's earned this."

Heat rose in Aaron's face. "Shut up, all of you," he muttered. "We have a job to do."

They moved on foot off the main roads, dipping through the streets in alleyways and keeping close to the shadows. "You know that we could have the MPs helping us," said Rista. "We don't need Noah on our asses even more than he already is."

"Better this way," Aaron answered with a shake of his head. "These two have been a step ahead of the watch from the start. They have to have a way of getting information on them."

"They're probably getting info from the Paradise-botherers," Durham offered. "The watch's movements aren't a secret."

"Good point," acknowledged Aaron. "That riot isn't a coincidence. Regardless of what they said to the populace, we don't have evidence aside from my conversation. We need to concretely pin the murders on them, or there could be big trouble."

Around the end of a wall, they watched a small crowd gather at a street corner, then disperse. "You mentioned that they're after some ritual site carved into the wall," Gavin muttered. "But I never saw it. What's so special about it?"

Aaron shook his head. "Not a clue. But they know more about magic than I do, and they're more than willing to kill for it. How much they know is anyone's guess; even more reason we need to take them in." They crossed the street. The site was only a few blocks away. "Be careful," he cautioned. "These two are as dangerous as nephilim."

"Maybe." Durham whistled softly. "But any bullet will work on these ones."

"Stop, you idiot!' Gavin hissed, but it was too late; she made to cross the street just as two dozen people rounded the corner. Aaron made to grab her, but was immediately spotted and fixated on by the crowd. They moved toward him in unison, an uncomfortable energy in the air. Gathering himself and putting on his most presentable face, he took the lead and approached the crowd.

"Please, all of you disperse," he said. "The streets aren't safe right now. We are in pursuit of a murderer."

A rock came from the back of the crowd and hit him in the shoulder.

"I insist that you all leave here now," he said, louder, noting that some in the group were holding weapons. They realized he was not human then and were momentarily cowed.

It was not to last, for their wariness was replaced with outrage when a woman called out, "I recognize him. He was there at the attack!"

"It was you!"

"That's why you're skulking about!"

"I knew you couldn't be trusted. You're the monster that attacked the brothers!"

Aaron took a tentative step backward, and another rock flew at his head. He knocked it aside, and the crowd stepped back, as if he had lashed out. Outrage fueled them, and they began to advance with uncomfortable speed. S-0 backed up, moving at a brisk pace, but not yet running.

"I'm going to put this down!" Durham hissed, grabbing Re-Human.

"No!" Aaron snapped. "We're not attacking them!"

The sound of the gun interrupted them. Sharp pain blossomed in his chest. Aaron looked down at the front of his jacket, where blood slowly leaked from the small-caliber round that had struck him in the sternum.

He touched the wound. It hurt, but only superficially, as the bullet was halted by bone. Not silver. His body was already beginning to heal.

He might have regained control of the situation, but before he could speak, Durham was in motion. She ran past him and closed the distance to the leader of the group, the one who had fired the small handgun drawn from his sleeve. He was a large man with broad shoulders and a nose that looked like it had been broken repeatedly. Durham dropped him with a single blow, slamming the hilt of Re-Human into the side of his head and sending him heavily to the ground.

Someone screamed, but this only emboldened the crowd. Rista pulled Aaron backward. "Go!" he said. "We'll handle it!"

The crowd surged forward, and Aaron leaped out of the way in order to avoid them, eyes trained on the nearest alley. He rounded a corner and sprinted through the adjacent gap in the old buildings, ducking rusted pipes as he crossed the next street in order to avoid being followed. He made his way westward, feigning entry into one of the smaller side roads that led to the guard post. Instead, he doubled back and returned on his way to the objective, hearing the crowd's voices grow more distant.

Aaron made it to the road in question, walking it slowly, taking note of the distinct lack of people there. He saw the alleyway from a distance, scoping it out before making his way to approach it. He turned the corner and passed between the buildings.

The beating of a calm heart. A deadly whisper of metal in the air. Aaron pressed flat against the wall, barely avoiding the nail that buried itself in the cobblestone. Drawing his foot back, he smashed into it with his full strength, snapping the weapon off at the silver tip.

Oris stepped out of the shadows in which he had hidden himself with superlative skill. "Hello, Captain White. Come to chat one last time?"

Aaron took note of his clothing. Oris still wore the same white cassock as before, but the signet of Paradise was tucked beneath it. His dress shoes had been traded for boots suited to combat, and at his waist hung an assortment of equipment. Aaron's first impression was of holy weaponry, as would suit a paladin, but that was not the case.

Though there were sleek, subtle instruments that he recognized as belonging to the Church, there were also some he did not. Trinkets, baubles, and other items with no discernable purpose, including stone idols, animal skulls, and gleaming feathers.

"We'll have plenty of time for that," he stalled. Fishing into his jacket, he pulled the small bullet that had struck him free from the mending skin. "You're being surrounded as we speak."

"Doubtful," Oris dismissed. "My followers have made sure of that. They were supposed to keep you away, too, but this works just as well."

Aaron took note of the sweat on his brow and his lowered eyelids. Even more than before, there was something about him that was slipping.

"You're scared."

"More annoyed, really. I thought you had activated it."

Aaron made a note of each word. "Well, I definitely did something."

Oris took a step forward. "No more games. No more lies. If your words won't tell me, then I'll use your blood instead."

"Like the others?" Aaron replied, digging for information like trying to pull free another bullet from himself. "Dead for something you don't even understand!?"

Oris's expression softened, though just for a moment. He sank slightly lower. "Regrettable, but necessary. I took no pleasure from it, nor will I from this. But it must be done."

Aaron's hand twitched, his pistol weighing heavily on him. The other members of S-0 always carried two sidearms, one for humans and one for anything else. He had never done so.

"These bullets were made for nightmares, but they'll work just fine against you."

A tilt of the head. "Then why haven't you done so already? Can't kill me, is that it?"

"Nobody would mourn it, but that isn't why. I don't *want* to kill you. I don't want to kill anyone, least of all a human."

Oris smiled sadly. "And that very sentiment will cause you more pain than any other. Meaningful change only comes from the destruction of what is. Your master would agree, I'm sure."

"Maybe," said Aaron. "But I'm stopping you here, and you won't be leaving without a scratch. It may not be my place to sentence a human, but Lady Baal will have you. Say a prayer if you like. That's my final courtesy."

The smile vanished. "Put no faith in God. Put faith only in corruption, for it runs deep."

Aaron drew his sword and advanced. Oris drew another nail and thrust it toward the center of his chest. Aaron parried, then retreated when Oris crushed a vial in his hands and attempted to spatter him with blessed water.

Forward again. Oris deflected three consecutive swings, cold and efficient. Adjusting his stance, Aaron swung the flat of his blade, knocking the nail to the ground. Oris drew and threw a dagger in the span of a heartbeat. Aaron twisted out of the way, but the delay gave Oris time to release a small cartridge from his waist. It bounced on the cobblestone once before Aaron heard a click, his only warning to prepare himself for the explosion.

The stun grenade produced a burst of light and sound that overloaded the senses, but Aaron pressed himself to the side of the alley to dodge the attack that followed, knowing Oris would be similarly affected. The swing of the nail tore six inches of fabric from his sleeve. Instinct compelled Aaron to strike with his free hand, but his mind fought it. *Don't risk it,* he told himself, n*ot against this one.*

His senses returned to him, and he inspected the tear. The silver had not touched him, though a patch of his skin beneath was now exposed to the air. The thought made him uncomfortable. Oris released a breath, his accelerated heart reverberating in Aaron's mind.

"It's not too late. We could heal you, too. Your body and your mind."

A pit formed in Aaron's stomach. The apprehension was only smothered by his body's desire to crush his enemy.

"Why?!" he shouted, feeding more strength into his blows. "Why do any of it?!"

He battered Oris's defenses with a series of strikes to force him to expend his strength. The paladin was as deadly a foe as any nephilim, but Aaron was the captain of S-0, and every member of his team was an experienced soldier who had earned their place in life by hunting those who would have made them prey. Aaron knew exactly what a human was capable of with nothing more than focus, training, and unflinching willpower.

This gave him an advantage other nephilim wouldn't have: He didn't underestimate his foe. Just as he would train against Durham, he kept the pressure fast and intense, never giving the human a chance to collect himself. Aaron didn't overextend or even commit both hands to his attacks, but relied on brute strength to turn the tables on the man and force him to do what he desired of Aaron—to overreach.

With a forward swing, he knocked Oris off-rhythm. The paladin reached for his cassock, but Aaron was ready for it. He caught the hand, locking his grip around the man's wrist. Carefully loosening the mental restraints on his strength, he pulled Oris off his feet and hurled him into the nearest wall.

He fell to the ground coughing. Aaron planted his sword in the ground. It was a calculated attack with enough force to crack ribs and concuss, leaving Oris easy prey to be taken captive. Aaron kicked the nail across the alley. *I won't take a chance with you,* he thought, reaching out for the paladin's bicep. *One squeeze and I'll break your arm.*

"You're smart," Oris hissed between breaths. "Not arrogant like other nephilim. But you're crippled in body and mind. You're not strong enough for what's to come. Not strong enough right now."

Aaron stared at him in shock, his hand still outstretched, an inch from the paladin's arm. It was caught, however, in Oris's free hand, like Aaron had done moments before. He pushed, but the arm didn't budge. *What?* he had time to think before Oris slammed into him with a headbutt.

Aaron reeled backward, vision flashing different colors from the impact. When he found himself again, Oris had stood up and calmly walked toward him barehanded. He drew back an arm, the strike simple and predictable. Aaron had all the time in the world to bring up his own to block it.

The force of the blow caused his whole body to buckle. It pushed him, his boots scraping helplessly against the stone beneath as they failed to find purchase. Before the disbelief could even register, Oris struck him with an uppercut. The air was driven from his lungs, and a wave of nausea overtook him. Oris wasted no time grabbing him by the collar and throwing him headfirst into the wall. Brick cracked, and his head split open.

Aaron struggled to pull himself to his feet. His head throbbed and tickled as his skin knit together, but the real damage was deeper. He could feel it in the way the muscles in his chest spasmed and the way the world spun despite his standing still. Oris had retrieved his nail and charged at him with another thrust. Aaron didn't try to block, instead twisting out of the way to avoid the frightening strength behind it. He diverted it into the wall and then backhanded the paladin. This time, he used more force, and against an ordinary human, would have knocked out half his teeth.

Oris didn't react, except to snarl and swipe at him, cutting Aaron's cheek. Shocked but not stunned, Aaron responded with even more force and struck Oris with a knee that should have collapsed his lungs. Oris stumbled backward, clutching his chest where the blow had landed, but recovered almost immediately and attacked once more.

Aaron blocked as many strikes as he was able, but Oris's strength was more than equal to his. He desperately avoided a fist that broke the brick it impacted, and he punched the paladin in the face. It should have taken his head off. Instead, it split his cheek, but Oris's expression was one of melancholy. He grabbed Aaron's arm, pulling him forward and retaliating with a punch to the jaw.

Aaron's vision flickered. When it returned, he was on the ground. A human was overpowering him. The idea of the situation was almost as absurd as the reality was agonizing. His breath came heavily, and he tasted blood. "What are you?" he croaked.

Boots came into his field of view. "I would ask you the same thing," Oris said, reaching toward him. A hand closed around his wrist, tearing the sleeve away and lifting it to examine. "So much damage. What could have made you like this?"

Oris's head snapped to attention, and he released Aaron, letting him drop to the ground in time to catch the knife that had been thrown at him. Oris looked at the newly arrived Durham with a playful smile, only for it to vanish when Rista stepped into view, gun leveled. Oris ducked the first shot and received a glancing blow from the second, but the handful that followed struck home. He fell backward into the side of the alley.

Durham ran forward, drawing Re-Human, but Aaron interjected. "Wait!" he called, still struggling for breath. "Don't kill him!" She looked at him in confusion, and her eyes widened. Her posture relaxed, and she sheathed her blade, moving toward him instead with Rista at her side.

She helped him to his feet with a nod. Her mask was torn, and Rista had a scratch on his cheek, but otherwise, they appeared unharmed. "Where's Gavin?" Aaron asked.

"He's fine," Rista assured him, keeping his eyes on Oris. Durham examined Aaron's head, her hand coming away stained red. "What the hell happened to you?"

"I'll be all right," he said. "I just need a minute. It's healing now."

He reached into his jacket and grabbed his flask, taking a sip from it to accelerate the process. His neck twitched, sending a shiver through his body.

"He's strong," Aaron said. "Too strong for a human. I don't know what he did, but we need to be careful. Get Dalton on the line and tell him to treat Alexander with extreme caution."

"I guess he had a few tricks up his sleeve," said Rista, examining the paladin's slumped form against the wall. Oris coughed, blood and spit staining his white garb. "But he's wearing silver. He's no nephilim. Speaking of, I might have hit a lung. If you want him alive, we need to move him fast."

Aaron lurched forward, strength beginning to suffuse his limbs once again. "You're right. I'll take him. Don't get too close."

He stood over the downed paladin, who looked up at him with the same easy smile he'd worn when they met. Blood from his wounds was starting to leak through his cassock. Rista shot well. They needed to work quickly and keep him conscious.

"Stay with me, Oris," he said. "We'll take care of you."

Oris coughed again. "If only I had met you earlier. You truly are a gentle soul."

Aaron leaned down, intending to lift the paladin and bind his hands. It was this opportunity that Oris took, eyes sharpening with focus.

"It's a shame."

He rose to his feet in an instant, body contorting as if he were being pulled upward rather than exerting his own strength. Oris struck out with his hand, aiming for Aaron's throat with a bullet-like jab. Only Rista's intervention saved him, pulling back and out of the way.

Then Oris twisted. His arm struck Rista at the junction of his neck and shoulder, sending him a dozen feet with the terrible sound of cracking bone. He flew, then tumbled, then struck the corner of the street and was still. Aaron stared in horror, and the paladin looked down on him, saying no more, but drawing a long dagger instead.

Durham didn't hesitate, but drew Re-Human and attacked in a flurry of sweeping strikes. Oris blocked each with the flat of his much-smaller blade, accruing cuts from each but showing no signs of being bothered by pain. He lashed out with a vicious swipe and forced her to retreat, overwhelming force clashing with supernatural skill.

She narrowly avoided his fist before dancing around his guard and slicing into his shoulder. Oris laughed, raising his leg in a kick. Durham blocked the blow, but it sent her backward into the wall. With the distance created, she drew and leveled her pistol at him, eyes full of murder, and he charged her. She shot three more times before he could close the gap. They didn't even slow him down, and she twisted out of reach, avoiding his grasp by inches.

Oris charged again, and Durham raised Re-Human to meet him. They clashed as Aaron pulled himself to his feet, legs barely holding him up. His head swam in agony, and he lost his balance, falling against the stone wall. Beneath his touch, the inscriptions pulsed with his heartbeat, as if alive.

Durham sliced into Oris's nose, but he was able to grab hold of Re-Human. With a single hand, he threw her back into the wall, the collision knocking her prone. He was different now. His breath was coming faster, more labored. Beneath his skin, Aaron observed his veins pulse visibly, a subtle glow of fiery orange seething in his blood. It crept along his arms and up his neck, the faint light flickering in tune with his twitching muscles and facial tics. Grimacing, he adjusted his grip on his knife.

"That weapon…to think Sitri had come so far and so quickly. I'll have to examine it later," he said. "Still, you aren't useful."

Any words Aaron might have said were replaced by a thoughtless roar of fury. Abandoning restraint, he launched himself at Oris, tackling him from behind and throwing him to the ground. His body ached, but he paid it no mind. It didn't matter that the world flickered between reality and illusion. It didn't matter that past and present collided in his mind. He smashed his fist into the stone where the paladin's head had been a second before, pulverizing it into sand and deflecting the retaliatory strike. Grabbing Oris by the shoulders, Aaron picked him up and tossed him backward, driving him into the wall.

Oris didn't flinch, instead narrowly dodging the follow-up blow that shattered the structure around it into pieces. Crumbling brick and mortar created a moment of distance, and Aaron used it to grab his sword from where he had planted it in the ground. It breathed in his grasp, responding to his urgent rage. His vision flickered, the man before him replaced by another he didn't recognize as the strange magic ticked within his mind. Wielding it with both hands, he raised the sword high and then brought it down in an overhead blow that shattered Oris's blade and severed his arm beneath.

The paladin's eyes went wide, a muffled scream in his throat, but Aaron didn't stop. His swing sent the tip of his sword off the ground and out of his hands. He let it go, instead reaching out and grabbing hold of Oris's chest with such force that his fingers sank into the skin, cracking ribs, sternum, and clavicle in his crushing grip.

They stared at each other, both in shock. The utter stillness of the moment, mixed with the alluring warmth on his skin, snapped Aaron from his frenzy. Oris clutched the stump of his arm, dark blood seeping between the fingers of his remaining hand. His breathing was ragged, but he didn't hesitate except to draw on whatever strength he had left. His arm shot outward, revealing a second knife from where he had hidden it in his sleeve.

Durham slammed into him with her boot, knocking him backward and pulling Aaron's hand from his chest. Pistol ready, she shot him until her magazine was empty, then discarded it and grabbed another. Oris staggered backward, cassock now more red than white. His injuries were horrific, yet still he didn't fall. The veins beneath his skin glowed bright as hot metal.

His eyes darted back and forth, desperate but still focused, calculating. They passed over Durham, who was halfway through loading her second magazine, and fell on Aaron. He blinked, slightly slower than normal, and sighed.

"I see now. Of course, it would work for you. Good fortune, Aaron," he whispered. "Beware. Soon, they will come for you."

Then he ripped his cassock, revealing a row of black canisters at his belt. He tore at them, and Aaron realized what he was doing. He stepped forward, shoving Oris backward across the alleyway, and then turned, wrapping himself around Durham.

The explosion lit the world, drowning it in light and sound for all of a single second. When it faded, Aaron's mind was able to focus again. He was bleeding, a dull pain in his lower back. He cataloged the injury. It hurt, but not excessively. Shrapnel had shredded his vest, but it did not penetrate deeply. He could feel his body working to repair it, an uncomfortable sensation like a swarm of insects under the skin. Durham struggled to her knees, clutching one of her ears with her free hand. She opened her mouth, speaking experimentally, and wincing at the sound.

"Surrender complete?" she asked.

He wanted to smile but couldn't bring himself to do so. He smelled her blood and saw the dark stain running down the sleeve of her left arm. He began to speak, leaning forward, only for a wave of nausea to hit him. He caught himself on a hand before he could faceplant in the cobblestone, but the effort reduced him to wheezing. The strength that had propelled him against Oris had vanished, leaving him empty save a fading echo that left him wondering how he had managed it in the first place. Still, he tried to stand to help her.

"It's fine," Durham insisted, pulling her sleeve back to reveal a gash across her forearm. "He just grazed me. Worry about yourself."

He shook his head. "We need to get Rista. We can still—"

But he couldn't finish that thought, as he was interrupted by the sound of a suppressed gun. It hung in the air, leading the entire world to a state of unnatural stillness to Aaron, but only for an instant before his back exploded in flame.

Aaron had been touched by silver on several occasions, and it haunted him to recall any of them. Ordinary wounds could hurt him, of course, but they were generally tempered by the fact that his unnatural body would immediately begin to mend. Silver was different. Its existence was anathema to his nephilim soul and felt like nothing short of glowing hot metal pressing into his flesh. More than simply pain, it was a hungry void, tearing a wound in his spirit and sapping his strength from him all the while. In a way, it made him more human. It was absolute, impartial, and inanimate.

What struck him then was not the same as ordinary silver. It was excruciating. It drained his strength. But this had intent, and it carried malice. All his senses cried out at the violation. A high-pitched ringing filled his ears, and his head shuddered with a sense of vertigo. He smelled as he tasted, his throat dry as if coated in charcoal. The colors of the world flashed in shades of red that he did not know existed. But above all, he burned.

He fell forward onto Durham, a scream involuntarily leaving him with his breath. She pulled him to the side, emptying her reloaded pistol into the haze from which the shot had come, and forced him into the hole he'd broken in the side of the alley. The smoke from Oris's final act dissipated, revealing a woman with blonde hair ducked against the corner of the alleyway. She was flanked by two others, though Aaron only recognized her as one of the acolytes who had condemned him at the church. He tried to place her name, but couldn't do so as a wave of agony ravaged him. He twisted and reached, desperately trying to rid himself of the blessed bullet, but to no avail.

Durham fumbled with her injured arm, searching for another magazine to load her pistol. She reached for his gun as well, but couldn't pull it from his hip. He tried to speak, but no sound could leave his lips beyond a gasping, wordless plea.

She spared him a single look of compassion before her face contorted in hatred. "Who the fuck are you!?" she snarled. Opening one of her knives, she threw it into the air, and another gunshot rang out.

It seemed quieter than before, with the furious ringing in Aaron's ears.

Aaron heard a cursing voice, muffled and farther away than it should have been. "You monsters…they were the only ones that could save us!" Durham stared down the alley, taking in details with instinctive speed. Aaron's back arched, and his hand shot out, cracking off another brick.

Another gunshot. Durham inhaled. She looked at Aaron's sword, testing its weight, then shook her head.

Though speaking brought him even greater pain, he mustered the will to force out the whisper. "Leave me."

Durham didn't acknowledge him. The distant-sounding voice of his attacker rang out again. "You'll all die! You'll die and burn in cold emptiness forever!"

"Not today," Durham hissed.

She grabbed a fallen brick with her injured arm, bracing herself and throwing it up at their attackers. The woman fired, but her eyes were drawn to the projectile, and with that hesitation, Durham made her move. To any other, it might have been suicide, but its simplicity was its strength, and she carried it out with no hesitation.

Durham crouched low and sprinted straight forward, moving faster than any human should have been able to and letting surprise and panic keep her alive. She lunged downward, throwing another knife as a distraction until she achieved her purpose. Her hands closed around Re-Human.

Aaron blinked, and the world skipped forward a handful of seconds.

Then Durham was wrenching the blade free of the woman's side. Blood splattered the alley wall, and his attacker screamed. Durham continued, quick as a nephilim and merciless as a nightmare. There were two more behind the shooter, and she opened their throats with a single slash each. They hit the ground together, their lives ended in the span of a single breath.

The world flickered, and the next second, she was kneeling over him.

What followed was less coherent. Aaron's body twitched and shuddered against his will. His breaths came shallowly. Words lingered in his ear like musical notes, muddled by his own fleeting consciousness. *Easy. Good. Sorry.*

The air was cold on his skin. Aaron's chest was exposed. "Jacket," he muttered. "Where's my jacket?"

He hated his body. There was no fat on him, and the muscles of his arms and chest were sunken and emaciated. They drew inward, making him unnaturally thin. His translucent skin looked like it was stretched over him and covered in a litany of scars. Every breath threatened to split him open. He wrapped his arms around himself, trying to cover the sight, but it did little to help. He looked up. Durham's form was blurring, but he made out her eyes and the shape of a knife in her hand.

"Hold on," she said.

Then he closed his eyes and didn't open them again.

–CHAPTER 19–

TO LIFE

Swimming beneath consciousness, fragments of time and memory blended. Aaron walked in gilded halls and picked through the ruins of a once-noble castle. Voices laughed and wept at his presence, but their faces were shadowed and indistinct. He could only try to pick words from the insanity, and none of them made sense. Then he was on his knees, bloody and exhausted. A voice spoke down to him.

"Do you want me to save you?" it asked. *"You can take revenge on everyone who hurt you."*

"They're dead now," said a voice that was not his. But it was a lie. There were too many to count. Anyone. Everyone. Reason was destroyed by caustic hatred, and the voice screamed into the wastes.

Aaron woke abruptly, drawing in a heaving breath. His muscles tensed and shuddered, trembling with energy but seized and immobile. He bit his tongue. To his relief, the pain that had sent him into unconsciousness was gone. He focused on his breathing, in and out. Slowly, painfully slowly, he reasserted control of his body.

A hand falling on his shoulder nearly caused him to jump to the ceiling. He hadn't even noticed Gavin at the bedside. His hair was a mess, and he was in need of a razor, but he looked otherwise unharmed. "Glad to have you back with us," he said.

Aaron exhaled, drawing strength from and savoring the contact. Taking stock of his position, he was grateful to see he had been covered. The ruin that was his body was draped in a loose robe, ideal for concealing his form. Only the left sleeve had been rolled up, and though far from pretty, his arms were a magnitude better than the withered husk of his torso. A needle was fed into his exposed skin, and while his throat was dry, he didn't feel the gnawing hunger that often accompanied healing.

"How long has it been?"

"Just a day," Gavin answered. "You were in bad shape, but Durham managed to get the bullet out of you without roughing you up too bad, and they got you treated quickly. Doctors had to cut some of the burned flesh, but you've been on a drip of something or other, and your wounds closed up after a couple of hours."

Aaron shifted in place. Sure enough, the motion didn't cause him discomfort. All that remained of the haunting agony was a dull ache where the bullet had entered him.

"What about Durham?" he asked. "What about you?"

Gavin sat up straighter. "Minor injuries, both of us. Durham says that if she hadn't read the instructions, she would've been red as roadkill. I got off easy. The crowd was meant to separate us, but I got them under control."

"Did you kill them?"

"I should have," Gavin said darkly, only to flinch at Aaron's expression. "But no, I didn't. Much as I'd like to say I did it for you, I figured we might learn something from them. No luck on that front, meaning it was for nothing. I'm sorry I wasn't there to have your back."

Aaron pulled the needle from his arm, watching the puncture bleed for a moment, then heal. It hurt, and he wanted it to. "Don't apologize, it was what I wanted. They were just victims, manipulated by killers. Maybe I should have just let Durham handle it. If I had... I was weak, and Rista—"

Aaron blinked. It didn't make sense. It couldn't. He had spoken to Rista just minutes ago. The man had given Aaron permission to call him by his first name. He smiled at him and offered to help. He saved him, and then he died.

The hand on his shoulder gave a squeeze. "Don't," Gavin said. "Anthony knew what he was doing. He made the choice to fight because he knew that he could, just like he chose to trust in you. We still need you, Captain. Durham told me what happened. The story with Alexander was similar, and the watch failed to take him alive, even with Dalton. Lady Baal ordered an emergency meeting of the senior staff, and that includes you. It'll happen tomorrow, following Rista's funeral."

"You weren't going to tell me he was up?" Durham chirped as she entered his field of view. Gavin just shrugged, shaking his head, and she leaned on him in place of the adjacent chair. She stared at Aaron, her expression unusually reserved. "You look like shit."

"More than usual?" he asked, feeling the air on his skin and becoming more acutely aware of how exposed he was. "Where's my jacket?"

"Right here," Gavin said, draping the oversized coat on the foot of the bed. "Grabbed it from the barracks, but you're down one. That bullet messed you up."

"Burned right through your clothes," Durham said. "However it felt, it wasn't silver, meaning those priests did something special to it. It's been collected for examination to figure out what. Whatever it was, it worked."

"It was worse than silver," Aaron replied, testing the movement of his limbs. "Worse than anything I've ever felt. Maybe the gun was special. Did you get it?"

"You don't remember?"

"Only pieces," he admitted. "You saved me. There were others there. Did you—"

"I carved them up like animals," she said. "And if you start crying about it right now, I'll punch you in the face."

He expected it, but her stare, spiteful and pitiless, was still saddening. "I just think you—"

She punched him in the face.

The blow hit right between the eyes. His head snapped back, the world flashing different colors as his senses righted themselves at the assault. That was to say nothing of the pain, though it was blessedly brief in comparison to what he had recently endured. Durham's strength, with the benefit of her pact, was greater than her size suggested.

When he saw straight again, Durham was flexing her hand with a scowl. "That hurt. You're dense in more ways than one," she grumbled.

"Poor technique," Gavin said. "You know better."

"The mark will take care of it. Besides, it's worth it to drill through his thick skull." She waved him off and drew closer to him. "You are so stupid, you know that? Do you have any idea what my pact feels like when you're on a mission? We're looking out for you while you're wasting your time over pieces of shit that would spit on your grave! I know…I know you're trying to make a difference, but sympathy and I haven't been on good terms since I was eating rats in the undercity.

"*This*," Durham said, pointing at the spiderweb of scars on her face, "is what the world will do if you let it. There are not enough important people in my life to waste mercy on traitors. And if you want to rise above this hellhole, then you need to stop letting it drag you down!"

Their faces were inches apart. Durham's heartbeat was almost as loud as his. It was only then that Aaron considered that she might be afraid of how he perceived her actions.

"I won't," he said, putting a hand on her shoulder. "But Alice, we're the same. You, me, Jaycen. We might have come from different places, but we had nothing. We made ourselves from nothing. I just don't want anyone else to have to live like that. That's why I have to try… It might be crazy, but I know I can do it *because* I have you watching my back. And I may not always like it, but I'll never ask you not to be who you are. Thank you, both of you, for being there for me."

Durham relaxed at that, adjusting her position and nodding with a look of vulnerability unsuited to her. "Well, good. You're welcome."

"After the bullet, it all gets hazy," Aaron continued. "The last thing I saw was you holding a knife before I passed out. Was that it?"

"Pretty much. You're a tough one to cut into, but I managed to get the bullet out. You're lucky it got caught on your shoulder blade. If it had penetrated any deeper, you'd probably have lost a lung or your heart and died before we could get help. That's when Lady Baal showed up." She laughed at his bewildered expression. "I guess she had the same thought you did, that one of them would make for the site of the first kill. The bitch that shot you actually survived me ripping her guts out and tried to get back up. Baal smote her on the spot. That crazy light of hers, what's it called again?"

"Entropy," Gavin said, using the proper title.

"Stupid scary," Durham said. "Nothing left but dust. Annihilated the gun and the magic bullets in one go. Seemed a bit overkill, but I don't know what else we could've done. Half of that cultist was painting the wall, and she was still coming at us. Oh, and speaking of the wall, you wrecked it."

One casual hammer blow after another left Aaron stunned. "Pardon?"

Durham smirked. "Yeah, they're not too happy about it. You punched right through the brick while trying to pound Oris's face in and knocked off about half of the whatever-it-is. But hey, at least we took pictures! Maybe this was a bad time to mention it."

"I really am good for nothing," Aaron muttered, clutching his head.

He remembered it more clearly – the moment he'd made contact with the strange markings for a second time. The rush of strength and vitality that it granted him, as well as the anger.

"Was Sitri able to make something of it at least?"

Durham made a sound halfway between a choking dog and a tortured cat. "Well, she didn't say much while she was there. Mostly just stared dramatically. Helped me lug your heavy ass back to the base, though, so that was nice; she is crazy strong. What? Don't look at me like that! I'm not a musclehead, and you're giant."

"A giant scarecrow, maybe," he grumbled, forcing himself upright. Gavin tried to hold him down, but Aaron moved him with a light but unstoppable push. "I've lost time already. I need to get back on my feet."

"You're hopeless," Gavin said, but helped him nonetheless.

Aaron stared at his thin arms and skeletal chest. The anger at his own weakness intensified, and he threw the coat on with haste. Before he could button it closed, though, Durham put a hand on his shoulder.

"What happened in that fight?" she asked.

He tilted his head. "What do you mean?"

"I mean, you should be dead," she asserted. "At the end, right before you knocked his lights out, Oris stabbed you in the gut."

"His knife missed me," Aaron said.

"No, it didn't," Durham stated. "I thought I made it in time, but I didn't. There was a hole in your shirt, and the knife was broken on the ground. It was a silver knife. I don't need to tell you what that means."

He rubbed his temples, not understanding what she was getting at. "Well, I don't have to tell you that I'm not dead! I don't know what to say, Alice. I got lucky. We could use some of that."

"You touched the wall," she said as if that explained everything. "It did something to you, just like when we were there with Dalton. Aaron, you need to keep quiet about this until we have a better idea of what that thing was."

"I can't just withhold that information."

"You are so dense!" she snapped, grabbing him by the collar. "Listen to me. You have people out to get you, not just those God-bothering freaks. Sitri doesn't control everything around here, and there are plenty of the brass who don't like what you represent. They think you're trying to put more power in the hands of the rogues, and they *will* hurt you if you let them. Don't give them an excuse!"

"Fine! Fine. We'll keep it to ourselves, at least until we know what it is. We have bigger problems to worry about, but once we know more, I will tell Lady Baal." Gavin stared intently after Aaron conceded, and he shifted the topic. "Is everyone else all right?"

Gavin nodded. "They're fine, maybe finer than you'd like. Dalton's got them writing up reports in your absence. You'd best get ready, because you're expected to speak at the meeting tomorrow, and most everyone there wants your head."

"Just most? Things are looking up, then." The words hung in the air, Gavin responding with a slight smile. Durham, however, remained somber. When he took notice, she looked between them. "Are you going to tell him?"

"Tell me what?"

Gavin shook his head. "Give him a minute to breathe."

"He needs to hear it," she insisted.

"Am I invisible?" Aaron exclaimed. "What's happening?"

"Happened," Durham answered. "It's already happened. We think it was a week ago. All the shit with Oris and Alexander kept us out of the loop, but our people didn't even know it until it was too late. We've lost Alvas."

Aaron froze. He couldn't understand. He hoped he was mishearing, and grasped at that hope. "Lost it?"

True to form, though, Durham didn't acknowledge the attempt. "It was attacked, Aaron. The outpost was breached. Its wall went down. Everyone there is confirmed dead."

"That doesn't make sense! Alvas is our southernmost position. We just cleared out a pack of nightmares down south and repelled a swarm at the city gates! What could possibly have threatened—" Then he realized it. "It wasn't nightmares, was it?"

"I'm sorry, Aaron," Gavin followed. "But we've got eyes there. The meeting isn't just to discuss the paladins. It's also to figure out what to do about Roman Sterling's attack on our border, and if I know Lady Baal, then there's only one answer."

–Chapter 20–

On the Brink

Following the revelation of Sterling's attack on their southern border, Aaron had little time to waste. He met with the members of S-0 only long enough to gather their reports for the coming day. Normally, he found such work to be tedious, but he was grateful for it then. Any distraction from his thoughts was a mercy.

Unfortunately, it wasn't enough, and dread ate at his mind. Sterling. Lord Roman of House Sterling. His was not the meteoric and ruthless rise to power of Lady Baal, but he was equally famous. His family had been wardens of the eastern frontier for as long as the Baals, and they had never known a challenge to their reign. Shapeshifters were nephilim boasting the greatest physical strength, and the Sterlings were the mightiest of the shifters.

They were a house of tradition, with deep ties to their land and to Paradise. Sitri Baal's acceptance of nameless nephilim as soldiery was an unprecedented, almost heretical act, but the Sterlings worked in the opposite extreme. Where other noble nephilim families would employ smaller houses to serve them, the Sterlings abstained from such a practice. Instead of having weaker, though still respected households serving beneath them, they simply took any shapeshifters they encountered into their pack and viciously attacked any interlopers, nightmares, nephilim, or otherwise.

Strength was all that they required, and none had been able to match them for thousands of years. Roman himself was the oldest living warden in the East, several centuries into his reign. That he would make such a drastic incursion could only speak of a surety of his ire or a justification for his actions.

It was that very idea that haunted Aaron. Even as he studied the potential foe, he warred with his own conscience. *It was the right thing to do,* he told himself. *We knew Silas would show himself. If we hadn't acted, the entire village would have been massacred.*

The sound of Eric's cane substituted for knocking, stirring him from such thoughts. "Historical attacks, nephilim files, and now the Sterlings," he said as he cracked the door to the study. "You're running me ragged."

Aaron rubbed his neck, stiff from being hunched over for hours. "I am sorry about that."

"That was a joke," replied Eric as he approached. "Compared to chasing nephilim, this is the easiest gig of my life. It's how I know I made it."

He placed a book at the end of the table. When Aaron reached for it, he found it was held in place by a metal flask. "What is that?" he asked, knowing the answer already.

Eric drew up a chair, reclining with a slight groan as he sat. "What do you think? Normally, you hear me coming. You need to recover. Unlike me, your life's on the line out there."

Aaron stared at the flask for a time. It was perfectly sealed, and none of his senses could determine its contents. Nonetheless, he knew them, and his body reacted. He fought it for a time, but, seemingly of its own accord, his hand reached out and grasped it. His fingers unscrewed the top, and his arm brought it to his lips.

The gore ran hot down his throat, and every cell in his body thrummed with renewed strength. He endured the ecstasy in silence, but nothing could restrain his relief. When it was done, he resealed it, noting that his fingers had contorted the metal out of shape. Just like that, his strength was restored. So easy. He was whole again, and Rista was dead.

He set the flask aside and asked quietly, "Does it disgust you?"

Eric, who had watched the shameful sight calmly, answered, "I don't think it matters."

Aaron searched for expression in the same stoic face that all of the members of S-0 wore when watching him feed. "What if I said it mattered to me?"

Eric just shrugged. "I'd say you shouldn't look for validation in your coworkers like that, and I'd rather you not make me a source for it."

He reached out and collected the empty vessel. "May I speak freely, sir?"

"I'd like you to know you always can. I know what—" Aaron bit his tongue, looking for a better term but not finding it. "I know what I am, and I know what it means to you, and the other ordinary people. There are a lot of nephilim that Lady Baal took in who aren't in it for anyone but themselves. I'd like you to at least trust that I'd never do anything to…just say what you mean," he said. "Please."

Eric nodded, tapping his cane on the floor idly. "You remember how I got retired? Siren. Damn bitch pointed at my leg and said, 'break,' and it did. The pact healed it too fast, and it didn't set right. How many insane monsters did we put down before a word took me out of the action forever?

"Even with Lady Baal's blessing, we're fragile. And we have nephilim walking the streets like it's supposed to be normal. Nephilim that would kill us if it suited them. People are right to be afraid of the monsters she's unleashed, and sir, they're right to be afraid of you. But I'm willing to roll those dice because I've seen how bad it can really get, and you can't reason with nightmares.

"I'm older than most of the rank and file now. I know what things were like before Sitri came to power. The fact is, life here's better than it's ever been for folks like me. It's hard, and nobody gets through it easily. Take what you can and be grateful you have it. Unlike us, you have all the time in the world if you can keep yourself alive."

He stood, stretching his weak leg with a wince. "Now, I believe you have somewhere to be."

Aaron stood as well, thanked him for his words, and was off.

The service was brief, as they tended to be. Aaron had not attended many funerals; doing so required connections he simply didn't have. Those he did attend were always military. The ceremony took place in the castle's atrium for a small assembly of those who knew of Rista's exploits. S-0 was not to be recognized by the public so as not to advertise the existence of rogue nephilim. As a result, many of his greatest triumphs would remain unknown. Those in attendance were of rank and prestige: captains, commanders, some other special forces units, and, of course, S-0. All of them waited in respectful silence for the one who would carry out the deed.

The halls of the keep heralded her arrival with the sound of metal crashing against stone. It was strange to some that she wore steel greaves at all times. Aaron had asked her about it once. She had told him that a ruler should have nowhere they fear to tread, and that their enemies should hear their approach. It was a confidence he couldn't relate to, but it certainly had an effect. All were silent as she took her place between the willows that framed the central path through the atrium. Showing no indication of the discomfort it caused her, Lady Baal stepped into the sunlight.

She dressed in a gown of obsidian linked with gilded steel chains, finely etched bracelets wrapped around her arms like snakes. Her hair was the dark of a moonless night against porcelain-white skin. Her eyes were emeralds set in ink. With high cheekbones and a proud, imperial gaze, her face was the sculpted beauty of a doll, and as far from human. That otherworldly majesty that marked her as a higher breed of nephilim was unmistakable, and everyone who looked upon her stood straighter so as not to embarrass themselves in her presence. Then, her lips parted, long fangs glinting in the light as she spoke.

The voice was as unearthly as her appearance, a resonant contralto that lingered in the ears and left the listener desperate to hear more. Though spoken softly, each word smothered all other sounds in the air and echoed in the mind like a song.

"There is no shortage of those who give their lives for our freedom," she said. "We know them, fight with them, love them, and say our final farewells to them. We celebrate their memories in the lives we lead after they are gone. But this is not a celebration. The priests of Paradise believe that the soul is the only thing of worth, and that once it has departed our world, the rest is inconsequential. I, for one, do not share this belief. While the dead should serve the living, courtesy must not be forgotten. We should give something back to those who gave everything for us. You are all aware, no doubt, that you may choose the site of your burial, should you wish it, if you fall in the line of duty.

"There is precious little I can grant the dead, and Anthony Rista humbles me still. He did not wish for burial, and instead offered his mortal remains to be put to use. By now, his body in its entirety will have already been harvested and distributed to the nephilim who fight for our cause. Though he slew the vilest of traitors in life, in death, he shall give strength to those who serve us. I wonder if that was his intention, or if he simply did not wish to cause undue inconvenience in his passing."

She smiled sadly. "Well, I am not one to be outdone. His name, as with all of our fallen brothers and sisters, shall decorate the memorial overlooking the river where the public may observe and pay their respects. In accordance with one who has distinguished himself in service to his people, I would also have his name etched into the walls of this castle, so that future generations would know who kept it standing."

She gestured with a hand to the far wall of the atrium. Gazes followed, coming to rest on the cascading series of names carved into the stone at the heart of the keep. There were hundreds written in the stone, a list that had started at eye level and worked its way up and across the once smooth structure in honor of those who no longer could see it. At a distance, the work almost looked familiar. But Aaron's eyes could see the details, the minor cracks and dents from the craftsmen's handiwork. It was not the same as the inscription.

Lady Baal's words once more enraptured the audience. "It has been over a decade now since I returned to this frontier. A decade of fighting. We have suffered. Not just for the mistakes of my predecessors but for my own. Anthony Rista paid the price for a future wherein we might live freely. He was not the first, and he will not be the last, but he was one of us."

Her voice fell to a low whisper, and she turned to face the great Atsali tree that reached to the heavens. Its ivory leaves were lined with crimson veins, and each bough trembled slightly as if saturated with energy.

"I have always admired these trees," she said, taking slow, careful steps to approach. "Ancient, strong, beautiful. So resilient, they dare even the nightmares to touch them. We struggle against it with all our strength, but in the end, we all return to the earth. Let the earth bear this mark, then, in one of its living children."

She reached out a hand and placed her finger against the edged bark. There was no sound, but Aaron could clearly see the long thorn protrude at the contact, piercing the skin of her finger and drawing blood. Then her pearl-white skin was illuminated with viridian light. It grew outward, running along her arms, legs, and shoulders before flickering about her in branching geometric patterns. The light of entropy that was her magic set the skin tingling and harshly stung his eyes. Even prepared for it as he was, Aaron's legs nearly gave out beneath him at the invisible pressure of the spell. It lasted for only seconds, and when it faded, the near-indestructible tree was cracked and leaking amber sap, its bark marred in the likeness of Rista's name in elegant calligraphy.

Little was said after that. There were hints of quiet conversation, mostly related to Rista's achievements, but most simply took a moment to approach the Atsali tree and offer it a moment's respect. S-0 remained silent. Aaron tried not to let it distract him; they were human and he wasn't, and so he didn't presume to know their thoughts. But unlike him, Rista had never been different from them. He thought he saw Moore wipe at his eyes, and Sif turn her head away in a moment of silence, but Aaron felt the distance between them more acutely than ever. Though appropriately somber throughout the whole affair, it was only Dalton he saw shed a single, nearly invisible tear.

The man's face was stone, but in his hand, he held a sheet of folded paper. His finger twitched. His trigger finger never twitched. When Aaron asked what was written on it, the response was as he expected.

"Not important," Dalton replied, stuffing the crumpled note into his pocket. "Anthony had some…choice words for me recently. I was just wondering if I should take them to heart."

Aaron wanted to continue the conversation, but Dalton directed his attention to Lady Baal. She stared at him intently from a position of more comfortable shade. Her black sclera, not unlike his, made the brightness of her irises even more pronounced. No words were spoken to convey her wishes, but she turned wordlessly to exit the ceremony. Aaron took her message and excused himself, sharing a nod with Gavin and Durham before he did.

He, alongside several other attendees, climbed the stairs of the castle in silence. He didn't mind the ascent, taking the time to steady his heart and mind for what was to come. The group made their way toward the room in which he had been scolded by Constantine not long ago, where they were stopped at the door by a pair of Lady Baal's praetorian guards.

Each wore a heavy jacket stitched, lined, and ornamented in the geometric runes of their mistress. Wrapped around their wrists and necks were heavy bandages, some of which hung loosely from them. Their faces, where they could be seen, were either callused or worn away through constant exposure to magic.

Lady Baal's entropy had eroded their flesh, leaving blotchy scars over their bodies. One was a thick-necked boulder of a man with a chunk of his scalp shaved away and sporting a decorated eyepatch. The other was a young woman, barely out of her teens. She had lost half of her ear and the corner of her lip, white teeth showing through the gap that the damage created. They stared straight ahead, emotionless and silent, not acknowledging the growing party assembling before them.

The doors opened with a groan that grated on Aaron's consciousness. Lady Baal herself sat at the head of a large oak table. To her right loomed General Gallem, coal-black eyes scanning the room as one might after breaching a hostile encampment. At her left was Valentine, who leaned close to whisper something to her that even Aaron's hearing couldn't pick up.

"Enter and be seated," she commanded. "We have much to discuss."

There was not enough room for everyone to sit at the table, and so Aaron volunteered to stand. It gave him the excuse to rest in the background, though he knew he would be called to speak. He took note of several of the names gathered. Constantine was present, as was Sietz. Barnes, who controlled the city's gates, was also attending, as well as no fewer than five commanders of noteworthy outposts to their northern and southern borders.

Two other nephilim were present. The first was Helena. She had tied up her wild hair and dressed in a button-up shirt, but that was the limit of her presentation. She sat, absentmindedly brushing at the scars ringing the dark skin of her arms. Her bright eyes shot from person to person with the speed of an animal, but her lips showed only the hint of a wry smile. Aaron also recognized the other one, but not by name. It was well over seven feet tall, hunched over but still towering over the guests. The manticore wore only a long kilt, wrapped around its waist in a thick length of rope hanging with the mark of Baal. Its body was a cross between humanoid and leonine, bipedal, and covered in sandy fur. A great mane framed its catlike face, while curled around its legs was the barbed tail of a scorpion. Despite how far its face was from human, Aaron could still see it grin.

When Aaron looked away, Lady Baal was already staring at him. "Let us begin without delay. I would first offer my commendation to Captain Aaron White and the members of S-0 for their efforts in tracking and putting an end to these recent crimes. You continue to distinguish yourselves as the first and greatest of our defenses against these special class threats. I would also commend Captain-Commander Sietz of the

City Watch. You kept order in a time of unrest that courted calamity: This city thanks you."

Aaron inclined his head in acknowledgment, observing Sietz do likewise.

Constantine shifted in his chair. "If I may, Lady Baal, I must note negligence by both parties. Though their investigation did eventually lead us to the killers in question, it was not until many losses were incurred, both civilian and military." His eyes moved between the two of them. "Also, their objective was apparent from the first crime, if they had been more thorough."

Sietz remained cool at the accusation. "I accept full responsibility for the lack of insight at the crime scene. That was an inexcusable error on my part and a failure of my duties. I do not expect anyone to cover for my mistakes, but I am grateful that the missing link was eventually discovered." He gave the slightest hint of a nod to Aaron. "That said, the investigation into the identities of the murderers fell under the responsibility of Captain White of S-0. My hands were tied."

Aaron took a breath, gathering his courage and steeling his will. "Captain-Commander Sietz is correct. He offered my team assistance in any capacity we required. Though I coordinated with the forces of the city watch, I refused to bring his officers into the investigation under the flawed assumption that we were still dealing with a nephilim, as the prey patterns indicated. I had a failure of imagination in that regard. My intention was to not create a panic by mobilizing so many men and women inexperienced in combat against non-human foes, nor to play into the hands of what I believed were deliberate provocations and not coverups of the real intention of the killers."

Eyes shifted back to Constantine, who didn't press the issue as Aaron had expected. "Of course, I acknowledge your expertise on the hunting of nephilim. However, I question your attempt at confronting the two. Why did you go to the church to question them alone?"

Aaron had hoped to avoid that particular question. However, before he could fumble a response, Lady Baal spoke. "I believe I understand Captain White's choice. At that point, there was no evidence that the paladins were the culprits, and though he entered the church garden alone, he was accompanied by Lieutenant Dalton, Second Lieutenant Durham, and Sergeant Rista. They assisted you when you were attacked, yes?"

Her gleaming eyes held him in place, and though he wanted to speak, he merely nodded.

Constantine betrayed no emotion at her defense of his actions. "No casualties occurred at the scene, thankfully. But in light of our failure to take the two alive—"

"The matter is closed," Sitri said with a dismissive wave of her hand. "The paladins were prepared to die, and the agents of Paradise never do us the courtesy of dying easily."

Aaron winced at that, the memory of the fight with Oris returning to the forefront of his mind in all its bloody details. His hands tightened their grip on his coat, avoiding anything that might break in his grasp.

"If I may, my lady, can we even be sure that's what they were?"

All eyes returned to him. General Gallem's expression changed for the first time since the meeting had begun. "What do you mean by that, Captain?"

Aaron met the man's stare, careful not to overreach his stance. "It's just a...suspicion. In light of my experience combating Oris, I don't think we should be so hasty to identify them."

"That they were abnormal is no secret," General Gallem replied. "Say what you mean."

Aaron took his chance gratefully. "I anticipated that one of the two 'brothers' would return to the site of the first murder. My hunch was correct, but he was prepared. Oris had followers in place who started a scene, separated me from my teammates, and prevented them from arriving until I'd already engaged him. He was dangerous, of course, but nothing I couldn't handle. I disarmed him and was preparing to incapacitate him so that he could be safely taken in and questioned. I threw him into the wall. He was concussed. I might have heard his ribs crack."

Helena grinned. "Get to the good part. Then what?"

"Then he wasn't," Aaron said. "He stood up like he was unharmed. He nearly beat me unconscious with his bare hands. His strength exceeded mine."

The room was silent. Aaron had half expected someone to laugh at him; to call him useless or a fool. But be it by understanding the seriousness of his words or the intensity of Lady Baal's presence, nobody did such a thing.

Sietz was the first to speak. "My men were with Lieutenant Dalton and the rest of S-0 when they encountered Alexander. They told a similar story. He killed every person he could lay his hands on: six in total at the site of his death, with their necks broken or holes punched through their chests. It matches the state of the murder victims. Deadeye shot him clean through the throat, but he still kept moving. It was worse than using normal bullets on nightmares."

"Let me make sure I'm not mishearing this. A human overpowered you?"

Aaron stared directly at Constantine, not flinching before his inquiry. "He did. At first, I was careful not to kill him, but as he showed powers far beyond the realm of a human, I was forced to respond. I struck him with all my strength. It should have gone straight through him. Instead, he shrugged it off. We shot him half a dozen times; it was like firing blanks. He killed Anthony with one strike. That thing, the inscription—"

He bit his tongue, remembering Durham's words and not speaking any further. Lady Baal's words came to his rescue, however, with their next declaration.

"Occult sorcery." All eyes were on her immediately, her perfect features marred by a curl of her lips and the glint of a bright fang. "You are fortunate to be alive, Captain White, and we are even more fortunate that you lived to report this to us."

"Magic unbound by pacts or inheritance," General Gallem growled. "Free of all of the restrictions that those systems provide, but also without their safety. Its applications are limitless and powerful beyond reason, but the church of Paradise has stamped out such things for millennia. The miracles they perform are fueled by the collective faith of their followers. Lady Baal, how can you be certain this is one and not the other?"

She nodded as if this were expected, and Aaron had the distinct impression that they had already had the conversation. "Their interest in the blood of their victims tells it. Magic bends and breaks the rules of this world, but one thing is always true – you can't make something from nothing. There is always a price, and that price is paid in the soul.

"Even nephilim do not dabble in magic lightly. The houses of old place restrictions on their arts to focus them, but also to protect their wielders from such power going out of control. As you said, the Church can access magic, but it's limited by the rigidity of their faith. There is another reason so few humans practice the mystic arts, and a reason the Church takes such a strict stance against them. Human souls simply cannot take the strain of prolonged use. Without another source of power, you're simply cannibalizing yourself."

Constantine shifted. "But they *are* capable of doing so. It might be taboo in Paradise, but the frontiers have always been less strict. The human servants of Eydis Nero were well-versed in the mystic arts."

Lady Baal's features twisted, a wave of hatred working across her face. A sudden chill racked those present, but the moment of blazing anger was gone in the next moment. When she responded, serenity had already returned to her.

"They did, but we exterminated all such practitioners. Now, any magic worked in this nation is done under strict supervision. Even in such cases where those humans were versed in the spellcraft, they were always augmented with power bestowed by Eydis and her brood.

"I always found it strange, the condemnation I received for taking in so many nephilim. The pursuit of magic has caused far more atrocities in our history. For all their bluster, the Church is right about one thing: it only takes a taste of such things to reduce a faithful soul to drinking the blood of children. It's a matter of power, first and foremost. We nephilim feed ourselves with fragments of human souls and then share our powers with humans. We increase our reach, and humans can utilize abilities that don't risk extinguishing their being. The powers we bestow, like our own, are finite and will run out if not maintained.

"We can't be sure of exactly what the two were capable of, but given the nature of the murders, it's clear that they called on these powers to misdirect us. For Oris and Alexander to strengthen their bodies beyond the realm of a nephilim like Captain White, and to do so repeatedly…it must have been killing them. But that might not be true. Perhaps the deaths were sacrifices for such power. With the two of them dead, it's impossible to tell."

Aaron thought about how Oris had appeared in the garden. He couldn't say if his health was deteriorating, but something was clearly amiss. Before he could consider it further, Sietz spoke up. "Have we made any progress on deciphering the site? Or at least, what's left of it?"

"The inscription, if you can call it that, was damaged in the encounter with Oris," Sitri answered. "However, we have images from before the event to refer to. At the very least, they are nothing that I am familiar with. If they are runes of some kind, then they aren't of

Baal. I've sent these to a contact with more knowledge of the arcane than anyone on the frontier. We're awaiting his reply, though it may be some time. From now on, the site is under permanent watch, with at least one nephilim there at all times."

"Then we return to Captain White's insinuation," Gallem declared. "With what we know, do you share his suspicion that these weren't paladins at all? I, for one, am not convinced that they aren't of the Paradise Church. To me, their actions have the stench of executioners."

Aaron's head snapped to attention at the word, and Lady Baal drummed her fingers on the table, nails clicking against the wood. "A fair suggestion. The executioners are some of the mightiest and most deranged warriors in Paradise. They're trained to kill nightmares and nephilim, but more often hunt humans: betrayers of the faith. Their knowledge of the occult is unmatched. You aren't wrong to suspect them as such, but I remain skeptical. Though they fought with skills comparable to them and a depravity that speaks volumes, circumstances don't lead me to believe it was the work of the Church."

She gestured to Sietz, who cleared his throat before speaking. "Despite its horror, Alexander's death was a public affair, and that has a benefit. Much of the work he and Oris achieved in turning the citizens was undone. It also gave us the necessary grounds to detain those envoys of the Paradise church who have entered our western border. To our surprise, all those who had entered submitted willingly. Yet these envoys insisted that they sent only one ambassador to Spearhead, one who does not match the description of either Oris or Alexander."

"Perhaps they went rogue," Helena offered. "Paladins and the executioners have done so before."

"It is possible," said Constantine. "But even if they were rogue, why come out here? All of the agents of Paradise that were making headway in the frontier have had their work undone. And for that matter, if these two were investigating that 'inscription,' why do it the way they did? There's more to this than just the Church."

"I agree," Aaron said. "At the site, before we fought, Oris mentioned using my blood as well. It seems he was going to try using nephilim blood next, indicating he never succeeded in what he sought to do. I believe the site was only part of a greater plan. Chaos was their objective, first and foremost. If it wasn't, they wouldn't have needed to play the part of paladins and incite the populace to unrest. For one thing, there are far easier ways of acquiring blood in this city: ways that don't require them to become wanted fugitives and put the guard on high alert."

He chose each word carefully, wanting to inform the room of the danger, but not implicate his own encounter with the magic. It seemed to satisfy the room, as several nodded in agreement with his words.

Lady Baal spoke again. "Valid points, all, but let's say what we know for certain. The power they wielded was real. To me, that says the power they sought was real as well. And they absolutely did not seek it alone."

"I ran every background check I could," Barnes said. "It both supports and undermines the Church's stance. They had exceedingly well-made forgeries of official documentation, including a false letter of introduction from the primary church. This looks like it was planned months, maybe years, in advance. But how could they have done so in anticipation of the Church's arrival on the frontier? Who would be capable of recruiting, arming, and training these men, then providing them with high-end mystical knowledge and some archaic black magic?"

Constantine stroked his beard. "A difficult question when we wonder about the scale of our investigation. You have no shortage of enemies, Lady Baal. I can think of a number who would like to see your power destabilized. For practicality's sake, we should take Vergil's words at face value for now. He was of the opinion that these actions were as much to hurt the Church as it was to hurt us. Paradise is full of enemies, but they're cowardly and far away; too far to attack without concrete evidence, which we are unable to gather ourselves. I believe we should focus on the immediate possibilities; Talos from our north and Sterling from our south."

Maciolek, who managed the closer towns, smirked. "This doesn't look like a scuffle at the border, Const. This is espionage and terrorism. How do you connect the two alleged paladins to either lord?"

Constantine did not hesitate. "Talos is a dragon, and the most magically knowledgeable force in the frontier. Sterling has been at war with us before, and has over a century of experience as a warden. Moreover, this…site of power was located in Oldtown, part of the original city before Spearhead was reclaimed a decade ago. For these men to know about it, they would need to be informed by someone well-connected to the affairs of the eastern frontier. I think we should consider the timing of this attack."

Maciolek's expression soured. "So, Sterling?"

"I think it's worth considering more seriously," Constantine replied. "Sterling is insular and untrusting of outsiders, with a hatred for the nephilim Lady Baal recruited. He lost territory to us in the past, and could have been waiting any number of years for the Church to make a move. He has the knowledge and the resources to do so, and above all else..." His eyes flicked toward Lady Baal, betraying just a hint of frustration. "He just launched an unprovoked attack on a military base in our territory." His stare then shifted toward Aaron, lingering just long enough to get his point across.

There was silence as Lady Baal pondered. "Alvas was a watch post established as a warning system in case Sterling attempted to move against us. We weren't aware of its fall until we investigated following a failure to report. Roman had the advantage, but he didn't move forward. A warning? Constantine raises a fair point. His stance has always been far more confrontational than Talos's."

"We are prepared to counterattack Sterling," said General Gallem. "If he advances again, we can take him by surprise. We target his pack and bring down his children, or better yet, take them hostage."

"We should be careful," Constantine said. "We may bite off more than we can chew. According to Lady Baal, his firstborn, Thalia, is almost as powerful as he is. We confirmed at least one of his children was at Alvas, but there could have been more."

"Should it begin, we need to be wary of an attack from Talos," remarked Sietz. "Are we prepared in case of his involvement?"

"Ethan Talos is a tyrant but a coward," Lady Baal remarked. "So long as we are bold, we can take this victory before he musters the fortitude to capitalize."

Gallem stared forward, eyes distant, but his lip curled in the hint of a sneer. "We can prepare an ambush: Send an advance force under the guise of repairing Alvas, and then, the moment Sterling or any of his children show themselves, we take them then and there. Strike quickly enough, and we destroy his momentum."

Lady Baal paused in thought once more, head tilted but eyes remaining in a fixed position. "A decisive strategy. I offered Roman a formal declaration the last time we came to blows, but he has struck without such courtesy. This time, we'll be more proactive."

"If it's the case, we should start moving forces into position in case of a wider-scale counterattack."

"What about his forces in Paradise?"

"The Hell breach weakened his position as much as anyone's. He won't be able to rely on aid."

Aaron listened to them speak back and forth for another minute, dread growing all the while. The more they spoke of tactics, weapons, and supplies, the more it grew. He knew the consequences of speaking without purpose, but far more than those consequences, he feared the anguish of staying silent. Finding a moment to speak, he interrupted. "What if we're being too hasty?"

All eyes, human and nephilim, returned to him. Their expressions ranged from surprise to accusation. Some tilted their heads in curiosity or disdain, and some turned to Lady Baal for guidance, but none questioned him. He took her attention as the most important. She looked at him with quiet interest, and he took it as an invitation to speak again. "It's far too premature to say that this is Sterling's doing. We don't know what motivates him any more than we know what motivated Oris and Alexander. But we lose the chance to find out if we declare war again."

"This response does not require him to be connected to Oris and Alexander. It is preparation for a counterattack should he enter our land again," she said calmly.

"An ambush of him or his children will be war," Aaron answered.

"I'll remind you that he killed our people," interjected Constantine. "He crossed into our land and attacked *our* post. We have a force attempting to destabilize our government, one that may very well be connected to him. Our focus should now be on killing this aggression before it can escalate further. Sterling backed down before, and we will force him to do so again."

The room was silent. Lady Baal's eyes moved between them, curious, but silent. Aaron chose his words carefully.

"We don't know who Oris and Alexander worked with, but don't you think it's possible that just as we are discussing this attack, Sterling might be doing the same? As you said, he's insular. Do you really think he would have commanded those two? Coordinated their arrival with the movements of the Church, slay their ambassadors, and replace them? I don't think so. I think it's far more likely that he might have encountered the same situation and assumed the worst of us in turn. Preventing this from escalating is important, which is why we shouldn't take action that could lead to a war on multiple fronts. This is a chance to initiate a dialogue with him and get real answers. It might be our only chance."

"That all sounds great," Sietz said, looking unimpressed. "But that is a dangerous mission, Captain White. Whoever goes to meet with Sterling might not come back."

Aaron didn't hesitate. "Then send me."

Sietz sighed. "I thought you might say that. Sterling might be more inclined to hear from another Nephilim, but you don't have the experience to speak for us, unless Lady Baal disagrees."

All eyes were once more drawn to her as she stared at Aaron with her gemlike eyes. "Sterling is insular, but that leaves him isolated. As a warden and as a commander, he is extremely orthodox. I believe it unlikely he would slay an envoy sent in good faith, and I am unconvinced that he is the benefactor of Oris and Alexander. But that is not a guarantee. The fact remains that he attacked our base and killed our people. Captain White, what you are proposing is to march into his territory and interrogate him. You believe you can do this and come out alive?"

He exhaled his trepidation. "I believe it's worth risking my life for what we can gain."

She nodded, as if this was the expected response. Light danced behind her eyes as she spoke, her words weighted with authority. "Colonel Constantine, I believe that our southern border is in need of reinforcement if an organized campaign against Roman Sterling is to be reinitiated. In the meantime, something to occupy his attention could be beneficial. If Captain White is incorrect, he has bought us valuable time. If he is proven right, then we may avoid a conflict altogether. Those do seem like the best outcomes. Do you disagree?"

Constantine looked at Aaron, then at her. "I don't, my Lady. However, the captain will likely die if his prediction is incorrect. He is a valuable asset, but not one I would recommend for his political acumen."

"Perhaps not," Sitri said, "but neither is Sterling, at the end of the day. He is a simple man, one who respects drive and strength. False words will not sway him, but when I was a girl, he once told me that a single soul with strength of will can overturn the whole world. I approve of this mission, Captain White."

She paused, and Aaron realized he was meant to speak. "Thank you, Lady Baal," he said. "I will not fail you."

"No, you won't," she said, her eyes shining with viridian light. "Because this is conditional. If Sterling is revealed to be responsible for the actions of Oris and Alexander, or shows you a sign of hostile intent toward your person, your mission will be to kill him, then and there."

Her words struck him dumb, but she did not relent.

"The hand that brings peace does not hesitate to eviscerate those who bring war. If there is to be war and Sterling has determined it so, then your life there will be forfeit, Aaron, as will Dalton's and the rest of S-0. If you wish to stake your life, then I would have you prepared to kill for it. Should these conditions come to pass, you will fight until you die, and kill as many of his people as possible before you do."

He didn't turn away, half afraid of the expressions of those around him and half afraid of what she would do if he avoided her gaze. With no other options, he nodded, clenched his hand, and spoke clearly.

"As you wish."

–CHAPTER 21–

MOONLIGHT VIGIL

Aaron paced the dark halls of the castle, practicing his composure. He shifted his shoulders and straightened his back, putting on a demeanor of confidence and control, but the thought of his upcoming meeting chilled him, and his charade failed to fool even him. It was childish to be so shaken. He'd spoken with Lady Baal before. But the call to speak one-on-one in her personal study, the very day after she'd assigned him his mission, was unsettling.

Considering it further, he doubted it could be more tense than when he briefed S-0.

The news was met with utter silence. The team stared at him with wide eyes, mouths open but bereft of any words. It lasted almost an entire minute. When it looked like it might break peacefully, with him preparing to speak again, he had managed a single *"I—"* before being cut off.

"You what!?" Sif screamed. "Sterling…Roman Sterling?!"

Moore rested his head in his hands. "This is a warden. We're supposed to fight him? Is that a joke?"

"Only if things go south," Lenz had offered, wincing as if even he didn't believe it.

"They always go south!" a chorus of voices had reprimanded. It was the most emotional Aaron had ever seen them, even when lives were on the line. In light of their response to Rista's death, it was almost enough to anger him, but it was their lives after all, and he held his tongue.

The members of S-0 had the mental fortitude to slay nightmares and the skills to kill nephilim. That they were so shaken was a testament to the depth they were in. Their closeness to Lady Baal meant that they had a better idea than most what a warden was capable of, and several had seen Lord Sterling himself in the battles the two had fought in the past. They understood the magnitude of their mission, and they were frightened.

Gavin had whistled, a too-wide grin on his face. "A warden of the frontier…How many people in the world can stand on even footing with Lady Baal? You never struck me as the guy to punch up."

Durham had laughed at that, having summarized the entirety of her feelings on the matter when she threw Re-Human at Aaron not five minutes before. Dalton was the only one not to let his emotions show.

"If Lady Baal approved it, then it was bound to happen eventually. Better to think of it as unavoidable. Now, all that's to be done is to prepare for the mission. If you have objections, you'll have to take them up with her."

That quieted the room very quickly. In truth, Aaron had objections of his own. But it was his idea, and in the face of his request being granted, he hadn't possessed the courage to air them. It wasn't long after that he received the summons.

He wondered what she would say. Was she going to provide insight into the lord? Point out a weakness or a change to the plan? Or, as he suspected, was it to chastise him for his behavior in enemy territory that led to the attack? He thought endlessly about the possibilities of her wanting him, but eventually settled on the conclusion that overthinking the matter was only going to make things worse and that the best course of action was to simply take the opportunity for what it represented.

At least, until he made it to the castle and his nerve failed. And so, Aaron spent an uncountable number of minutes pacing, worrying, and otherwise thinking of all the ways it could end poorly for him. It was only the passing of a guard that gave him the push to move forward, not out of any real courage, but for fear of looking insane.

The door to her office was a looming maw. Aaron could sense her within; she was too proud to hide her presence. The weight of her soul radiated, scraping against his skin like a cold blade and ringing in his ears, all while drawing him closer. She was a primal force, like gravity. He bit his tongue, took a breath, and knocked once on the door before opening it.

"Aaron, it's good to see you."

"Lady Baal," he greeted, careful to bow as he entered. She was not looking at him, however.

Instead, she was writing something at her desk, and after a moment, she discarded a paper to appraise him. A score of candles were lit throughout the large office while the light of the full moon shone through the floor-to-ceiling windows behind her. It dyed the room in hues of icy blue and ruddy orange except for her eyes, which shimmered verdant green as they met his.

Her voice, as ever, was hypnotic. "Your strength is returning."

"You can tell?" he wondered. She continued to stare at him, and he adjusted his collar, careful to avoid looking like prey.

She brushed at her hair, eyes scanning over her work once again before answering. "Your appearance changes very little, but your posture no longer bleeds weakness. Is there still pain?"

"Not anymore," he said, his shoulder tensing reflexively at the memory. "Your doctor cleared me."

With a slight flourish, Lady Baal began to write something on the paper in front of her using a gilded pen. "Very good. Elizabeth is the best I know. She was the first to treat the nephilim under my command after I returned from Paradise. She may not know what you are, but you'll find no finer treatment."

"She certainly wanted me to come back soon." He shuddered, remembering the look in the old woman's eyes. There lay a curiosity that bordered on insanity, and a resemblance to nothing short of a starving beast. "Almost looked like she wanted a piece of me for herself."

Lady Baal hummed acknowledgment. "That does sound like her. If it's any comfort, she's hounded me quite persistently for samples of my person as well. She was a good acquisition, but quite obsessed."

It was no comfort at all. "I see. Well, it's good to know she takes her work seriously."

When she did not respond, Aaron searched around the room, eager to find another avenue of conversation. His eyes were drawn to the candles. They weren't there when he had last seen the place. The light they gave off was unusually bright and even, closer to electrical bulbs. When he took a step closer to examine them, he noticed a peculiarity. The fire that was lit did not flare upward but extended evenly, forming a perfect sphere. Within that miniature star was not just the orange and yellow of ordinary fire, but flecks of black, white, silver, and gold, winking in and out of existence with each passing second.

"What are these?"

Her voice carried over behind him. Though she hadn't moved, it sounded as if she were whispering directly into his ear. "You noticed. They're lit with holy fire. In poor taste, perhaps, but they don't burn through the candlewick and they produce a more even light."

"But why use them here?" he asked, approaching the flame, which did not flicker or otherwise react to his breath.

"Technology has been lost and rediscovered over the millennia," she answered. "But mystical knowledge rarely dies so easily. Though it's a power of the Church, it is a gift to humanity, and I would have it for my people as well."

Aaron reached toward the flame, pondering an odd urge to touch it. He shook his head at the lunacy of burning himself for a third time in so many weeks. "Forgive me, Lady Baal, but that's not what I meant. I mean, why here? Why your office? You don't need the light."

He turned to see her standing, leaning against her desk. The light dancing behind her eyes shimmered, and she slid a golden ring onto her finger.

"I have these candles because a ruler should be comfortable in the dark, but cannot rule from it." She picked up a similarly regal bracelet and slid it onto her forearm. "In order to achieve what I desire, I must operate in the light, even if that light might be uncomfortable for me."

Aaron thought of the people who had tried to attack him in the street; the words they had yelled as he tried to pursue the men who were killing them. Then he thought of Oris and their conversation in the garden.

"Yes, operating in the dark is not enough. But you're a nephilim. Would you say that you're acting out of your nature?"

She examined her nails. They bit deeper into the joints of her fingers than a human's. Unlike his, hers were naturally pitch-black, almost opaque. "Difficult to say. I was born to rule. It never concerned me how I did so. I acted only as I thought was right." She crossed the room, her steel greaves echoing her every step. "I have many blessings, but I should have some disadvantages as well, don't you think?"

She produced two glasses filled with burgundy liquid. Returning to her desk, she offered him one. He accepted, slowly. She watched him as he lifted the glass to his nose and inhaled. A mix of floral and citrus stung his nose. "Wine?"

She drank from her glass, the color staining her lips red. "Of course. I know how stubborn you are, though you're free to have a taste of mine."

She lifted her glass toward him, and the scent that touched him was much, much sweeter.

"No, thank you," he muttered.

She fixed him with a look of mild disappointment before adopting the appearance of sipping absentmindedly from her glass, all the while her eyes remaining trained on him.

Aaron fought the temptation to toy with the hilt of his sword, knowing the consequences of rudeness. "Lady Baal, at the meeting, why did you lie? I made it clear in my report to you, I was there alone. Durham was alerted by her pact to the danger and followed her intuition. Constantine was right, I didn't consider the consequences."

"Why were you there at that church, Aaron?"

He could only answer with the truth. "I was investigating a lead."

"And what lead was that?" she asked. "You said you only confirmed their involvement during your conversation with Oris. If you were there alone, then it wasn't because you suspected them. So, why go there at all?"

Aaron choked on his wine, stifling the response that followed as he realized he hadn't thought of an answer. "I wasn't there for them," he admitted. "I needed to confirm something with a different follower of the faith. The caretaker, Leah."

She blinked for the first time since he entered her office. "Did you suspect her?"

"No," he said immediately. "I knew she was innocent. I just needed her insight."

"You knew she was innocent?" Sitri pondered. "How so?" Her tone was light, almost playful.

Aaron sensed he was being trapped. "I trust her."

Lady Baal laughed, high and loud like the peal of a bell, and though she raised her hand to cover her mouth, he still caught a glimpse of her fangs. "And there you have your answer! I trust you, Aaron."

He stared at her; he hadn't thought she would say something so sincere. She tilted her head, studying him in turn.

"Is that so hard to understand?"

It was, and he couldn't reconcile it with his own feelings. "Is that why you had Constantine lie? Is it why he said the attack was unprovoked when you knew it wasn't?"

"Roman could have attacked for any number of reasons." When his expression made clear his thoughts on that idea, her face settled into sternness. "You acted in your capacity as my agent to exterminate the rogue vampire Silas. Your actions in pursuit of that goal are inconsequential compared to Sterling's transgression here, and to compare them publicly would have done more harm than good. I asked Constantine to keep any accusations to himself. It was a request, not an order. Though he may not have enjoyed it, he did so because he believed it was the best course of action."

The explanation was too convenient. Experience told him it wasn't everything. "But why go out of your way like that for me?"

"You can stop with all of that," she dismissed. "We're friends, aren't we?"

"I...don't think we are." For a second, he was too surprised to check his words. His heart skipped a beat remembering who he was talking to, and he frantically backtracked. "I mean, that doesn't seem right, does it? I didn't think you were allowed to have friends."

Her green-in-black eyes sharpened. "And who decided that?"

"Nobody, I suppose," he reasoned. "But to be friends is to be equals in a way. There's a difference in station between us."

"A fair point," she admitted. Aaron expected an argument or rebuke, but instead, she stared into her glass pensively. "There is a relationship of sovereignty that sets us apart. But then, you're friends with Alice Durham, no? Jaycen Gavin as well. They answer to you; would you not call them your friends?"

"Maybe, but in the field, we put that aside. We look out for each other because we have to."

"Then I don't see how this is any different. We are nephilim, separate from the humans we fight for and from others like us. We see the impossible and want to make it real. There is kinship in that, something closer than blood. And, as we are not in the field right now, I fail to see any issue." He fumbled for words, uncomfortable in the moment, and she traced a finger against her glass. "You are unique, Aaron. You resist what serves you because you are unaccustomed to progress. I'll help you and make it simple. We are friends because I declare it so, and that is that. And if we are speaking to each other plainly, as friends might, then I insist you call me Sitri."

He smiled at the absurdity. "Is that how you make all of your friends, Sitri?"

A smirk of satisfaction played across her lips. "Of course. Who could refuse me?"

She gestured to a chair, and he took a seat, removing his blade and resting it against her desk. "I have to ask; are there any outside of your rule that you call your friends? Someone you could call your equal?"

Sitri sat against her desk, posture relaxing in a moment of candidness. "There's one, I think. I met him during my exile. He's bold, fearless. Unbearable at times, really. A hopeless know-it-all. But he did challenge me when I needed it, and he gave me some advice that I didn't want to hear when I needed to listen."

"He must have been quite a monster to get away unscathed."

She grinned, no doubt having expected such a remark. "Hardly. He's a human."

"No!" His laughter was more from incredulity than humor, but still reduced him to coughing. When he recovered, Aaron looked up to see her glowing eyes illuminated, a hand outstretched toward him. He straightened himself, nodding when she asked if he was all right.

"Fine," he replied. "Better, in fact."

"That was not from the bullet. Your body shows no signs of improving?"

He looked down at his jacket, imagining the skeletal form hidden beneath. "Still like death. No matter how much I eat, it doesn't change. I can only heal back to *this*. But I can move and fight without issue, and that's all that matters, I suppose. As for that friend, I'd like to meet him someday."

"You may someday soon. I'd planned to bring him here and show him what I've created. But now, all this business with Sterling, and this latest incident, it may have to wait." Her lip curled, exposing her fangs again. "This was inexcusable."

Aaron watched the change in her demeanor, carefully measuring her change in emotions as her fury bled through. "I'm sorry. I should have done more."

"You have done enough. Nobody could have predicted what those two were capable of." Sitri rose from her position, setting her empty glass aside. As she did, Aaron glanced at her desk. Several stacks of paperwork were filed neatly, held in place by weights in the likeness of matching wings. A map of the East was imposed against the wood, and off to the side, three insignias carved in the crests of the houses Baal, Sterling, and Talos. Catching his eye, a small set of pens aligned with one another, black with golden trim. Next to them, a paper covered with ornate lettering.

"This is like what you did at the Atsali for Rista," he remarked. "Calligraphy?"

"Just a hobby," she said. "Elegance in all things is a mark of status."

"It's very good," he said, examining the delicately styled letters in greater detail. "Smooth and steady-handed, almost like wire. The strokes are so precise, you must need a sharp point to achieve it."

Her eyes widened. "Very good," she said. "And you're right; a sharpened point instead of a flat allows for a leaner stroke. Not quite as easy to read, yet that is somehow more appealing, no? Art should not be appreciated quickly. I didn't know you were familiar."

"I…There was a man with black hair and brown eyes. He taught me how to…"

He fought as hard as he could to remember. A disciplining hand struck his wrist as he laid out his strokes of ink on vellum. A cool breeze entered the window from outside, where it rained without reserve. He smelled living earth, fruit, and flowers; yet his mouth tasted like death. "I can't remember who or where. All I have are the actions."

"Truly fascinating." Sitri stared into the darkness of night, out at the landscape that would have been invisible to anyone else. Seeing her do so, he thought back to the first time he could remember meeting her.

"I wasn't like that, always," Aaron muttered. "When I awoke in Paradise in the ruin of that castle, I remember feeling purpose. I knew I had to come here. But I also remember feeling hollow. There was an infinite…hunger, and it tore my mind apart until there was nothing left. I can never escape. I can only put as much distance between that state and myself as possible."

She looked at him, luminescent skin shadowed into a grim mask. "Many came to the East when I offered a life outside of savagery. We may be able to survive abhorrent conditions, but life to rogue nephilim is as unpleasant as it would be for a human. Countless have lived and died just like that. It's what makes adjusting them so difficult, but also what makes it so meaningful."

"Is that why you humor me?" he asked. Lady Baal didn't respond at first, and he continued. "But I'm not like other nephilim, am I? I lived in a castle. I had a family...I just can't..." He exhaled. "I woke up alone, and I knew I had to come here. But something is missing from that memory, something not right."

"There's very much that isn't right in the world, Aaron," Sitri said in reply.

"Yes, you're correct." He didn't attempt to argue. He knew it would be pointless. Instead, he returned his glass with the other, setting it down with care to not cause any damage. It was as good a time as any, he thought. "Sitri, I want to talk to you about what we saw when we were out in the wastes."

"The nightmares?" she said, surprising him. "Yes, I heard. Constantine was skeptical, but that is his way. Though he may not believe it himself, he is taking steps to investigate."

"That's good to hear," Aaron said, put off by her acknowledgment. "But still, I was hoping you could put in a word for me. I've been doing research into prior examples of abnormal nightmares. There's nothing conclusive yet, but I can't shake this feeling that there was something else off about them."

"They are aberrant, after all," she said with a smile. "One war at a time, Aaron. There are more pressing forces working against us."

"That isn't enough."

She stared at him, her face showing more curiosity than surprise. He shifted in his chair, acutely aware of the pressure that his sixth sense perceived emanating from her. His grip on the armrest tightened, wood creaking in protest.

"I..." He bit his tongue. "Sitri, it's precisely for that reason that we need to act decisively now. Those things appeared at the border between Sterling's land and ours. They could already be in our territory, and with the nephilim concentrated here, if they get farther...In the reports, I read words written by your mother, and she said that—"

"She was a fool!"

The words were harsh, biting, and spoken with absolute authority. They were cold, but not as cold as her eyes. Her lips were drawn back, the corners of her mouth slightly upturned. To a human, one might call it a smile. But Sitri was not human, and the teeth that showed her as such were plainly visible in the terrifying face of the beast that stared at him. The air whined and whimpered, reality bending as magic flickered into being beneath her skin. Aaron froze, a pressure at his throat sharper than any fang. He was unable to even breathe for fear of what it might result in. The cold claw of fear gripped his soul at her rage.

She held the mask of terrible fury for a time, but be it by her will or some unknown trigger, it fell from her, and her face returned to the image of refined beauty that she preferred to present. Lips pursed, she shook her head in disappointment, but her next words were gentle.

"Tell me, Aaron, do you know why Paradise does not stand against me, despite my actions? I killed Eydis Nero, another warden, and they did not punish me. Why?"

"She struck first," Aaron answered. "She tried to wipe out the Baal family."

Sitri shook her head. "She did, but that is not why. Eydis bled our support away, harrying our borders and weakening us to nightmare attacks. We lost the ability to hold territory. Not every human is capable of holding their wits against nightmares, and if you lose your best and brightest, as we did, you can face a catastrophic collapse of infrastructure. The pact between nephilim and Paradise forbids wars of annihilation between competing wardens, but Eydis never pushed too far. She simply poked and prodded and let the monsters tear us apart. She wasn't condemned to death for such actions; she was condemned because she didn't contribute soldiers to the Hell Breach."

Her lips twitched, flickering between bitterness and begrudging respect. "It was a clever strategy, I admit. She trusted that the other houses would sort out the calamity, and that once it was over, all others would be too weak and wounded to protest. The other wardens would have their own concerns, and Paradise's humans would live to death and forget their grudge before being able to take action. I leveraged that when I proposed being allowed to destroy her family and take their lands for my own. But do you know why Eydis Nero ever had the bravery to attempt to usurp us in the first place? It was my mother.

"Even before the breach, we were weakening. A century of leadership, and Lilith achieved no more and no less than her predecessor. She took a mate below her station, a commoner whom she uplifted for love over merit. My father was a skilled enough warrior, but he did not have the influence to strengthen us when we needed it. Then he died in the breach, and Eydis smelled blood. I begged Mother to show our strength, to push back against an incursion against our honor and our lives. Do you know what she did? She exiled me, her own heir, to wait and watch the doom of my house from Paradise. Then she died, and I was left to pick up the pieces. The only solace I take is that my exile gave me the chance to find new allies, ones unafraid to fight for a place in the world."

She traced the edge of the map beneath her with a claw-like nail. "Her words are dust in the wind to me, Aaron, and I have greater concerns right now than the fears of a dead woman. With respect to you alone, I will take responsibility for these nightmares, but the more pressing threat comes first. Settle this with Sterling, and I promise you that we'll see it through together."

It wasn't perfect, but it was as good as he could have hoped for. And, as with most things with Lady Sitri Baal, it brooked no argument. So, Aaron didn't press forward. He nodded in acceptance, inclining his head in a bow.

"Thank you," he said.

She smiled, her inhuman hatred vanishing like smoke. "You don't need to thank me. You need merely uphold the terms of your pact. If you wish to be a lord, then you must show a lord's strength, and I can't have you dying just yet."

–Chapter 22–

Together Alone

From her office, Aaron made the silent walk from the castle, disregarding the armed guards at the exit to trek down to the city alone. He noted the sparseness of the streets despite their usual tendency for nighttime activity. No doubt, the deluge of tragedy had spoiled such an attitude in the populace. But then, that might have been wrong. *What do I know about what a normal person thinks?* he wondered.

Nothing, of course. Yet Aaron knew so little of the wants of nephilim, too. The wardens and nobles were so revered, it had never occurred to him that Sitri might not share that reverence. But to hear her disgust for her own family was something even more. It had been a scathing reminder that Lady Baal was as far from him as he was from the humans who looked at him with fear.

His wandering found him in the park. No birds chirped in the night, but the fountain babbled quietly, forming a pleasant ambiance that he had always appreciated. The area had been cleaned up quickly following the atrocity it had played host to. Hopefully, it would return a sense of normalcy to the people. Too much time had passed since they had been "blooded," as Durham might say, and that had left them more sensitive to the attacks. The carefully maintained green was meant to be a place of comfort, of beauty. Aaron took a seat on a bench, deciding he should be the first to enjoy it as such, and there he sat, taking in the sensations while his mind replayed the decisions that had brought him there.

It was in that contemplation that she found him.

Aaron saw her before he heard her. That was a feat of strength only a handful of humans had ever achieved. Were his eyes not suited for the night, he would have undoubtedly mistaken her for a stray shadow.

Perfectly calm, she moved neither quickly nor slowly. Her motion became a part of the environment, ignored and forgotten. Her black cassock was fine camouflage in the dark, but her auburn hair was unmistakable, falling past her shoulders like autumn leaves.

"Leah," he greeted her approach. "Just who I was looking for."

She detached herself from the cover of the trees and stepped into the light. "Glad I could accommodate you," she said softly.

He smiled. "Not that I'm ungrateful, but a few days ago might have been better."

She was dressed as ever he'd seen her and bearing no apparent injuries. Her hazel eyes always drew his attention, a deep chestnut-brown ringed with a hint of jade green. They were vibrant and alert, but shrouded in dark circles as they always had been. Her angular face gave away little of her feelings, and her posture was reserved and stiff. Still, there was a strength and sureness to her bearing, and her stare was as striking as Lady Baal's had ever been. She was unique, and he couldn't take his eyes away.

"Did you know I'd be here?" he asked, curious but hardly invested in the question.

She shifted from foot to foot. "I've…been waiting for you since you left the barracks." Her eyes went down to her hands. "That sounded better in my head."

That made him laugh. He was too exhausted to play it cool. "I'm glad you're all right," he said when his breath had calmed. "I really am."

She took a seat next to him on the bench. He followed her gaze to her hands. Like him, she preferred to wear gloves, though in reverse of his own, hers were pure white and scrawled on with prayers and words of protection. They rested on her lap, serene yet restless.

"I'm sorry about your friend."

"I'm not sure I ever could have called him my friend," Aaron replied. "Maybe at the very end, I think. It doesn't matter anymore."

"When their lives are ending, people no longer need their masks," she declared. "You should cherish it."

"I'm trying," he said, his hands suddenly feeling very heavy. "It happened so fast. It's still happening so fast; it feels like he's already been forgotten."

"That's a tenet of Paradise as well. Regret poisons the soul. It slows you, festers into bitterness and spite. We should live in the present, not the past. Did he practice the faith? I'll do a reading for him if you like."

"The Recitation of Sins?" He shook his head. "I don't know if he practiced. I hardly knew a thing about him, all said and done. I've never enjoyed the idea of the rite. It always seems wrong to remember the bad things someone's done after they die."

"We speak them aloud to be rid of them," Leah said. "Once we've let them go, we can remember the good ourselves. Burn away the corruption and let the flowers grow anew, it's said. We can't throw our lives away for those who are already gone."

When he didn't reply, she twitched, her face contorting as if she had realized a grave mistake. "I'm sorry. In the first place, the tenets of Paradise should never bind you."

Still, he had no response. He knew, of course, that Leah's words weren't meant to hurt him. But once again, the reminder of what he was not, rather than what he was, stung. She sensed it too and pivoted the conversation. "You said you were looking for me. Was it just to talk about your friend?"

He chuckled. "I was hoping for help. I'd been looking for you since Oris and Alexander arrived in the city. At first, it was just to introduce you to my friends, but when things escalated, I hoped I could get your thoughts, like before."

"I'm so stupid," she muttered. "When they arrived, I hid, fearing the arm of the Church. Even when I heard about the other towns, I still believed it was best to keep my distance. When you spoke with them, I thought you might have been investigating their intentions, so I stayed away."

"I talked to them, but each time, I was hoping for you." He tilted his head. "Wait, you saw me and I didn't notice you? I really am hopeless. What do they even keep me around for then?"

They shared the laughter.

"Actually, Carmen talked to me," Leah answered, a note of sadness creeping into her voice. She smiled at his stupefied expression. "She used to visit me. She doesn't practice the faith, but she was curious to learn, like you were. I went to offer her my condolences shortly after you visited. You made quite an impression."

"Did I?" he wondered aloud. "It didn't seem so."

"You did," she insisted. "You showed her a different perspective, something she didn't think possible before. That counts for something. I didn't think you'd tell her so much about you."

"I hate telling it," he muttered. "It reminds me that I'm missing something important. I hate thinking about what came before, but neither can I let it go. I just wanted her to *understand.* But trying to force that rarely works out for the better."

He glanced at her, noting her hands shifting restlessly. Her thumb and forefinger were pressed together tightly, as if holding onto a blade that wasn't there.

"I saw the mark at the sites of the murders. I thought you might have discovered something."

"No," she answered. "Nothing. I just said last rites. After I spoke to Carmen, it seemed like the right thing to do. I know better than anyone what the Church is capable of, but I never imagined they could do something so ghastly! I should have followed them. I should have dug deeper. I should have…"

Aaron took the reins before she could torment herself further. "What would you have done had you found out?"

She took a deep breath. "I don't know. But I know what I should have done."

"They would have killed you," he said. "They nearly killed me. They weren't just paladins, if that's what they were at all."

She rubbed her wrists, and in the glimpse of her forearm, he caught sight of twisting scars that he knew ran deeper than flesh. "You think they were executioners, don't you?"

He knew what the answer meant to her, and so he was grateful that he could speak to her honestly. "Some people are of that opinion. I think it's something else."

"They could be." Her words were barely more than a whisper. "The executioners were meant to be unbreakable warriors: martyrs in all but name that give everything to preserve order. They kill their own humanity first, then the enemies of the faith. But it's harder to damn your fellow man than it is to kill a nightmare or nephilim, and more often than not, the ones who became executioners did so because they enjoyed it."

"The more I think about what they said to me, the less I understand," Aaron said. "But I don't think any executioner would have used magic like that, and whatever they were after was something different than just blood. Something evil is coming, Leah. When we were out in the wastes, we found a new kind of nightmare. They were smiling. They were… speaking. They didn't burn at the touch of silver, and there's not a shred of doubt in my mind that there's more of them out there."

Her mouth moved in a silent prayer, hand touching the signet that hung from her neck. "Have you told Lady Baal?"

"It's all I've been trying to do since I got back," he groaned. "But it's one thing after another. Just a mountain of tragedies, piling on themselves. We can't keep up. *I* can't keep up. Now we have the attack from the south. So many people fight and die already, how can everyone be so eager to kill each other?"

"Oris and Alexander were enough," she agreed. "But to think Sterling would attack as well… I've heard that he isn't like Lord Talos, but he's territorial. When Lady Baal came to power, he didn't hesitate to do battle with her, even after she exterminated the Neros. But it's been a standstill for years. What could have possibly set him off? And what will Lady Baal do in response? Aaron?"

She had noticed before he realized it himself. His hand had clenched around the metal arm of the bench, twisting and contorting it around the shape of his fingers. He cursed, releasing his grip on the ruined segment. He fussed and fidgeted, trying to shift and hammer it back into place in an increasingly fruitless effort.

With each new application of force, the metal cracked and groaned and shaped itself into new and more obvious imperfections. His frustration grew quickly into anger, and without thinking, he dropped his palm onto the degraded work. It snapped off like broken glass, leaving him with nothing but an unspoken scream that he desperately fought to contain. And still, Leah observed him quietly, seemingly undisturbed by the childish and demeaning destruction he unintentionally wrought.

"It was me," he whispered. "We chased Silas to the south. The others wanted to go back, but I couldn't let it go. It was Sterling's territory; a village under attack, not even a town. I knew what it meant. They tried to warn me but…How could I just sit there and watch? How could I listen to all of their screams? They practically chased us out when they learned what I was, and everything that followed is on me."

He clutched his head, more aware than ever to keep out of his hands anything that he could break. But he broke almost everything. "We're going to meet with him to try and set things right. But I have no idea what to do. No idea what I should have done…"

She covered her smile with a hand. "You know I'm poor at conversation," she said with a shake of her head. "You are definitely worse." He looked at her in stunned silence while she brushed at her hair, shifting in place with discomfort. "That also sounded better in my head," she said sheepishly.

"Maybe that's why I have so few friends," he muttered, reclining against the bench.

"And maybe that's why two killers did more for the faith in a week than I accomplished in years. Nobody's perfect."

Just like that, he laughed again, the motion forcing him back to an upright position. He closed his eyes, imagining the myriad of better paths he could have taken, only to be snapped out of it by a pressure on him. It was a foreign and unusual sensation, so much so that he nearly jerked away. But when he looked down between them, he saw Leah's hand over his.

"I know what it's like to fight so hard for something, only to feel like you've made things worse," she said.

"I know."

"But it's all meaningless if you start to doubt your ideals," she continued. "Question yourself. Question everything. But you have a good dream. You should chase it, and don't mind if it's covered in blood and shit or if people curse you for it. I believe in you."

A breeze stirred the nearby trees, tugging at their hair and clothes. He felt the heat of her hand even through the barriers between them, and wondered if she found it cold. If so, she didn't show it. A tightness gripped his heart, and he stood. "I should go," he muttered. "The last thing you need is to be seen with me now."

She smiled at him, something warm and open and foreign to them both. "I think I'll stay a while longer. It's a beautiful night."

He nodded, turning to walk away from her in hopes the heat in his face didn't show. Before he could take more than a few steps, she called out to him.

"Aaron?" He looked back at her, cast against the moonlight and still as a statue. "Feel free to stop by when you make it back," she said. "I promise not to be so hard to find. You can tell me all about how you got the better of Lord Sterling."

He returned her smile, shrugging with a wave as he stepped into the night. "Count on it," he said, hoping it wouldn't come to that but holding it close as the promise that he would see her again.

Acknowledgements

This is a place I never thought I'd get to, but I always hoped.

First, a thank you to my mother, who encouraged me to take up writing in the first place and whose support for me has been unrelenting my entire life.

Thank you to my father and brother, who I love very much but am absolutely certain are reading this book for the first time despite my best efforts. We'll see if a physical copy does the trick.

Thank you to my friends, all of them, who are better than I deserve and deserve the very best themselves. A particular thank you to Jake and Shakti, whose feedback has been invaluable in helping me shape this into the best story it can be.

Thank you to Michael Waitz, who not only edited but also referred me to my publisher. Thank you to Mikael Carlson of Warrington Publishing for taking a chance on me and making this a reality.

Lastly, I would like to thank anyone reading this sentence, because it meant that you cared enough to learn about the village in the background that helped make this happen, and that means something special to me.

About the Author

Mason has a love for dark fantasy in all its forms. Be it comics, games, or books, he is always looking for a new world to obsess over and characters to follow into danger. His debut novel in The Desolate series, *Inhuman Intentions*, hopes to treat you to the same tense anticipation he enjoys.